ANATOLIA
and Other Stories

Anis Shivani

Black Lawrence Press
New York

Black Lawrence Press
www.blacklawrence.com

Executive Editor: Diane Goettel
Book Design: Steven Seighman

Black Lawrence Press
8405 Bay Parkway C8
Brooklyn, N.Y. 11214
U.S.A.

Published 2009 by Black Lawrence Press, an imprint of Dzanc Books

First edition 2009
ISBN-13: 978-0-6152818-2-7
Printed in the United States

TABLE OF CONTENTS

For Mehnaaz

Who Makes It All Possible

DUBAI

After thirty-five years of living in Dubai as a guest worker, Ram Pillai, prone more often now to a weariness of the bones, if not yet an ache of the heart, is leaving Dubai. He must bid goodbye, before the end of the week, to his greatest benefactors. Some of them have died, and others wouldn't remember him. But most are still around. The former Bedu might have lost all visible traces of estrangement from the city of lights and arguments, the once-green Emirati with an eagerness to spout off knowledge of "the way the British used to manage things" might no longer show such insecurity, and the abaya-wearing native women might walk with a little more pep in their step and a little more stiffness, but you can't tell Ram that in all the ways that matter, Dubai isn't still a shy bride, a virginal flower, a shadow in search of itself, and that only coaxing and coquetry work, force of any kind the banned substance in this most seductive of the Emirates.

His decision is somewhat sudden, as his friends in the labor camps have already claimed, but wasn't it always inevitable? It's neither as simple, nor as complicated, as the conviction of impending mortality. He's only fifty-five, even if the strong Gulf sun has sapped the strength out of his body and soul. His years of hard labor were few and long ago. Still, how real is his good health? He doesn't know. He also doesn't know where he'll go back to in India. His devout father and mother, in the Kerala village he came from, are long dead. Over the decades, he's had news that his small fishing community, off the Malabar Coast, has nearly emptied; the young people have gravitated to the larger towns, much as he, in 1972, packed his belongings in a small bundle to leave for Trivandrum, resolved to quickly earn the money to pay a recruiting agent the necessary fee to secure a coveted place among the shiploads of people embarking then for the wealthy Emirates. Something tells him he must leave Dubai before he's made to; why, after decades of never having had the slightest run-in with the authorities, he should fear this, he doesn't know.

The mistakes of judgment Ram made in his youth, added to the complications of having overstayed his original two-year work permit, have long ago ceased to bother him. He has justified his silent bargain to his own satisfaction. Law and justice are abstract constructions, generalities which concrete facts usually make a mockery of. At the public library, which Ram has begun to frequent in recent years, he's become fond of Santayana. He has a difficult time understanding such philosophers, even in accessible translation, but he is more than ever convinced that self-sacrifice is not the Holy Grail orthodox belief makes it out to be. Still, Ram's past is beginning to rear its monstrous head when he least expected it, as his heart becomes less supple and his body a less wieldy instrument. If only he could tell someone! If only there were someone to unburden with! But he hasn't whispered a word of his secret to his most trusted friends. They know Ram has some leverage whereby he can remain in Dubai unmolested, in an "illegal" status, for a lifetime, but out of respect for his apparent sadness, they've observed limits in inquiring what advantage he's acquired.

Not even Friday makes Dubai really slow down; still, the traffic on Khaleej Road, heading into Al-Hamriya Port, is thinner than it is the rest of the week. Instead of taking a bus, Ram is driving today his old brown Datsun; it's rare for a worker living in the camps to own a car of any kind, but Ram has been discreet enough not to have bought a newer model, although he has enough savings to easily afford one. This way, fewer questions will be asked. Also, having a car of some kind allows him to occasionally park along the main shopping boulevards, without too many probing glances; his actual status, as a laborer of long residence, should be self-evident: he's not trying to pass himself off as one of the Indian professionals, welcome for their limitless credit cards at the shopping plazas, received by the salespeople almost as well as European and American shoppers. Also today Ram has taken a long bath, wondering if in India water will be as plentiful. The camp he lives in is so close to the city that it's almost not outside it anymore, and because it acquired water and electricity as early as two decades ago, it's debatable if it can even be called a camp. Rumors that Ram's camp will be demolished for the city's expansion needs have been rife for years; Ram has never paid attention. Workers he knows from the real camps, farther out and without any real facilities, where eight or ten to a room is common, have always kidded him about his "privileged" status; he's tried to take it in a tolerant, grandfatherly spirit.

Already, well before noon, the most devout among the Emirati worshippers are making their way to the Grand Mosque, their flowing white dishdashas starched and sparkling, their headscarves tightly tied by the black aghal. It used to be, at one of Ram's first jobs, at a construction site on Sheikh Zayed Road, near the present Golf Club, that he would sometimes accompany Muslim workers to the mosque, despite his own

Hindu origins; Islam, like Hinduism, has had little attraction for him, but it was either that or, instead of the hourlong Friday prayer break from the dusty screaming site, taking only twenty minutes for lunch at one of the hot roadside tandoors set up for Indian laborers. The mosque is the only place in Dubai where national and foreigner, citizen and guest, rich and poor, stand side by side, see each other's faces without feint or filter. In the mosque, all faces are empty of demand.

Al-Maktoum Bridge takes him to Al-Rasheed Road, off which he takes crowded side streets to get to his old friend Krishan's fabric shop in the ancient Deira district. Notices to tear down the ramshackle building which Krishan's shop fronts have been issued since the time the tallest building in Dubai was a few stories high, not even easily visible from the wharves. Krishan deals with a Muslim middleman whose job it is to pay off the busybody civil servants with nothing better to do than harass honest businessmen with vain threats.

In the early years there used to be mounds of spices outdoors—ah, pungent red chilies six inches long, bright as a new bride's smile, stacked impossibly high!—but the newest and poorest of Asians now prefer to buy indoors, in the spice emporiums. Other than the occasional Western tourist, there are few resident white faces in traditional shopping districts like Deira. Over the years, the brazenness of Western visitors in such neighborhoods has visibly declined; now they act apologetically, as if they owe their presence to the sufferance of their kind hosts, speaking politely with the Indians, Pakistanis, Bangladeshis, Sri Lankans, Indonesians, and Filipinos who're otherwise treated as invisible actors in fashionable Dubai.

"Memsahib," Ram says, tipping his cap, to a middle-aged European woman in a long pink dress, bargaining with a street vendor over "pearl" jewelry.

The fondness of the Westerner for expensive junk is limitless. These are the same people who patronize the Emirates' many museums, which have risen rapidly to mummify the extinction of the pearling industry, the Bedouin habitat, the obligations of kinship, as fast as these old ways of life are becoming dated. These are the type of people who spend entire days in the "heritage villages" in the Emirati hinterland, observing the feeding and milking of camels by the stern Bedu, and who can't tell that the many "forts" constructed along the Arabian Gulf, from Abu Dhabi to Ra's al Khaimah, are actually of recent construction, made to look like antiquities.

But Ram's forgiveness knows no bounds today. He is, after all, bidding farewell to the fond familiar sights. He expects whatever town he relocates to in India, perhaps after he's taken a young wife, to immerse him soon in its vastly reduced level of energy. And this isn't something entirely to regret. One gets old.

"Is brother Krishan here?" Ram asks Krishan's older son, Ganesh, inside the shop crammed with cotton and silk fabrics in every available cranny. Ganesh seems to be trying to fix the broken cash register.

Now thirty-six, for some inexplicable reason Ganesh has always resented Ram. Krishan never brought over his wife from India, although technically, once the shop took off, and especially after Krishan set up branches in Sharjah, an easy drive to the northeast, and then in Abu Dhabi, another short drive to the southwest, his income level was high enough to qualify him to bring over family. Krishan's two sons, who came from India on work permits when they were old enough, could have had a chance to bring over Indian wives had they petitioned the government, since they do run a business; but they've chosen to remain bachelors too. Why they've done so has never been entirely clear to Ram, and he tries not to wonder about the unsavory possibilities, including homosexuality, which, as he understands it, is rife in the labor camps.

"Not here today," Ganesh says peremptorily. "In Sharjah. Fridays, always dedicated to Sharjah. Mondays and Tuesdays, Abu Dhabi. Wednesdays, he goes over to Fujairah—maybe to set up a new shop there. If you need to talk to him about anything related to the business here, he won't know." Ganesh stretches his chest, sturdy as a block of bricks. "Ask me. Ask me anything."

The years of schooling in India have left little impact on Ganesh, as rough and crude as ever. Ram physically backs off. There is a smell coming from Ganesh, as of a raw animalism, that frightens Ram. He feels weak and vulnerable. "What would I ask you?"

Ganesh smiles monstrously. "I don't have to ask *you* anything. I know you're jumping ship. I heard already. From Mustafa, your old buddy. And Jivan. And Patel. All the Patels. Everyone knows you're abandoning Dubai. I wonder why. Why would a man still in his prime"—Ganesh shushes Ram's protest—"still able to earn at least a thousand dirhams a month, and no expenses, mind you, no family to support in India—why would such a man want to go to a home that isn't a home, where there's nothing to return to? What did India ever do for you? The future is here, man."

"I've lived here long enough, haven't I?" Ram is edgy, lost, defensive. "I was here when you weren't yet born. I've seen this city grow and grow, until it's—it's something I hardly understand." Ganesh snickers, which makes Ram even more apologetic. "I'm not anybody who matters. I've paid for my little share of this crazy development, this gigantic construction—with blood, sweat, and tears. Do I not have the right to retire?"

"Retirement?" Ganesh spits to the side. "Is that what you're after? I doubt it, man. What's the real reason you're leaving?" He becomes meditative, dismissing with a gruff wave of his hairy hand one of the shop assistants who is trying to get his attention at the door. "Everyone knows you never returned to India to renew your work permit. Not once. And you don't have a business, like we do, to keep renewing it here. Then how have you been allowed to stay? Wave after wave of deportation drives. I'd say at least a dozen major ones since you've been here. There's some mystery here, and it creates problems for me—for the community. We don't like people who distrust others."

"Your father trusts me well enough."

Ganesh spits to the side again. "My father's an old man who doesn't know anything."

"He's taken good enough care of you. He owns three shops now."

"And one more on the way. I know." Ganesh laughs viciously. "It's like having children…Look, I have a busy day ahead. Very busy. Come again tomorrow, if you're still in Dubai. My father will be here to check the accounts."

Ram's head feels hot and heavy when he steps outside amidst the bustle of pedestrians. What a rude son! Ram's own lack of family has never caused him to be so frustrated and angry. Perhaps it is the nature of the younger generation not to show respect as a matter of principle. Perhaps there is no real reason for Ganesh's animosity. But what a rude young man! In all his life, Ram has never spit like a village illiterate.

He no longer feels enthusiastic about his plan to fill up all of Friday with farewell visits, to Al-Khabeesi, Al-Baraha, Umm Hureir, Karama, adjoining downtown commercial districts where his old friends, who were good to him in the difficult years, prosper as merchants. In Hor Al Anz is a shop owned by the Lebanese Christian brothers, the Frangiehs, who welcome Ram and discuss, with all the gusto of harmed insiders, Sheikh Mo's—the ruler, Sheikh Muhammad's—follies in awarding contracts to large construction firms. The Palms, the World, Ski Dubai, Burj Dubai, these and other projects are discussed over mint tea as if the Frangiehs had a real stake in all this. Ram takes their idle resentment in good spirit, but why should he care about the devious strategies of rich builders? In Mankhool, the Naseris, Iranians, sell girls' dresses, and imagine their smart nephew, now being educated in Britain, returning to Dubai to start a joint venture in Dubai Internet City. And there are others, none of whom ever talk about leaving Dubai, for any reason. Even the worst-off among the labor camp residents, inclined to strike and riot in recent years, only want their living conditions to be improved.

The Friday prayer is in full swing. The city is on hold—as silent as it is possible for Dubai to be, although the non-Muslim workers at the innumerable construction locales are busy orchestrating their staccato clanging and banging to remind the worshippers what Dubai is all about. Ram decides to go home. His belongings after all these years are very few—mostly his spotless clothes, especially white shirts, bought at steep discounts from the better stores along Sheikh Zayed Road, after the end of the annual January Shopping Festival. His one persistent memory of India is of a secondary school teacher inviting him home for snacks and beverages to discuss ignored Malayalam writers. That afternoon it rained so hard even the boisterous children glad of the drenching went back inside their homes after a while. In the old teacher's courtyard, the leafy banana trees bent back in the lash of the rain, like old people sustaining crooked bones.

Ram stops at one of the disappearing traditional snack vendors by the Clock Tower on Abu Baker Siddique Road.

He buys a plate of fried plantains, then orders another to take home to his roommate, a Sri Lankan Buddhist who speaks only when absolutely necessary. Ram sits on the edge of the long wooden bench outside, watching the morose traffic. The desert compels human beings to keep reverting time and again to naturally slow rhythms, give up their robotic wind-up doll mannerisms. Ram feels in his pants pocket the one-way ticket to Trivandrum he's already bought. It is so silent unwanted memories return to him.

What happened was, a Sheikh ran over an old man, and Ram saw it.

He was the only one to witness the accident. At a building site which was then far from the center of the city, Ram was taking a break from operating the concrete mixing equipment. His back was giving him trouble. He'd thought his body was indestructible—hadn't he been the most athletic among his schoolmates? Was there a tree he hadn't swung from, a creek he hadn't swum in? The late afternoon prayers had been called, and workers—even Hindus and Christians— were reluctant to resume work. Just before evening prayers were called, the builder, a North Indian man who'd picked up fluent Arabic, would show up to inspect the day's work, and needlessly grill the workers about wasting materials. The hammering and buzzing were beating a nightmarish track in Ram's head. He walked a good few blocks away from the work zone, abruptly coming up against the beginnings of the endless desert. If he kept walking south, in the same direction, eventually he would collapse and die. A lonely desert death seemed at that moment a most noble one.

He heard the screech of the car—a sickening sound— and the slam of the brakes, followed by the thud of the falling body, lifted off the ground and thrown far away. He bent double, as if he were next in the line of fire. A Toyota had whizzed past him on the dirt track—what passed for the road leading into the desert—and slammed right into the old man Ram had noticed in the periphery of his vision. Soon a Sheikh was bent over the old man, whose body lay crumpled and twisted, a sack of disjointed bones. The man lying prostrate was a Bedouin, his leathery face testament to endless years of willful soaking of the sun. He must have tended sheep, goats, camels with the gentleness of the honest caretaker, known the difference between benign and malignant nighttime desert sounds, never lived in fear of stolen property or the taxpayer's intrusion. Now he was dead. A trickle of deep red blood squirted out of the left side of his mouth. Ram found himself bending over the old man, many feet from the edge of the road. Ram's warm breath was blanketing the deep wrinkles of the man's peaceful white-haired face. The Sheikh was crouched over the dead man too.

"It is my fault," the Sheikh said in Arabic, distraught. "I admit it."

Ram looked closely at the Sheikh's face, never to forget the least of its contours for the rest of his life. He was young. The light in his eyes suggested ambition, and even the horror of the moment hadn't been able to quite extinguish it. His lips were thick, and the trace of a wart on his right cheek only lent his handsome face more character. It seemed as if time slowed down—came to a stop—as the two of them cradled the dead man's body.

"It is my fault," the Sheikh repeated.

Was he sensing his young life go up in smoke? Did he have a wife, children? He wasn't one of the princes, that was clear. If he were, he wouldn't have been so afraid. Nor was he a Bedouin, he showed too much refinement for that. He was from the intermediate merchant class, who were the real energy in the Emirates, while the princes gave the orders

18

and the people at the bottom performed the grunt work. Ram tried to recall how fast the car was going. It couldn't have been going too fast. The road didn't make that possible. Yet how could the Sheikh not have seen the old man? Perhaps the declining sun had blinded his eyes.

"It is no one's fault," Ram said in halting English. "His time had come. Look how old he was. It is no one's fault."

The Sheikh stared at Ram for a while, as if wondering whether to take Ram seriously. Then, with huge reluctance written over his face, he agreed, "It is no one's fault. It is Allah's will."

"Yes, Allah—Ram, God...he was a very old man."

There was no shade to move the old man under, no tree, no cover. Everything that was done from then on was bound to be disrespectful. If Ram reported the incident, whether or not the authorities pursued the truth of it, Ram would surely be thrown out of the country. To leave the dead man there was sacrilege, countenanced by no religion or code of honor. And yet what could be done with him? The Sheikh could hardly dump him in his car and bury him somewhere else. If they left him there, the vultures would devour him before morning. He deserved a decent burial—his family, if he had one, around him. If Ram didn't report it, and if it came to light that he'd wandered off for a considerable time at the same hour, he'd be in much worse trouble than mere deportation. If only there were a grove of trees, some shade, to let the dead man lie in peace, and the police notified anonymously. Yes, that was it! Someone— perhaps the Sheikh himself—could make an anonymous report in a couple of hours, when the construction workers had quit. Ram wasn't stopping to think about the morality of escape. He didn't exactly know how the blood-for-blood principle worked among the Arabs in case of accidental slaughter, but it couldn't have been good for the young Sheikh.

"Go," Ram waved at the Sheikh, conveying to him in faltering English the outline of his plan. The Sheikh would have to promise to make an anonymous call to the police just after sunset. Ram would be nowhere in the picture. "Go!" Ram said more sternly, because the Sheikh wasn't showing any indication of leaving. Finally, the Sheikh seemed to sense the wisdom of the idea. What was done was done. Only the future mattered now. As long as it was only an accident, and the Sheikh wasn't at fault...and he wasn't.

The Sheikh made Ram write down his exact name and full address, his passport number and date of birth, on a notepad he got out of the glove compartment of the Toyota. Upon arrival in the Emirates, a worker had to turn over his passport and work permit to the recruiting agent or the employer, to be returned only at the time of departure. Ram remembered his own details. He never paused to wonder about the wisdom of sharing his identity with the Sheikh. Ram couldn't help but memorize the license plate number of the Toyota. He couldn't stop staring at it.

Then it was all over. He was back at the building site in a few minutes, and things went on as before. He had to go to the same location for a week more, but he never took a break, let alone wander over to the location of the accident. A few months later, when he went to his employer, the Indian builder, to ask him to renew his work permit, he was told not to worry about it. The labor ministry had already taken care of it. When the employer died in a freak accident a few more years later, many of Ram's fellow workers found themselves scrambling to arrange new employment; some had to leave the country. But Ram was immediately contacted by a new and better employer, who said the labor ministry had asked him to. Over the years, whenever Ram has been in a scrape, or about to get into one, a benevolent invisible hand has seemed to pull him out of it, and set him back on course again. Ram has no doubt the Sheikh who killed the old man has been behind it.

"Keef Halak." The greeting is issued in a commanding voice. "May I speak with you a moment—sir?"

Ram is finishing the fried plantains. He looks up to see a plump Emirati national wiping the sweat off his thick forehead, and staring at the remains of Ram's snack as if he finds it a personal affront for anyone to eat in the street. A gleaming black Mercedes is squeezed into the tight parking spot behind his own Datsun. Even before saying yes, Ram wipes off with his palm any imaginary dust and crumbs on the bench next to him, to make room for the stranger. He can be pretty sure who his interlocutor is.

"Shukran," the Emirati says, sitting down with his legs spread wide. He doesn't remove his dark sunglasses, taking in the construction clamor emitted from just beyond the horizon of the low-rising buildings in the neighborhood, as if personally approving the continuing spate of action at this normally lax time of the week. "Something about Friday, the end of the week—it makes you take stock of where you've been, where you're going. Doesn't it? Even if you're not Muslim. They say our ancestors were great poets. Every man a poet in his home. Imagine, pearl divers, impoverished Bedu, goat herders, dhow-builders, reciting poetry about the beauty of their mundane work. In touch with their essence, their being. A sweet, sweet harmony. But so much has passed away, so rapidly. In another generation—poof!—no one will have any memory of the ways of our forefathers." Then he laughs cynically, turning his face to Ram. "But this is all to the good. Sheikh Mo says we must be number one—in everything. There's nothing difficult about progress. Only cowards are afraid."

All this by way of prelude. Ram has heard about them, picking off troublemaking foreigners and journalists, instigating pro-Mo rallies and events, stirring nationalist fervor among students at the University in Al-'Ayn, gleaning information useful to the ruling Al-Maktoum family at all sorts of harmless festivals and celebrations, but he's never known for sure when he's been in the presence of one of them. They wear dark glasses, carry symbolic walkie-talkies, drive black Mercedes, and are supposed to have a tad more arrogance than the most inebriated of Emiratis. Not that these are precise identifiers. So he's finally in the jurisdiction of one! In other Arab countries there is a name for their type— in Iraq, Saudi Arabia, Kuwait, Syria, Egypt: mukhabarat, informers. Officially, Dubai doesn't have spies of any kind. Officially, sometimes even the police and the military don't exist. Dubai's only business is business. Everyone's at bottom either a businessman, or an enforcer of business norms.

"Does this stuff taste good?" the Emirati asks. "I've never tried it."

Ram immediately offers the untouched plate of plantains meant for his roommate. The Emirati makes a great show of enjoying the South Asian snack, licking the grease off his thick fingers. "Delicious. It tastes just like—bananas. But I guess that's what it is. Very filling." In quick order, he finishes the whole plate, barely taking time to properly chew and swallow. At the end, he licks off all of his fingers snappingly. Then he places Ram's finished paper plate over his own, and walks the few feet to the nearest trash receptacle, which happens to have on it a colorful depiction of Dubailand, Dubai's own Disney World. Returning, he says, "Well now, suppose you tell me how you've been keeping yourself busy this week? Name's Muhammad, by the way." His thick hand doesn't shake, only grips hard, and Ram feels as if he's offering his thinner hand in ba'ya, the traditional oath of allegiance.

"Ram," he says, as if there were any need. Ram wishes the Emirati wouldn't waste time with the useless small talk. There's no need for it. His heart should be thumping with anxiety, his pulse throbbing with fear—instead, he mostly feels curiosity. In his own drama, can it really be said he's been a full participant ever since he came to this land of madcap building up and tearing down? He raises his palm quietly, as if signaling the end of preliminaries.

"Not that we don't know. First, the one-way ticket to India. That always triggers an investigation, you know. Just to make sure everything's on the up-and-up. The travel agents are very cooperative. They have to be. I mean, even if a prince in the Al-Maktoum family took out a one-way ticket to Paris— cleanest city in the world, by the way, I love visiting it—we would make sure the Prince's state of mind was unobjectionable. Then your visits to your friends—and what a diverse group they are, if I may say so. Remarkable. For someone who got his start in the construction industry, to know shopkeepers, budding entrepreneurs, people who have a legitimate shot at investing in the free trade zones—remarkable!"

"I haven't worked in hard labor since my first years here…"

"And that's the other thing, the transition to clerical work, when you came here as a laborer. Almost unheard of— even if there's been little promotion. I asked my colleagues to come up with comparable examples, and there don't seem to be any, for non-Arabs. Remarkable."

Despite himself, Ram smiles. "Perhaps I've just been lucky. In the right place at the right time."

"No, my friend, it's more than luck. More than sheer resourcefulness, ingenuity, ability. Pretty nearly all your compatriots are blessed with these qualities. And they work hard, all of them work off their butts, but most stay in the same kinds of labor camps they were assigned to begin with—until the day comes to leave, which is nearly always involuntary. But you, my friend, are leaving voluntarily. Remarkable!"

"Is it a crime to leave Dubai?"

"Crime? Well now, now that you mention crimes—I wonder..."

"What is it you're trying to say?"

The Emirati looks away. His heavy cell phone tinkles, and he presses the mute button, not checking to see who's calling. He taps his right foot on the ground, his heavy leather sandal loose enough to almost fall off. "It seems they're taking three hours now for Friday prayers...Simplicity is better in all things. The simple recourse, the simple explanation, is usually the most elegant. But this principle is always in opposition to the momentum of complexity. Things assume momentum sometimes for the most curious reasons, the most fragile circumstances—coincidences. Yet the momentum for anything has a time limit. People's patrons—for instance— meet their maker. They die. Their time comes and goes. Then what happens to those they patronize? They're on their own. Simplicity, you see, returns to its rightful place, and harmony reigns. Beautiful!" Then he abruptly turns to Ram, his face turning a harsher hue. "On the afternoon of September 4, 1974, were you mixing concrete at the construction site of Zaytoonah Mall? For an Indian contractor named Suleiman Shah? Were you on the road to the desert for more than an hour at the time of the 'asr prayer?"

So he knows everything, Ram thinks. Defense will be useless. The young Sheikh is probably no more. The strings that have been manipulated on his behalf probably no longer have a puller. Has the Sheikh died recently? He would only have been a middle-aged man. Ram feels sorrow overcome him. "What do you want from me?" he complains. He thinks of his Sri Lankan roommate, silent and contemplative even when an employer withheld his wages for two months. He was so undisturbed that the superstitious employer became perturbed and not only paid him the back wages, but also gave him a bonus worth two more months of wages, and promoted him. The world is crazy that way. If you place no demands on it, mostly it goes along with your wishes. They say in India, the monsoons have assumed a most erratic pattern, compared to when Ram was a child, regularity being the byword then. Kerala gets far less rain now than it used to. The tea plantations are suffering. The fish aren't as plentiful on the Malabar Coast, and they don't taste as good. This is what he has heard.

"Hayyak. Come, my friend. Let us not waste time." The Emirati rises, with a hint of what Ram thinks is shame at his overwhelmingly dominant position. "There's an old building nearby. Functional, unremarkable. On the other side of the creek, on Oud Metha Road—between Old Trinity Church and St. Mary's Catholic Church. Most people think it's a watch repair factory. It's an interesting place. We do a lot of good for Dubai there. People volunteer all sorts of helpful information. We live in a world where information is the cheapest but also the most expensive commodity. And so we think of this building—and you'll meet some terrific friends of mine there, real veterans, very good friends—we think of it as the nerve center of this metropolis, in some ways. In everything we try to discover the principle of simplicity converging on similar tracks. In the end…well, you'll see."

Ram gets up, a little of the fight returning to him. He'll deny everything. They have no proof. Whoever has looked out for him all these decades will surely do so again. They just want to make sure he stays in Dubai. Why this would be so, is beyond him, but as long as he remains safe here, he will be fine with staying. He will make that willingness crystal clear at the very beginning of the next interrogation.

"You'd better leave your Datsun here. We'll take care of it."

Muhammad politely holds open the front passenger door for Ram to get in. It's the first time Ram has ever sat in a Mercedes. It's true what they say about the smooth ride, the solid suspension. It's as though there is no movement. Muhammad turns on the radio, to an FM station broadcasting classical Arabic music. Ram likes being behind tinted glasses. The pedestrians don't know who's riding inside, the most beautiful or the ugliest person. While they've been talking, Dubai has resumed its frantic pace. The pensive moment of the Friday prayer has left little trace on the speedy movements of the population. They cross Al-Maktoum Bridge over the creek, get on the road past the old Dubai Radio & TV building. A striking blonde Westerner is walking on the broad pavement, in a skirt far too short to be tasteful in the Gulf. A young Arab in spotless white dishdasha and headgear seems to be trailing her, although at a respectful distance. There will be no rude wolf-whistles, no overt harassment, as in uncouth India.

Ram looks over at Muhammad's inscrutable face. "Did you know there are almost no incidents of reported rape in Dubai?"

Muhammad smiles. "I've heard that. I've heard that."

MANZANAR

August 2, 1942. Would I have been safe had I never met the camp director and his alluring assistant? At first the rumor was that the camp director had contracted hives. He is a man of many allergies, numerous pains, baffling energies. Sensitive to criticism, he keeps his face hidden. A few days under a doctor's observation will check any man's pride. The camp director's semiofficial busybodies used to swagger around the barracks, looking into alleged instances of uncleanliness or sloth. It seems they have restraining orders now—or maybe they got tired of the game. We have not heard the word "Jap" from one official since February. Should I be thinking it was all unintentional and will be corrected soon, when Mr. Roosevelt and Mr. Stimson realize what a gigantic blooper they've committed? Some say they were grossly misinformed about the Japanese threat. I say it doesn't even ascend to that level. Some things register on the Caucasian consciousness. Others—well, they just flit on their noses for a second, like pestering flies, then one swipe of the hand is enough to bring oblivion. Back to the camp director. I'd say on the whole he has been magnanimous. Perhaps the jailer acquires the characteristics of the jailed. It's the only way he knows to keep things at a low boil. Make the jailed think the jailer is not that different in his humanity. By this criterion, the camp director would also have to be obsequious, slanting, germane, officious, incongruous, bootlicking, niggardly, calculating, inscrutable, pessimistic, opportunistic, practical, scholarly, jettisoning, spying, suspicious, bemused, oratorical, etc. Ha! How much do I focus my researches on the camp director, the man with the heavy shoulders and the wasted camouflage jacket, whom no one seems to be able to call by his name? Orders of magnitude less than on his flock of assistants, especially the Quaker lady from Iowa designated to spread cross-cultural understanding. More on her later.

August 6, 1942. The dust storms have kicked up again. We were greeted by them five months ago. At that time I thought it was pure hell. Anything—death, mutilation, suffocation, drowning—would be better than to feel the sting of dust in the throat, the eyes, the nose, the lungs for days at a time. At first people walked around with blankets over their heads. This did no good. The tarpaper covering the barracks walls is thin, penetrable, only false cover for the gaps and slits that branch across the wood like veins on an old man's leg. In the middle of the afternoon, when the execrable noodle slop from the mess hall has been digested by the weary stomach, one squats in the middle of the apartment (I prefer this dignified word to cell), knees raised to the ear, hands over head, listening to the detested soundtrack of the wind. The wind groans a dirge for time lost to fatal error. How was it we thought we could become fully American, one hundred percent American, unassailably patriotic American, and get away with the illusion for so long? Forty-two years in my case. "Jim Hosokawa, renowned Issei intellectual and community leader, founder of at least five literary journals for exile-minded Japanese over his lifetime, restrainer of hotheaded Kibei too enamored of the emperor's charms, one-time manager of the most dignified hotel on the Seattle waterfront, importer of teas and herbs, exporter of machinery, shipper, wholesaler, middleman, broker, insurance maven, and icon of extreme moderation in all things worldly and Olympian; family-oriented though single; lover of children, animals, waifs, naïfs, streetwalkers, medicine men, tribal elders, middle-of-the-road politicians, Mr. Roosevelt's New Deal before it became old, improbable dances, and peace in the world; and the single most important moderating influence on the Japanese American Citizens League, even if this last fact is so deeply buried in the past, it might as well not have been." Some profile. Forty-two years of forgetting and not wanting to remember, then suddenly I'm forced to remember. Old Japan, mist-shrouded Kyoto temples, houses frail as matchboxes, narrow streets that one traversed with the head down, cosseting aunts and wise uncles, and always a profound silence, which prevented coming to terms with history. It is this forgotten past we are forced to live up to. The problem is, our memories are not what they used to be. America has softened us up.

August 11, 1942. I meant to say something about the Sierra Nevadas in connection with the endless battering of the wind (a wind so almighty it seems to emanate from the heavens), the limpid blue and marigold shyness of the Sierra Nevadas, standing guard over the desert, but I find myself becoming inarticulate every time I contemplate the majesty of these mountains. I honestly don't think I've seen anything like them in nature, and I've been all over America: Colorado, Wyoming, the Dakotas, Idaho, Montana, New Mexico, Arizona, and of course Washington and northern California. When the sun rises, incrementally burnishing the closest peaks, Mount Whitney and Mount Williamson, it seems as though pure gold spreads over them like water, like angels painting the surface with billions of tiny brushes, spilling nothing, losing nothing. I meant to say that one begins to look forward to the bedlam of the mess hall, the adults slipping easily into children's roles (always wanting more, more, more of the inedible swill), the children acting grown-up and recalcitrant, as though in possession of secrets of abuse and torture denied the adults. I meant to say that one walks with one's head held high, and for a moment, as the sun and the peaks do their dance of inseparable inclination, the camp perimeter with its watchtowers, the distant barracks of the camp director and his assistants, the fields in the valley where former store-owners, executives, and part-time poets labor for twelve dollars a month, are all erased. One's stomach rumbles, hunger leans its head inward, and it seems possible to greet women one's own age, removed from sexuality and intimacy, as though with the Eastern veil one ought to have experienced in old Japan but never actually did. Of course, all this is on days without dust storms.

August 17, 1942. My next-door neighbor is a woman three years older than me, also single, also noiseless like a mortally injured rat. I share twenty-one hours of enforced quiet with her. Is it too much to claim that I know her unique smell as well as I have ever known any woman's? Miyo Yoshida is not what you might call handsome, let alone beautiful. Her haunches are too wide, her eyes tiny buttons of opaque misreaderliness. Still, she is sweet, or am I going sweet on her?—more or less the same thing. We're both lucky to have private apartments without having children. We could easily have been made to share quarters with other people our age. And to end up next to each other, with only a thin partition between us. Imagine my agony in helping to build the divider, when I already knew the identity of my neighbor! This seems ready-made for comedy—or tragedy, depending on your perspective. Our first day as neighbors—a day of violent dust storms, of course—Miyo asked how long I thought we were going to be here. "As long as the war lasts," I said. "Only that long?" she said. "What about after the war? Will we ever be allowed to go back into the world to pick up the pieces? This lasts for ever. This is the end of our lives." We all have the same thought, but no one speaks it, certainly not the adolescent hotshots running the *Manzanar Free Press* with all the bells and whistles of a real newspaper: internships and assignments and self-censorship and advisories. The "editorialists" for the camp paper opine that "we must be ready to resume normal life when conditions permit it" and not allow the well-known phenomenon of prisoner's despondency to take root among us. Prisoner's despair, among the Issei and Nisei? Already, for anyone over twelve, evenings are crammed with social activities. People dance and sing their hearts out in the uncountable clubs set up for the purpose. As though young boys and girls don't already suffer from raging hormones, we must create endless avenues for them to get closer to each other. Don't mistake me. I'm no prude. But this degree of exuberance, in our present condition, suggests something of escapism to me. And baseball! The Japanese have always loved baseball, but now everyone from six to sixty is on a baseball team, or more than one, and afternoons are spent in a froth of physical self-appraisal, as though we were getting ready to be shipped overseas to fight "the good war" and this was the best way to prepare. You see, motives and ends are everywhere confused and disorderly.

September 4, 1942. Miyo has taken ill and spent the last week in the camp infirmary. It's a long walk there, past the majority of the camp's barracks, as though to minimize the number of visitors. It's right next to a small school for the children of camp administrators. I have heard that the two Caucasian doctors in charge, both from the Midwest, are selflessly devoted to their Hippocratic oath, upset with Mr. Roosevelt's policies toward the yellow races, and not afraid to express their opinion. On my visit, the infirmary, which seems to have succeeded in importing the necessary equipment, feels almost abandoned, though I know there is an epidemic of diphtheria among the children and quite a few of them must be confined here. Miyo looks pale, drained of all energy, inhabiting a blur of nostalgia, as I would have expected. "Hosokawa-san, you should not have bothered," she feebly protests. "The walk is long, and the dust." She worries about my fickle knee—one of numerous minor ailments I keep in abeyance. "The dust isn't bad today," I reply, pulling a chair to her bedside. A Japanese woman of her social status—widowed, admittedly, but not immune, as no one is, from rumor and innuendo, especially under such desperate conditions—ought to feel some anxiety about the hospital visit of a single man, but Miyo seems calm, if a little shy at first. I don't know why she is hospitalized. I presume some undisclosable "female trouble" likely to overcome a woman of her withholding nature, disinclined to make friends or express joy and sorrow even under the best of circumstances. (Later, I will find it was heatstroke and wonder why I never alighted on this obvious explanation.) Her eyes sparkle as she props herself higher on the white pillows. She tells me about her husband. He was a mailman in San Francisco, often chosen as employee of the month. "We only had one child," Miyo says without explanation, "and I have always regretted not having another." She describes idyllic picnics in Marin County, visits to her sister-in-law's children up and down the California coast, from Monterey to San Diego, and even a memorable visit by her parents-in-law from Tokyo, who after six months in America declared that their son's long-ago decision to emigrate to the New World was blessed and sane after all. "Did you never marry, Hosokawa-san?" She already knows the answer, yet wants details. "No, of course not," I say, caught off-guard, hemming and hawing, before being rescued by the end of visiting hours. I wish I had had a box of chocolates or something similarly sinful to give her, and promise myself to buy her an exclusive brand through mail order. Back in my apartment, I continue to fear making noise even though there is no longer a neighbor to offend. One's body makes many noises, none of them appealing.

September 20, 1942. Sooner or later the call was bound to come. The camp director wants to see me in his office. Apparently his desert allergies have been suppressed well enough for him to put on a public face again. During his relative marginality, the camp has gained massively in efficiency—or the appearance of such. Nisei block leaders who rose spontaneously to take control, often in the interest of their own narrow agenda (blockheads, we call them), have been replaced through systematic selection procedures. Subject to discipline now, their replacements always seem to be canvassing for votes, recruiting new constituents, trying to walk both sides of the fence on the sickening question of loyalty. Our blockhead ignores my presence, as he does that of everyone older than thirty. Friendship with a certain type of Issei man, from this youngster's point of view, cannot possibly help his political cause. I hear that bathroom shenanigans have been cleaned up. In the beginning, young women particularly, but women in general, tried to go late at night or early in the morning, and just hold it at busy hours, because of lack of privacy; the handheld cardboards and newspapers were hardly sufficient partitions while one did one's business. But now the blockheads have assigned trustworthy middle-aged women to monitor the flow of people in and out of bathrooms.

No more hanging out and leering at the private parts of women one's mother's or grandmother's age. A few weeks ago no one seemed excited by the prospect of enrolling children in the camp schools, where we heard there would be heavy doses of indoctrination in American civics and citizenship, and very little of science and math. Better to keep the children busy with sports and recreation than accustom them to the low standard of education here in camp. After all, when they get out and go back to schools in the real world, not to mention colleges...But reality is sinking in now, and refractory parents and children are to be whipped into shape. There are to be no truants, no dropouts, no holdovers. All those capable seem to have signed up to work on the farms, bringing the Japanese people's legendary agricultural skills to bear on the war effort, and there seems little audible complaint about the token wages. The rest are going to be nurses, teachers, baseball coaches, dance and festival organizers, choirboys, pastors, members of committees dealing with the camp administrators, assistants to the Military Police, trash pickers, mess hall supervisors—in short, any designation to lift one out of the nameless number, 10437 in my case, by which we are otherwise known. All chiefs and no Indians. Such pitiable delusion! Such childlike gullibility! I must be the only one not known to have close friends. The blockheads and committee runners are bound to be suspicious of me. I am looking forward to having Miyo Yoshida resume her silent perch on the other side of our thin partition. In her sleeping breaths there is a rhythm I recognize as my own—faltering at just the same moments, without external stimuli; breaking stride at every incipient nightmare.

September 24, 1942. As I was saying, the camp director wants to see me. I ignored the first request. When the blockhead asks me about it, I tell him I forgot. The next appointment must be kept. The director is a generous man, but he is not to be trifled with. I decide to overplay my hand, to show contempt that way. I dress in the only suit I managed to bring with me, and decorate the lapels with every symbol of Japanese authority and allegiance I can muster: the pins awarded by the Japanese American Citizens League, the trade association ribbons, the honor society badges. No American flag, no symbol of obeisance for me. The director's office is at the southern end of the camp, guarded by the two tallest watchtowers, which were built by Japanese volunteers in March, soon after the exclusion order went out. Unlike our own tarpaper barracks, which let in sand and wind no matter how hard we try to cover the knotholes and gaps, the administrators' offices are sturdy buildings. Without knocking on the door, I enter and am greeted by the sight of several young Japanese girls typing away like mad—probably reports compiled by the anthropologists from Berkeley and Stanford who've been crawling over the place, or individual estimations of each of us: "So-and-so is more than ninety percent guaranteed of loyalty. His links to Japan are few, he hasn't left America since 1924, and he is not known to have made any pro-Japan statements to his neighbors or friends. A good candidate for early resettlement." My pride in my race and culture—whose rituals I haven't seriously observed since my early twenties— goes up several notches. This is despicable. Hiring the enemy to do the dirty work—the Japanese would never be so dis- honorable. Long-forgotten phrases to this effect, in literary Japanese, swim through my brain. Will these girls not stop typing and look at me? Pictures of Mr. Roosevelt and Mr. Stimson plaster the walls. In similar makeshift buildings the more militarist sorts are plotting annihilating revenge against Japan. I imagine the false camaraderie on military bases and compare it to our own sordid cheerfulness. "Won't you please step in, Mr. Hosokawa?" says the director himself, popping out of his office and clasping my hand. He is a squat, pale, almost hairless Midwesterner, with the unease of a Chicago boy in New York. His inner sanctum gives the appearance of a scholar's venerable study, with no sign of the actual work he is doing. I hear the click-clack of the typewriters working in unison, the drumbeat of my ego's death. Melodramatic? I could have built a theoretical case for the director wanting to recruit me as an informer—an *inu*, a traitorous dog the blockheads would warn their charges about, a marked man, subject to a beating outside the mess hall on some quiet Sunday afternoon, but I can see the strengths and weaknesses of my abilities in true light when the need arises.

September 25, 1942. A day later, I still wonder what made me soften toward the director. It was as though the symbols of Japanese confidence on my suit wilted at the sight of the unflappable man. I say unflappable, yes, because his unease, I soon figured out, is directed more at himself than at us internees. He is an efficient man, looking for the most direct way to get things done. I suspect this will be his downfall, but for the moment, the facility with which he speaks of the psychology of the Japanese prisoners he has been assigned on short notice to administer silences my rebellion. I understand he was never the first choice of the War Relocation Authority to direct Manzanar, but the men they preferred were already closely involved with the war effort. He knows how desperately we Japanese care about education, even in these cramped conditions, with no clear idea of how we will ever come out of this confinement. He knows that we Japanese would rather save face than admit humiliating mistakes. He knows that we Japanese hold the Constitution in higher respect than any Caucasian of comparable education and worth. He knows how uninterested we are in returning to Japan, even the Japanese-educated

Kibei, who are thought by their past gestures to have shown the most inclination to being loyal to Japan. He will use all these facts against us. Against me personally. "Mr. Hosokawa, you are an interesting case," he says, tapping his cigarette against the ashtray, after the preliminaries (health inquiries, the suggestion that I get a general checkup at the infirmary— "a must for a man of your age, over sixty, I presume") are out of the way. "In the beginning, we counted on you. You were one of the instigators of the Manzanar Cooperative. When others resigned themselves to doing without some of the necessities of life, which can be had so easily on the outside, you, with a few others, had a vision. You figured, why not tap into the savings of the Japanese, to build a cooperative venture? The co-op is the biggest success story of the camp so far, in my opinion. Of course, your interest in the enterprise declined precipitously once the idea was off the drawing board. You didn't even stand for election to the board of directors last month. Now it is run entirely by young Nisei. We needed a reliable Issei man of your impeccable credentials to take charge. Frankly, I'm disappointed. Mighty disappointed." At that moment, a gentle tap on the door announces a welcome interruption. It is one of the director's assistants, fresh from the Midwest (aren't they all, these administrators?), a big-boned Iowa blonde named Jane Thompson who, like the director, seems to have a fluid capacity to learn about all things Japanese. We had already heard her once in the open air, when she lectured the assembled ten thousand people (or as many as could make it) on the virtues of the American ideal of citizenship: "Remember, you are being tested, and it might not always be fair, but do not refuse the burden of responsibility. In some ways, it's like starting over. It's beginning with a clean slate. Look on the positive side." I felt alternate surges of attraction and revulsion. She was one of those Caucasian women I wanted to ravish on the spot, leaving no trace of her dignity. But a man of my weak physical drive (fantasy far outpaces actual event) was disturbed enough, when she picked me out of the audience to congratulate me on my entrepreneurial initiative, to crush any thoughts in her direction. I became much warmer to Miyo after that. Now here is Jane Thompson again, apparently not coincidentally either. "Hosokawa-san, so glad to see you. It has been a long time. I hope you are handling the cold well enough? It is difficult, there will be snow soon, so all things considered this is not such a bad time...Have you come to us with a new idea?" She rubs her hands as though in anticipation of some organizational breakthrough, and I can only mutter excuses. She stands for a while, talking about the great progress the schools are making—the Japanese volunteer teachers assisting the professionally trained Caucasian teachers are coming off excellently! "I hope to see you again soon, Hosokawa-san. They're showing *Casablanca* at the administrators' recreation hall next week. You are invited, if you care to come." When she leaves, the director makes a long speech about how he is against the whole idea of categorizing individuals' guilt. Either the race is guilty as charged, or not. "Don't tell me you can divine people's souls and identify potential, would-be traitors. Either the Japanese are loyal or they're not. I don't believe in spying into individuals' pasts to predict patterns for the future. If I were to listen to the bureaucrats in Washington, three-quarters of my time would be spent doing just that." He throws up his hands.

October 15, 1942. They have stopped making camouflage nets. Men are working in the fields, growing turnips and cabbage for our use, for the war effort, refertilizing the dried-up Owens Valley, in the sight of the snow-capped Sierra Nevadas, which look on in disbelief. Men who used to be lawyers and accountants—at least some of them—and men who owned the most productive farms up and down the West Coast, now work for twelve dollars a month, unless they're in a supervisory capacity, in which case they earn sixteen or nineteen dollars a month. There are no instances of rebellion, no disobedience, no attempts to run away, of course. Where would anyone run to? Men are busy planting flowers outside their barrack "homes." Men have built beds and drawers and cabinets and desks and tables and chairs from junk wood. Men have become carpenters who before had reservations about replacing light bulbs. Men have created, out of straw, many serviceable blankets per capita. Their wives show their pleasure in cooing voices after the evening meal, when something of the nostalgia for home is recovered, the dust and cold be damned. The radio plays Gershwin late in the day, and the children repeat their lessons in controlled voices. The co-op thrives as Sears and Penney's merchandise invades the pristine loneliness that was Manzanar in its early days. Men are building a rock garden with rare plants, a heart-stopping gazebo, and a pleasure pool with hideaway corners for flirting couples—the rock garden will have the most exotic plants procurable from Anaheim and San Diego, and chosen delegates will be allowed to travel back and forth between the camp and these cities. Men are listening more intently than ever to their block leaders, who want them to make up their minds once and for all: are they for Japan or are they for America? Men are singing in choirs, becoming converts to the Boy Scouts, closely following the war news, cheering every American advance in the Pacific. I am looked at with suspicion by all. People are talking to me less and less. If I keep this up a while longer, they will forget about me.

October 29, 1942. Miyo has been back in her room for a week. She pretends she is fine, hiding her paleness with makeup, but I can see she is losing her will. She can't afford to miss meals at the mess hall or the blockheads will be after her, but she eats very little. I save my share of apples and oranges and bananas, things I know she can keep down. "Miyo, we have to build you a new desk and a nice new chair so you can write comfortably," I tell her one evening. "If that makes you feel better," she says astutely. I have given her my record player, and we put on Haydn concertos, which I believe she has a taste for. She was a violin instructor for a short period after her marriage, before she had her son, who died of chronic bronchitis at a young age. Her husband had a fatal heart attack soon after. Through the shifting veils of the music, I perceive her intense loneliness. It is there as a talisman, as something by which she can live. "Miyo, people are beginning to be allowed to resettle. They can go to Chicago, New Jersey, Virginia, places where we might be able to live without suspicion and doubt. Would you want me to put in an application on your behalf with the camp director?" She has mentioned a nephew on the East Coast, but she says, "I'd be lost outside California." She laughs sheepishly. "I wouldn't know what to do. Would you, Hosokawa-san? Of course you would. You're a man of the world. I'm afraid I'm not so adventurous anymore." Her gnarled, thin hands are busy doing nothing in her lap. I wish she were preoccupied with knitting, anything to take her mind off her illness. It would not be polite for me to ask directly what her ailment is, but I found out from a nurse that it is a serious case of low blood pressure associated with general physical weakness. I worry about the coming months. The freezing wind is whipping against the tarpaper barracks, and the possibility of real winter, with the Sierra Nevadas looming like whitened monsters, is too frightening for us spoiled Californians to contemplate. My bones don't remember winter in Japan—so much of my life before eighteen remains only in rough, uneven patches. I remember Father and Mother and their reticent kindness; I do not remember as well the stultified Japanese landscape. I was a boy in Japan. I have been a man only in America. In those early days in Seattle, Caucasian girls would fall in love with me after only brief conversations. I had something of the roustabout in me, but couched in purely intellectual terms—dangerous, but safe at the same time. If Japan produced this mixture, I wouldn't know about it. I would say America crystallized the attitude. The last concerto has been over for some minutes. Miyo says, "Tell me, Hosokawa-san, when you evacuated, did you have time to dispose of your stuff?" Because she's asking, I know she must have been unable to take care of hers. "I was mad as hell," I reply. "I could have tried to strike bargains with greedy neighbors. Given away a piano worth many thousands of dollars for two hundred or less. My Studebaker for a hundred. Instead, I just gave things away. To all the bums on the streets of south San Francisco. At least they didn't pretend they were sorry." The rage that overcame me in those days, when I understood for the first time how attached I was to the undiluted American gospel of private property, returns in a brief glimmer, and I shift uneasily. I was cured of the anger when I spent a month at Tanforan Assembly Center, sleeping in a horse stall, taking showers where animals used to bathe, and eating food fit for cattle. I realized they wanted me to get angry, to lose my patience, so I stopped thinking of the past. "And you? What about your house? Your furniture?" I ask Miyo. She looks sad. "I trust my neighbors to look after it all. Till we return. They are a good couple. Good Christians. They knew my husband and respect him still." How does one console a Miyo Yoshida? I feel like a bumbling fool and soon leave. But the next afternoon I'm back at it, bleeding away, with well-intentioned stabs, whatever is left of our dignity. The more we talk about "what happened," the more we become what they want us to become. But I can't help it. Miyo is in and out of her room; she seems to pay return visits to the infirmary as though seeking old friends there.

November 12, 1942. We are told the man was shot because he was trying to run away. Run away where? Where on this vast continent can he hide? We are allowed to work in the fields without any fear that we will run away. All the time now, promising young men and women are being resettled at colleges in the Midwest and on the East Coast. Soon we will be allowed to serve in the army. The *Manzanar Free Press* can't write about the shooting. Not until passions have cooled. The man who was killed by the watchtower guard was old. He was probably trying to get his dog, which had wandered past the fence. The guard says he shouted at him twice to stop. The man just kept walking away, wouldn't listen. He was hard of hearing, almost deaf, some say. For days the air has been riotous. I keep waiting for an explosion of nerves in the mess hall. Even the latrines seem more hostile than before. Accusations back and forth of who's *inu*, who's trustworthy, who's loyal to Japan, to America, who fits into the Issei, Nisei, Kibei categories. The worst off are the mixed-race children. You see some of them in the mess hall, the shyest, loneliest of the bunch. The Japanese parent, who must be interned, has usually, but not always, been accompanied by the Caucasian parent. So we have some Caucasian inmates, usually women, in the mess halls. Who are they loyal to? Meanwhile, the flowers outside the barracks, the furniture inside, the shapeliness of the rock garden pond, these increase by the day, as do the *Manzanar Free Press*'s editorial exhortations to study hard, work hard, play by the rules, and reclaim American citizenship that way. There are some union types trying to stir trouble all the time: why are we being paid such pathetic wages for such high-standard work? The blockheads don't like the rabble-rousers. Soon there will be riots if the blockheads get too stern with the labor leaders. Reconciliation committees are sprouting up all over the place. So many Japanese factions to manage in this little city of ten thousand in the loneliest part of Owens Valley! I ought to be, by rights, on several of these committees. I am asked by one of the camp director's assistants to offer my services teaching American history to fifth-graders. I decline. I am asked to serve as liaison between older residents in my block and the camp director's office, one of the few Issei they want to have in this capacity, since the blockheads are almost all Nisei. I can take the concerns of people of my age straight to the camp director, bypassing the blockheads' often petty politics and excessive deliberations. I decline again. My own health seems to be fading. My bowel movements, for the first time in my life, have become irregular. The showers are too cold, and I avoid them as much as possible. I feel tired at odd times of day—for instance, soon after consuming the increasingly Japanese-style meals at the mess hall. I am giving away some of the furniture I made in the early days of camp, when it seemed important to keep busy. At last I take a trip to the rock garden on a day when many others are there. The atmosphere is as festive as the Fourth of July, as though people expected to be emancipated soon. Mr. Roosevelt, free us from this ignominy, restore to us our humanity! Ah yes, I can see the great man in his infinite wisdom listening, our father mercifully just toward all of us, able to hear our minutest whispers and needs. Miyo still won't talk about her husband or child. Letters come from her nephew in Philadelphia, but she doesn't comment on them. Her own letters are delayed because the camp administration censors them. I have written no letters to anyone on the outside. Some former business associates might feel sorry for me, and knowing who they are, I want no part of their sympathy.

December 1, 1942. I have not written about the larger part of my emotional life over these last months since the meeting with the camp director. It seems I suffer from the Japanese sense of shame after all. I have been a traitor, a collaborator with the enemy, the very *inu* the Nisei blockheads suspect me of being. When Jane Thompson asks me to see *Casablanca*, I do show up at the camp administrators' recreation hall. If you look respectable and old enough, you can go, though not every camp resident would have such smooth sailing. I go to see it not once but every day for a week, until she comes. Then she is quick to acknowledge me. "Hosokawa-san, would you care to have a drink? I really want to talk to you about ancient Japanese religious customs. Perhaps you can stay a bit?" I am full of hope and cheer, as in my adolescence, when the attraction of Caucasian women made me see the world in a rosy glow. I may have acted younger than my age with her, like a foolish kid who has no knowledge of the real basis of relations. She looks younger and more beautiful after our first drink. Abandoning my reserve of the preceding days, I start talking volubly, so much so that the recreation hall soon empties—perhaps the others feel a deferential embarrassment—and Jane and I are the only ones left. I don't let self-consciousness stop me even then. The more garrulous I become, the more Jane seems interested, and interesting. I don't know anything about the Shinto rituals she wants to talk about, so without being prompted I volunteer my opinion of the different degrees of capability and loyalty of the blockheads I have encountered and the people of high status known to me at Poston, Gila, Minidoka, Topaz, and other camps. If I have acquired one skill through years of business dealings, it is to make quick, accurate judgments of character. I may have been thought an unobservant, passive, quiescent resident, but I have been keeping my eyes and ears open since spring, and I spill it all out to Jane. "Very good, Hosokawa-san, very good." She tries to turn the conversation to a professor of Oriental religions I am supposed to have studied with at Berkeley in the days of the Red Scare, but I am reluctant to follow on that digression. I leave in a drunken stupor that evening, full of choking desire, unable to control my suddenly blooming libido. I am a dirty old man—not that Jane is very young herself. This is when Miyo is still in the infirmary. I have started leading a double life. I take every opportunity to see Jane, and opportunity these days is plentiful, let me tell you. After *Casablanca*, Jane has made it a practice to come to the movies at the administrators' recreation hall every evening. So have I. She holds her liquor well, like a Japanese woman, and we outdo each other in drinking whiskey. The more she drinks, the more emotionally steady she seems to become. "Hosokawa-san, do you know how easily one can forget one's surroundings? We could be at the faculty club in Ames, stealing time from our mates and families. We could be heading to the research libraries after all this...bloviating, soapboxing, haranguing, whatever you want to call it." Trying to make my five feet eight inches stretch as tall as I can against her six feet, I say, "I call it cross-cultural collaboration of a very high cerebral order," and laugh deliriously. The camp director once in a while drops in on our conversations, he too acting as though this were a faculty club at some idyllic Midwestern land-grant college: "I may not be here much longer, as I'm sure everyone has heard." The *Manzanar Free Press* has been speculating about it for weeks. It is reflected in the director's unwillingness to make long-term commitments to the camp's patterns of life. He is always tentative, as though biding his time. "Manzanar needs stable governance, above all," the newspaper pronounces, to the acclaim of the blockheads, and old and young chime in with approval. In my desperation to keep Jane interested, I have started making up stuff about blockheads and about which men are for and which against joining the military, although I am careful to keep my fabrications realistic enough. If pressed too hard for details, I defer by saying I need to be more sure. It has become intensely arousing to spend time with Jane this way. She is a dishonored faculty wife, alone and distraught, and I am her savior. The days go by quickly, and I no longer mind being woken up by the harsh bells at 6:45 a.m., because I can start plotting my conversational maneuvers. Once, when I don't go to the recreation hall, Jane is concerned enough to send someone to ask after me. It would be impossible to take a stroll with Jane around camp or through the rock garden, a place I used to dread—strict rules against public fraternizing between Caucasian administrators and Japanese residents apply. But the way Jane and I socialize doesn't count as fraternization. It is all done in the scholarly pursuit of research and knowledge. I wonder why she doesn't consider that being seen so often with her at the recreation hall would hurt my ability to be a useful informant. Perhaps she has never taken me seriously after all. Perhaps it is as much an act on her part as mine. I promise not to feel shame about what I am doing with her. I have stopped being pestered by the camp director's office about my lack of gainful employment. That seems to be a closed chapter.

December 15, 1942. Yesterday Miyo Yoshida died. Already weakened by low blood pressure, not to mention heatstrokes and the abscesses in her mouth that wouldn't be cured, she was attacked by pneumonia and this time couldn't hold up. She was delirious two nights ago, crying for her dead husband (so I'm informed by the Nakamuras, a family of six, who have been allotted the space opened up by Miyo's death and will become my immediate neighbors, crying children and all), but I, after having drunk too much with Jane, was deep asleep and never so much as stirred. I walk all day long in the cruel wind, which seems alternately hard and soft, as though unable to make up its mind. Mount Whitney, with its foreboding visage, seems more threatening than ever. I know there are Japanese working hard in the fields, producing not only all the food for our camp, but enough to supply the locals in this part of Owens Valley and to help feed the other camps as well. They weren't considered the most productive farmers on the West Coast for no reason. I envy them—for a brief moment. I look at myself through the eyes of the blockheads: a no-good, elitist bargainer who finagled his way out of work. Of course, there is a monthly charge for refusing to join the work corps, but I can easily afford it. The rest of them, even men older than me, are dying to join any kind of work project to prove their usefulness. Miyo was a good woman. The Owens Valley soil will receive her body without protest. In Japan there would have been weeks of quiet lamentation, a necessary change in attitude among her relatives and friends, whispers about the somnolent reality of death, which is both fearsome and tame. The infirmary wears a cheerful look when I finally make it there in the evening. A successful mass vaccination of children has been concluded. Doctors and nurses, Caucasians and Japanese, sport a look of accomplishment. Nowhere in the world are doctors mistrusted. "Miyo Yoshida, she died yesterday?" I say to the doctor who used to care for her. She is an ethereal Japanese spinster in her forties, never able to speak above a whisper. "Yes, I'm sorry, we couldn't do anything for her. Her body was too weak, after all the—the suffering. You can blame the heat and the dust, which I do, but when she came here she was already compromised. It was only a matter of time." As if that makes it all right. "What about the funeral?" I ask, wondering what kind of service they will give her, Christian or Japanese. She seemed to believe vaguely in the utility of all religions. "She has already been buried, I'm sorry you didn't know that." Already? So this is it? "I'm very sorry, Hosokawa-san, it's how she would have wanted it," the doctor says to appease me. "I know she was very fond of you. But under these circumstances, our emotions must be—must be restrained..." I leave the infirmary an old, broken man, aged by years, the haughty blood in my face gone. I know because I catch a look at myself in the bathroom mirror. I have to keep stopping to relieve myself. The walk back to my apartment takes forever. Always I hear the sounds of children reciting their lessons in English to patient fathers and mothers, families muttering homilies in Japanese (children and parents have reverted to speaking far more Japanese than they ever did on the outside), families enclosed in a bubble of safety, even in the desolation of the Owens Valley, at the foot of bald Mount Whitney. "There is a letter for you among her possessions," my new neighbors inform me, delivering a pristine white envelope with my name on it. It is written in the kind of beautiful Japanese script that few Nisei could produce. "Dear Hosokawa-san, I can't begin to tell you how much the pleasure of your company has meant. I remember when you first helped me fill the mattress with straw, I thought your hands moved too swiftly and expertly for someone who had never done manual work. You were equally good with all the household tasks you gallantly offered to do. An old woman like me, with no one on the outside, is blessed with incomparable moments of meditation. As I reflect on the past, I see only a continuity of effects, one linked to another, as though the chain of inevitability were unassailable—and it is, of course. Into this chain, whatever generosity you offered me fit perfectly. When you first visited at the infirmary, I was pleased by your boyish shyness. I hope no matter what happens you will always retain this quality..." It goes on for several pages. She admonishes me to take care of my health, never to lose faith in the future, and to encourage others to fight for their dignity. No mention of property, assets to dispose of, or messages to be conveyed, which is surprising because the letter reads very much like a last testament. I spend the night running to the latrines with uncontrollable diarrhea. At 6:45 this morning the entire family next door is up with the bells, clamoring to get a head start on the day.

December 28, 1942. For the first time, I'm reading about the progress of the war in the Pacific with some interest, almost cheering on our boys. Jane has left the camp for Washington—to do what, I am not informed. She always warned me that she might have to leave suddenly, but I never expected that there wouldn't be a final meeting. My shame knows no bounds. Is it something in the Japanese character after all, some desperate need to please and conform, that makes us such easy targets for Caucasians? These are my thoughts on my better days, of which there are fewer and fewer. I am a regular visitant to the infirmary. A lifetime of suspension of assorted symptoms—back and knee pains, bronchial allergies, headaches, gastrointestinal difficulties—seems to have collapsed overnight. If they give me pills for one ailment, another immediately flares up. The doctor who used to treat Miyo greets me with more than the usual concern. I hate being marked out like this. Last Sunday I went to my block leader and announced my intention to work. I want to be in the fields. He is very reluctant to send me there. They have more than enough agricultural workers. Besides, it's tough work, hardly suited for a man of my age and demeanor. "Wouldn't you consider some committee work, Hosokawa-san?" he asks politely. "There is so much to be done, now that we're looking at the possibility of choosing increasing numbers of candidates for resettlement. High school and college-aged kids need to have their paths smoothed as much as possible. Schools and colleges to be contacted, scholarships obtained where possible, living arrangements made, and all of it coordinated with Washington, every little step, every little move. Meticulous paperwork is what will make our lives easier, from here on out. Will you not help us with this, Hosokawa-san?" I retreat equivocally, unable to give him a promise. Later at night, as the family next door cheerfully discusses plans for tomorrow—they seem to be in competition to see who can work hardest under the most challenging conditions, a perfect democracy of labor—I try to imagine myself filling out reams of paperwork to please the WRA's every whim. "Once a Jap, always a Jap," as congressmen and generals have said. My neighbors talk about the New Year's celebrations, which are going to be Japanese-style this time. Yes, I can volunteer to help with those. The coldest wind of the year sweeps through the spaces between the boards. I am not one for winter.

CONSERVATION

Smuggling Antoine Watteau's *La Perspective* out of Boston's Museum of Art proved less of a problem for conservator Nancy Liu than finding an honorable enough place for it in her studio. In early September, her small Back Bay apartment was liable to suffer from New England heat spikes without much of a defense. But despite her faltering attempts to keep the temperature at the ideal fifty-five percent relative humidity, the painting would be better off without Pamela Harrington's predatory grab. Pamela, the head curator, rumored to be in danger of losing her job ever since the fiasco of the millennium eve celebrations five years ago, when the freely invited disenfranchised population of Roxbury and Dorchester made a mockery of museum etiquette, had lately begun to take an inordinate interest in the minutiae of conservation. The Watteau had long been safe from the eyes of ambitious curators; it maintained its brown melancholy, uninvitingly distant, except to the eyes of connoisseurs who appreciated the timeless beauties of the art of the *fêtes galantes*, enchanting depictions of the leisured class talking and flirting. To bring the Watteau back to the center of attention, as part of a proposed retrospective on the French Rococo period, Pamela wanted to perform such a radical restorative operation on it that it would all but erase its distinctiveness. Nancy would never let such desecration happen, even if it meant the end of her fledgling career in conservation.

There it sat now, packed in a glass box placed on the cart used by museums to minimize the vibration and shock to the precious paintings, in the corner of her untidy apartment. For a Chinese woman, she was peculiarly slothful; she explained it as overcompensation for the ritualistic, even obsessive, cleanliness conservators had to maintain at work: laboratories where all sorts of instruments that poked and prodded at microscopic levels, without causing damage, were indispensable. She set up the array of humidifiers she had smuggled out along with the painting in her Volvo station wagon—lucky for that; what would she have done with a little Toyota?—and her instrument clocked in close to the desired fifty-five percent. She calmly set about cleaning her apartment for the next couple of hours, as if it were disrespectful to her beloved Watteau to have disorder so close to the masterpiece. In one particularly frantic outburst of bleaching and scrubbing the kitchen sink, she paused to appreciate the irony of it: Watteau was well-known for the slovenliness of his painting methods, letting dirt mix in with his pigments, not letting his paintings dry enough, not pausing to take things one at a time, unlike a conscientious painter's habits. The presumed flaws in his paintings existed in large part because of these haphazard methods; but hadn't the painter known that? Why should a lowly latter-day conservator go against the master's intentions and try to cure the painting of its alleged defects by removing all hint of anomaly and conflict from the surface of the painting?

She relaxed in the armchair her mother had given her, the day she was admitted to the company of elite conservators after finishing her coursework at Delaware. An armchair? To alleviate the pain in her back from stooping over heat vacuum tables, she assumed. She grinned widely, and almost called Henry Hamilton, her on-and-off boyfriend of seven years— she suspected she was a closer friend to Henry, paragon of Wasp morality, than his current girlfriend—to relate her escapade of the afternoon. "Miss, do you need help putting that thing in your car?" O'Brien, the security guard, had yelled from the museum steps. She had let him help her. "The trolley too, Miss?" he said as he got it in somehow in the spacious brown Volvo, exactly the color of the decomposing varnish they were always removing assiduously from the surface of paintings. She suspected O'Brien was half in love with her, model of Oriental rectitude as she must appear to this burly, romantic Irishman, and she wasn't beyond taking advantage of such human weakness. "John," she said to him, "if Pamela wants to know..." "What, Miss?" O'Brien grinned foolishly. "Nothing, nothing," she said, dramatically encompassing the massive portico and columns of the museum in her glance, as if she might never again see them. What she had done was commit robbery, grand larceny, worthy of being sentenced to prison for whatever period of time the stern Suffolk County judge would deem appropriate. How long before Pamela, or more likely the museum director, Günter Hinckel, a hooligan with even more avant-garde notions than Pamela, called her, the ritual warning before the police showed up at her door? Minutes? Hours? Days?

Still sitting in front of the glass box stuffed with layers of brown paper and sealed to perfection, she started feeling sleepy; other ironies of the situation came to her mind, blocking fear for the moment. She had once, at Delaware, squealed on a fellow student for extracting from a painting more than the minimum microscopic sample for testing; that remained perhaps the most embarrassing moment of her life. She had had a crush on her teacher, Charles Heflin, a Byronesque man in his fifties, who was reputed to drink to excess but showed up at work a sober Schopenhauer, and it was her way of trying to please him. Other than her perennially estranged boyfriend Henry, who acted older than his age, she had always fallen for much older men, with whom there was no possible hope of fulfillment, certainly not physical consummation. The easy explanation was the early death of her father, a man who had been in the last stages of his postdoc at MIT when he got ran over by a speeding bus on Massachusetts Avenue, and whose death prompted her mother to miraculously let go of her heavy accent and become an expert at not betraying her foreign origins in matters of food and clothing. The first thing to go had been the Confucian altar her father loved; much else must have followed. Her father would have loved *La Perspective*'s pause of time and momentum. There was nothing more profound in it than a group of well-dressed eighteenth-century young men and women conversing, playing music, strolling, with a glimpse of Watteau's friend and patron Crozat's mansion in the background, and yet it hinted at the complex harmonics that was Western civilization at the time and remained so.

With her eye on the hygrometer's readings, she fell asleep, weakened by the exhaustion and escalating intrigue of the last few weeks—Pamela had interrogated her techniques in excruciating meeting after meeting (wasn't Nancy too conservative? Couldn't they afford a dash of innovation?) and her fellow conservators seemed to shun her company even in the inglorious cafeteria—only to be woken by a pounding on the door. The police! The police were here! She rose with a start; she would deny everything. But how could she? The painting was right here. She would plead temporary insanity. That only happened in the movies. Oh Lord, she sighed wearily, and covered her head with blankets to block out the noise, refusing to open the door, which was still being thumped loudly by someone's fists: "Open up! I know you're in there! Open up!" But wasn't that a voice she recognized?

It was Pamela's turn to be interrogated. An attractive brunette of fifty-five, with a desperate need to say the right word at the right time, she thought she still retained the verve of her twenties, when she was an ambitious assistant to successive directors at the museum. The current director, whom she faced now, failed to find her unique. She squirmed and wiggled. Forced to leave her office, she often felt ill at ease. More than a quarter century in the business, and she could still feel like an impostor in unaccustomed circles, as with this bully of a man, this unreconstructed Nazi, whose ideas of wholesale reevaluation were alien to the American Protestant temperament. You ignorant totalitarian, you Gestapo scientist, you Mengele of the hordes, she wanted to scream at him. Too bad Günter Hinckel wasn't a large man; too bad he wore wire-rimmed frames on his eminently professorial face; too bad he was perceived as a worthy enigma among the youngest of her colleagues at the museum, a penetrable Dalí or Johns; too bad he'd never committed himself in ways that could be held against him and lead to his downfall. Perhaps Günter's Olympian nearsightedness was the correct mode for these times. The man knew nothing of the future.

"I think, Pamela dear, we might reconsider last quarter's attendance figures—ahem—comparatively, rather than in isolation?" Günter adjusted his spectacles closer to his beady brown eyes and, a smirk spreading over his thin lips, reclined in his thousand-dollar leather chair.

He was definitely enjoying this; it must substitute for whatever passion and sympathy he was missing in his own life. Pamela wanted to despise him with a fury; the last director had been a gentleman Wasp, averse to impolitic decision-making.

"How do you mean?" Pamela had been trying to learn the technique of letting the inquisitor speak more than did the subject of torture.

"I mean—ahem—not to keep harping on our esteemed competitors, but look at what they've been able to do. MOMA—"

"Günter, we're not MOMA—"

"Maybe we should be more like them? I have this philosophy, you see." He took another sip of the infernal black coffee he seemed to drink all day long. Pamela could see a distorted reflection of herself in the window. Her ears seemed a steppe marauder's, her hair an Egyptian mummy's. "It's not just about quantity." Günter had penetrated American cultural insecurities well. He understood this was a nation of self-learners never quite sure about the value of what they had picked up here and there; thus their disproportionate respect for institutions, which had yet to truly fail them. "The quality of visitors is what we're really after. Consider this magnificent city. Its unparalleled universities, its world-class hospitals, its eons of revolutionary history, its layers upon layers of cultural complexity. Surely not enough of the students at the private academies are regular visitors? Surely we're missing legions among corporate contributors, folks otherwise content to fritter away their time in popular pursuits, in the absence of gentle prods from—from the guardians of culture."

Pamela sighed and leaned forward over Günter's desk, knowing she was exposing too much pale cleavage, to let her eyes glaze over the vast array of figures on attendance trends—comparatively speaking, of course, both within the institution and outside it—that he'd compiled with the help of the bean counters. It was the same old story. The museum wanted more traffic, but of "quality," as Günter bluntly put it. The desirable traffic in Boston now preferred to go to the movies, or at best the opera and the symphony. Museums seemed destined to become relics, she felt sure in her most depressed moments. People treated art more and more like any other possession; they felt no real connection. She heard out Günter's spiel. Next week, it would be a rant on altering the composition of exhibition space, even more in favor of the catchy impressionists and post-impressionists than was already the case. Or making it a livelier, more interactive experience for the casual visitor, getting him engaged in the hidden processes of art-making, rather than seeing it only as a finished product. Or pushing the curators to get out more in the community, the mountain walking to Muhammad since Muhammad refused to come to it. Thank heavens, his riffs on Berlin as the hothouse of revolutionary artistic development, especially after German unification, were obsolete. He had acquired American citizenship recently; he was intent on nothing less than the mass uplift of his adopted nation's cultural capital.

"Günter, I must get back to work."

What he thought she meant by it was poring over financial records, statistical analyses, budget projections. What she meant by it was spending a little quality time in the temporary galleries holding the restored Steens, Brueghels, and van Eycks, the Dutch and Flemish masters for whom she was developing a greater and greater affection as time went by. The lightness of their presentation of daily life was unmatched by later art. If she had her way, it would be the less appreciated among the Old Masters that would get pride of place in the museum's publicity efforts. There were individuals in New England who quietly held on to relatively unknown gems; more than ever, she was going to push the acquisitions people—she'd been at the museum long enough that she had some say in every department, regardless of her official portfolio, even becoming elevated to de facto director during the frequent transitions from one directorial regime to another—to work harder with the local aristocrats to bring these paintings to the light of day.

"Of course, you must return to work. By the way, I saw Nancy, our delightful young Asian conservator"—Günter had learned to his chagrin that the term "Oriental" was considered insulting in this part of the world—"load up her station wagon and leave in the early morning. A vacation, is it? Or some top-secret assignment to an exclusive collector?"

"I've no idea what you're talking about."

"Of course."

He must think she had something hidden up her sleeve; let him. She was in no mood to clarify.

She descended to the graveyard quietness of the conservation labs on the second floor instead of heading to her own office down the hall from Günter's on the little-frequented third floor. The whole project of cultural diffusion seemed a contradiction in terms when one was in the presence of Old World cynicism, like Günter's. But she must not despair.

She had managed, over the years, to surround herself with a brood of lively young female conservators and curators and buyers and developers. They ranged in age from twenty-five to forty, were as often as not brown or yellow or mixed—although black still seemed out of her reach, the elite schools not yet attracting this part of the population in significant enough numbers—and treated Pamela like a surrogate mother, or so she believed on her best days. It wasn't uncommon for

Pamela to spend the afternoon listening patiently to one of her young charges, perhaps to some tale of romantic woe that both knew would come to no good, but for the moment had to be treated as an ongoing drama with uncertain outcome. She wore welcoming pastels, pinks and mauves, as often as possible, to lighten the onerous atmosphere the museum had acquired through sheer weight of history, and she tried to speak in the young people's vocabulary, which determinedly shunned any reference to abstractions during off-hours and casual conversation. One of these pleasant afternoon comrades, Nancy Liu, a totally dedicated protégée, had lately been inclined to brood. This must not be allowed to go on for too long; Nancy's obsession with defending the decrepit state of the Watteau that had come under her care was markedly unhealthy. But Nancy would pull through. She had all of her race's sense of pragmatism, compromise, practicality. A most delightful companion, if a little eccentric; yes, she'd pull through all right.

    This woman, this jack-of-all-trades and master-of-none, Pamela Harrington, gave him the willies. Günter shuddered, letting the draft of wintriness pass over. She was one cold fish, with none of the continual coyness he'd come to expect from German women. Germans knew how to live for the senses; this Pamela, she was the paradigm of an America so out of touch with the sensual life that it had to find false value in passionless objects. Ah, what could you say? At least they paid well, when they weren't sure they had the expertise to judge on their own. He much preferred the new Americans, like that clever Asian girl, Nancy, always ready with a double entendre that both put down and built up the American

Dream. He only wished Nancy wouldn't always treat him like a harmless uncle; but that was something to be expected of young American women, all of them: their assumption of the radical innocence of the world, except when it came to their own bailiwick. Then they were like ferocious lions, defending their turf, the women especially. Was Fragonard—not to mention Lancret and Pater—really that deficient compared to Watteau? Nancy tended to get carried away with her assignments; it showed she lacked an inner life that could give her the balance she needed. What had happened to the famous yin and yang in her case?

He stepped to the window, which gave him a view of Huntington Avenue. Sometimes he thought the population of Boston was at least half under the age of twenty-one. Miniskirted girls and grunge-haired boys ignored the sexual insinuation in the air as they got on and off the T, correctly postured like wooden puppets. His head barely reached the middle bar of the window: Günter was a short man, and he'd had his difficulties with the most attractive of American women; it was an unconscious slight on their part, but it was palpable nevertheless. The directors before him had all been humongous men of the Wasp breed, their shoulders popping out of their black portraits, their giantness manifest in their heads and ears and chins. That short men compensated for their height with unrestrained libido or egotism was a canard. He could have had any woman at the museum in his three years here. He'd had none. In his dutiful letters to Stuttgart, where his aging mother and father continued to live in some imaginary world where good and evil fought to the bitter end, he presented himself as a humble scholar tolerated by the high and mighty in the art world.

And this wasn't far from the truth. Without degrees from Heidelberg or Munich, not to mention the glamorous institutes in Italy and Spain where the children of the rich and well-bred seemed to gravitate like proprietors toward their rightful heritage, Günter had nothing but sheer will to credit for his meteoric rise. Along the way—regretfully—he'd had to let go of a first wife, a good Bavarian country girl, who couldn't keep step with his ambition, and a second one who would have been ruinous for his social reputation. Now he found himself attracted mostly to women twenty or thirty years younger, but he couldn't act on his instincts; certainly not in America. But this childish, petulant, myopic country had its advantages. True, you had to resort to sensationalism to get their attention, but once you had it, it stayed there without flag, until the next big sensation came along. Therefore, you had to come up with sensation after sensation. The boys and girls sitting erect on the trolley, they were all but waiting for someone to whack them over the head with a two-by-four; Günter would oblige.

With the conservative board of overseers—no doubt they were already regretting their decision to bring in a rank outsider to take charge—breathing down his neck, he had no more than five years, at best, to see through his agenda. It was a high-risk strategy, but what was at stake for him personally? Nothing worse than an honorable exit, when the committees poking into every corner of his business finally put the pieces of the puzzle together about the real character of Herr Günter Hinckel. If he had his way, before he was shown the door, he would do his best to reframe the logic and purpose of the museum in America. The museum had to be made to come alive again, but without cheapening its appeal. Not for a moment did he buy into Pamela's cynicism—the core of her character, once you got to it—that the idea of the museum was dead. She was conservative, like all Americans. He had to oppose this defeatism with every ounce of his strength. He was a young sixty-two. He could easily stand up to the morally vacant Wasps channeling emptiness his way. No, he didn't have any "demons" in his closet; he wasn't a Faust in thrall to some Mephistopheles, as these Americans always assumed a man who spoke beyond the constraints of the immediate surely must be. He, Günter Hinckel, had nothing to hide.

Soon, the exhibition area would be altered to accommodate far more pictures in the same amount of space, leaning more toward the Old Masters, as the museum brought out of cold storage a number of underappreciated classics, dusted them off, and let them live and breathe again. When he came here, there had been no story line, no consistent narrative, informing the presentation; the idea had been to cave in to the passion of the moment, so that everywhere there was lack of proportion, discordance with the true importance of particular art works in historical terms. He had fixed some of that, and would finish the rest of the job. Pamela, of course, thought the resistance to any popular craze of the moment originated with her; he let her think that. For that matter, Pamela's fellow curators, both those with superior degrees and those without, liked to believe that every day one was born *ex nihilo*, that nothing had existed before the day's scribbles crawling across the blank slates of their minds.

The intercom buzzed, and he was told that a famous banker—someone with a newfound interest in art—was here to see him. The visitor would be a gold mine: investors in the early stages of their passion usually were. It was an unfortunate part of Günter's job. He didn't think his underlings recognized how hard he had to sweat to keep the money flowing at the levels it must to have all the good things they were always claiming as a matter of right.

The banker delivered a well-rehearsed discourse on the necessity of the museum in civilized society: without learning the lessons of the past, one was apt to repeat them, et cetera. Herr Hinckel listened raptly, never betraying his rising revulsion at the improper hands large amounts of money always seemed to end up in. A hefty check was written—and gratefully acknowledged, with Old World charm.

When the hammering on her door let up—she thought in the end there had been male and female voices imploring her to come out—Nancy unplugged her ears, emerged from hiding behind the thick covers on her futon, and came close to a decision.

Fear was the hobgoblin of little minds. She would take her case public. She would resign at a press conference, she would call on sympathetic columnists at the *Boston Globe*, she would recruit art critics and historians at the famous schools in the area to her cause; and they would be prompted to rally on her behalf, because it was David against Goliath, it was the little woman standing up against barbaric mutilation, against popular will run amok. *La Perspective* would become the Bamiyan Buddhas of modern New England; wasn't this part of the country supposed to be slavishly obedient to tradition? But all she'd seen in the conservation business was the opposite. They'd become like the nineteenth-century defilers of the Old Masters, who painted over objectionable parts, genitalia and whatever else offended Victorian taste, to make the works uniformly bland, and who encrusted every painting in existence with thick yellow varnish, to create an artificial glow that would later turn into brown muck all but hiding the vibrant colors that had often existed in the first place. Today, it was the same contempt for the artist, even if the conservator's aggressive intervention was couched in the pacifying jargon of *reversibility*.

She wished she had more allies in the museum itself; unfortunately, it seemed as if most of her colleagues took her for so inoffensive a creature that they didn't want to hang out with her more than absolutely necessary. The head curator, Pamela, a woman Nancy had always thought was more suited to the touchy-feely women's magazine world, seemed to perform the rituals of listening, rather than actually listen. The director, Günter, went out of his way to make comments calculated to bring high color to any self-respecting American woman's cheeks; yet she preferred this kind of hand-to-hand combat to the artless battle cries of the American-born women working at the museum: how so and so's Katy or Devin had started walking or talking, how the kindergarten teacher had all but declared the child an artistic genius, how the foresighted fund for college had acquired unstoppable momentum. Her own love of paintings as works of beauty to be revered, rather than objects to be treated by conservators with all the air of laboratory chemists or biologists, didn't sit well with her coworkers; she understood there was a perception of eccentricity about her, despite her conservative bearing and manner, that couldn't be overcome at any cost. Her going public wouldn't surprise them.

She set about unpacking the Watteau. It took her a good half hour, as she made sure that there was no more vibration and shock than was unavoidable. The slightest movement, after transportation in her station wagon with worn-out shock absorbers, was undesirable. The moment she removed the stuffings, she had to sit in rapture in front of Watteau's miracle. Tall, stooping trees, a young man playing a musical instrument to a woman listening in total absorption, a few more couples walking or sitting or conversing, and that was it; considerably less complicated than the *Pilgrimage to Cythera*, held at the Charlottenburg Palace, or others of

Watteau's *fêtes galantes*, which managed to load worlds of myth and legend in the apparently carefree assemblages of people of leisure. Nancy was an eighteenth-century person, no doubt about it, carried away by the possibilities of wit and humor as ends in themselves, not as means to vanquishing your partner.

And was there a doubt that anything except the most perfunctory swab over it, to clean the darkening varnish a bit, would be but detrimental to the hypnotic quality of time and age and senescence lending irony to the tableau of repose unfolded in *La Perspective*? In laboratory analyses, her fellow conservators—important paintings were first assigned to individual conservators, their recommendations reconciled in favor of the boldest, most technologically creative treatment plan—had gone so far as to advocate removing a section of overpaint which Nancy happened to believe was Watteau's own work, not a later addition; scrubbing out pigment and ground blemishes that she thought were imaginary, or integral parts of the painting as it had organically evolved over the centuries; and perhaps even relining the painting, after removing it from its present support; in short, doing everything imaginable to remove its dark allure and leave it a Happy Days Are Here Again lightweight conversation piece. The reason why she'd never seriously pursued painting was an excess of reverence on her part for the great masters; every avenue of expression seemed to lead to self-deception: hence, preservation as the modern antidote to the dead-end creativity had run into.

Evening came, and she spurned the thought of calling her mother, whose accounts of her ailing stomach and aching joints, learned to the last note of imitation from women of her age, would perhaps push Nancy to catatonic disgust with herself, for being the spawn of such a tiresomely repetitive woman. Civilization turned in 1963, the year JFK was assassinated, and people fell into a desperate spree of self-expression, usually of their dire physical and subterranean needs, from which region of pity they had yet to emerge. The police hadn't come so far; perhaps the theft hadn't been noticed. But she doubted that; some of her fellow conservators—spies? agents provocateurs? informers?—were in the habit of lingering near her section of the lab several times a day, asking her inane questions about minor techniques they ought to know well. What was the best solvent for removing disfigurations in such and such a painting? Did she have a secret formula for filler when the binding agents in the pigment were particularly cumbersome? Would she recommend straightening a warped panel by setting up a grid to hold it, or replacing it altogether? All these years later, she was never sure if these questions were mockeries of her seriousness, or if her fellow conservators were earnest to such a simple-minded extent. To spend too much time around these technicians, who gave no indication of a warm human spirit animating them, would destroy the life force in her.

The fading daylight was now at a point where it seemed the perfect accompaniment to the gloom within humor portended by *La Perspective*. Over the next hour, as the natural light declined further, she began to see the painting in all sorts of ways forbidden to her before. It struck her for the first time that paintings ought to be appreciated in their natural habitats for some period of time, then let go of, consigned to the mists of time and memory: a sacrilegious thought of the first order for someone in her vocation, the very antithesis of every professional value she was sworn to uphold. In the artificial, permanently stable light and radiance of the museum, *La Perspective* was an object among objects, constrained from speaking directly to the viewer. But what if you had it in your home or studio, if you woke up to it and slept to it, if you let it address your shifting moods and attitudes with its endlessly fluid reinterpretations of itself? Had Watteau not striven for precisely such ambiguity? Weren't his studiously careless methods entirely harmonious with the indefinable meaning of his work?

When it became dark, she searched out a candle, and sat absorbed in front of the flickering painting. Still, the police hadn't come. If it was to be her last night of freedom, she might as well spend it appreciating the only thing she loved.

She fell asleep around midnight.

First she dreamed of a rare visit by her neighbor, Mildred, a bony, silver-haired woman in her eighties, who chose to live on her own despite the invitations of her sons and daughters to stay in one of their many houses scattered over New England. Mildred would understand. She used to work for an art gallery in the forties and fifties, in the early days of her marriage; that was when she met all the interesting people she still ruminated about, from her finite store of memories. But the dream didn't unfold that way. Mildred was aghast at Nancy's daring: "You mean, you stole this precious painting from the museum! You stole it! You had no right!" Even when Nancy elaborated on how the removal of the old varnish, which had become integral to the painting itself, would be dangerous, how the picture had better be left in its dark, murky, melancholic state, or else the false bright colors and vibrancies that would suddenly appear would be a lie to Watteau's intent, Mildred kept saying: "You had no right!"

Then there was a visit by her cousin, Paul, old enough to be her uncle, a "landscape artist" who'd been in a struggle for sanity with his Puerto Rican wife for thirty years; the pair had met in the late disco years, and acted still as if the world hadn't moved beyond the selfish generational conflicts

of that era. Paul at first seemed to listen sympathetically—
"Explain again the difference between underpaint and
overpaint"—but soon his eyes became glassy, and he rose
to wave his hands in front of the uncovered *La Perspective*,
like one does in the movies to test if someone is really blind.
After a while, Paul said, "You'd better call your mother.
She'd know what to do." Paul knew that Nancy's mother
was useless in talking about moral dilemmas; she would
inevitably want to defer to the authorities.

When Nancy's unsatisfying visitors were gone,
the figures in the painting started to come alive, moving
like disjointed puppets and talking in a childish French,
addressing each other with exaggerated forms of politeness,
all the coquetry of a classical civilization at its peak. The
girl listening to the man playing the guitar hitched her
skirt up too high for modesty, and fingered her cleavage.
The man at the left, who had been pointing his outstretched
arm toward the edge of the painting, to somewhere beyond
it, kept shifting leftward until he was entirely out of the
picture, taking the woman whose arm he was holding along
with him. The couple in the center retreating toward the
glimpse of the mansion in the back passed the last of
the tall trees and disappeared from view altogether. One
of the girls sitting at the right started sobbing—or she
could have been laughing—and saying all sorts of accusing
things about, of all people, Monsieur Watteau himself, who
had dared to intrude himself into the unbroken tableau
of worshipful silence which, as soon as it was observed,
dissipated into nothingness. Then Nancy woke up with a
startling question ringing in her ear: "And aren't you an
intruding observer too?" It sounded like a familiar voice,
from apprenticeship days.

Bob Hoffman was a tired old man even when he was alive.

In 1959, he'd officially retired from the museum, after personally having restored nearly all of the museum's treatable paintings; when he ran out of paintings actively exhibited, he started extracting them from storage, systematically going over them one by one. He worked steadily, usually took no more than a week over each of them, and always chose the simplest procedures over fancier ones: spit instead of solvent, if he could help it, leaving things as untouched as possible, never getting carried away by abstract discussions about the restorer's role in reviving the original aesthetic qualities of the work, and other highfaluting talk of that nature. In fact, he stopped subscribing to the professional journals soon after the end of the war, when it became clear that there would be an influx of restless men and women, who would otherwise be fighting wars of ideology, into the genteel professions, and nothing could keep them out. He watched the construction of the first true conservation labs, the arrival of white-coated, dead-serious men and women who took charge of perfectly healthy paintings as though to resuscitate them from fatal illnesses, and who never smoked or drank or had time for real conversation. He knew then his time had passed. He kept hoping that the powers above him wouldn't notice how busily he was restoring every possible painting even in storage, carefully dating and noting his treatments, so that for some years at least no one would have an excuse to touch them. His life's work would eventually be wrecked, he knew that; empty hands needed the devil's work to occupy them.

He'd died in 1973, after having spent the worst years of his life, the last ones, mentoring and tutoring the hotshot young conservators with Ph.Ds, who seemed to make twenty people's work of one man's, his mind increasingly bordering on the hallucinatory, the murderous, the hysterical. His estranged wife didn't come to his funeral. Neither did his two sons, both homosexuals, who had illnesses of their own to contend with.

Since then, he'd been unable to leave the museum. Like bankers, everyone—the director and the chains of subdirectors, the curators and their legions of assistants, and the newfangled developers and fundraisers and financial analysts who inhabited their own floor, separate from the other life of the museum, their computer keyboards happily clicking away all day long, as if churning out romance novels or mysteries—everyone left at five sharp, with a tolerant air of camaraderie, shoulders being clapped and hands clasped, as if the barbaric enemy had been kept outside the gates for one more day. So he would have the whole place to himself. He didn't abuse his presence, reading people's private letters, for example, or rifling through their drawers. Not that these upright burghers claimed anything of intrigue to whet his appetite. Mostly he wandered the corridors, the spaces between one exhibition gallery and another, unable to decide where to spend the night: French Baroque or Early Netherlandish, Florentine Renaissance or late Victorian; the moderns he studiously stayed away from, even if in his restorative work he had been as attentive to the failing Picassos and Ernsts as to the Old Masters. It was excruciating to make up his mind, but on the occasions when he was able to enter an exhibition space, he would remain in raptures all night long, in awe at the delicacies of choice the artist had exercised. Nothing in any of the classics seemed alterable, not a brush stroke, not a pigment shade. He would almost stop breathing, so immersed did he become in the sublime grandeur of works that seemed to have been created out of time, out of place.

Then morning came, and the busy bee workers returned, their lab coats and business uniforms spruce and spry. The women had become more like men, and the men more like women. They spoke of similar concerns, in similar tones, in similar vocabulary. All the races pulled together now, all were agreed on the moral values worth holding—which allowed unprecedented barbarities to go on unchecked, since officially nothing untoward was sanctioned. Some of the younger workers considered themselves more conscientious, but this late-blooming rectitude was useless against the onrush of the apocalyptic descent into single-minded uniformity; it was like the worried child's assumption of angelic attitude to try to forestall inevitable parental divorce: it wouldn't work. If he cursed the unimaginative director, a Teuton who acted as if it were still the early thirties, the known world unexplored in its psychic dimensions from pole to pole, if he cursed the simple-minded head curator, a painfully self-conscious spinster for whom the museum was her sole refuge from total physical and psychological breakdown, it would do no good. The replacements would be even worse. So he said a blessing, on everything and everyone, and disappeared at daylight, swallowed into the space where the night trains made the last of their crunching, squealing sounds, and where the sky's redness at dawn bled into the blank blueness that we took for granted as the stable umbrella over us. It was a sort of peace.

Another funding crisis, stemming from the state legislature this time, quickly unified the splintering forces at the museum within the space of a brief morning. The Commonwealth's financial contribution, although fractional, was critical; despite the avalanche of private funds, its symbolic importance was incalculable. Now the talking heads in the state house were disparaging the museum's elitism; the greater the effort to bring the museum closer to the people, the more it seemed to disillusion its overseers. The word went around that Günter had called a meeting in the afternoon to "get in front of the issue," to devise a scheme of proactive initiative rather than be overwhelmed by the momentum of events. Everyone was invited to bring their most radical, untested, exploratory ideas to the table; nothing was off-limits. The only criterion was: does this fundamentally alter the perception game? Pettiness was to be put aside, and there would be a lot of shared pizza and doughnuts, working-class food that was the currency of greased bonhomie in such quarters.

Günter had had bad news overnight. His parents, in tandem, seemed to have taken a turn for the worse; the doctors at the sanatorium in Stuttgart now felt confident enough to pronounce them with not more than a few months to live. He would go to Germany for a month, leaving Pamela in charge; surely, she would seize the opportunity to be acting director yet again, after mumbling a few appropriate words of sympathy about his parents.

Despite his short height, he strode as magisterially as he could down the corridor to Pamela's open office: she never closed her door, even during private conferences. Upon leaving America, Günter would predictably be overwhelmed by a sense of defeat. Some critical mistake in deliberation had occurred along the line, and could never be corrected. Away from the scene, he would become angry at the philistines in America running the show, and his own complicity in granting them cultural legitimacy. Europe only had culture as its exclusive preserve; it must not be too generous sharing it.

"Ah, Günter, I'm happy to see you," Pamela said warmly as his stony figure emerged in the doorway. "Overnight, there have been some developments. I mean other than the legislature's inanities. We might have lost a conservator and—and—a precious painting."

She bit her lip, giving him the brief version of what she had learned so far about Nancy's disappearance, along with possibly the Watteau; the guard O'Brien had had some intriguing reports to offer. She ended lamely, leaving Günter to make the next move. He was in charge, after all. The impulsiveness of women these days left her stunned; in her time, women sweated and fretted over every little household chore; now their sense of entitlement drove them to extreme steps in the workplace, knowing that the judges and juries would always be willing to cut them slack. She was quite ready to bond with Günter, join him in casting some heretical aspersions on the generic fate of womankind. She didn't always have to take her own species' side.

But Günter deflated her rising victoriousness by waving away the Nancy fiasco—Pamela hoped it would be no more than that; God knew they didn't need another set of bad headlines—and quickly summarizing the situation with his parents.

"Of course, I'd be happy to take over—I mean, hold the fort," said Pamela, "as long as you—well, you just let me know what you want from me."

Günter said he knew he could count on her, and then all the tension went out of the meeting. For perhaps the first time, Günter was able to talk about Pamela's past and background, her way of life, without embarrassment. Pamela responded likewise, happy to detect a glimmer of friendship in this unlikely source. They kept out of the discussion all friction about the relative allocation of exhibition space to the masters versus the contemporaries, Günter declaring at one point: "Everything we've acquired has been after laborious evaluation. It's all worth exhibiting. Any random order would yield fantastic results." He instructed Pamela to take control of the meeting that afternoon, after pooling ideas from the staff all through the morning. "And don't forget, publicity, good publicity, is the key word." Then he said he would be going out for a long walk.

It was only after he had left that Pamela got a gnawing feeling in her stomach: how empty her life was, how devoid of incident, event! Could she really blame Nancy, that hapless Asian girl, burdened by heaven knew what weight of tradition, if indeed Nancy had taken the rash action it appeared she had? O'Brien was a flighty Irishman, prone to exaggeration. She would have to evaluate the case on its merits—if it had any merits. For once, could she try not to follow protocol to the precise T? Couldn't she take a truly independent course, free of what she was supposed to do in the circumstances? She was so dismayed by the emptiness of her vanity—what did her past thirty-five years in the work world amount to? Should she have married and led a domestic life, as had so many of her friends?—that she delegated the organization of the meeting to one of her underlings, someone who had recently made the transition from the corporate to the nonprofit world, and was bursting with the manic energy such people brought with them. A short trip to the conservation labs would have confirmed or dispelled the rumors about Nancy's disappearance, but Pamela declined to move. She was going to be sick; like Günter, she should leave the museum for a while, be anywhere but in these claustrophobic confines.

Meanwhile, Günter was spending exorbitantly over baubles—mere knicknacks, with no intrinsic worth—at the galleries on Newbury and Boylston Streets. He'd done the rounds early in his Boston tenure, but since then rarely visited; the ignorance of the dealers had left him stunned. Today, he was ready to forgive everyone. His parents were dying, and he was sure this was no false alarm. They could have raised him to have a more flexible sense of right and wrong, but they were Germans of a certain generation, and couldn't be blamed. Walking without plan, it occurred to him that it wasn't possible to lose one's way in this oldest and most haphazardly constructed of American cities. Now, wasn't that remarkable?

Nancy slept until two. Once the decision had been made, sometime in the dawn hours, she had one of the most peaceful sleeps of her life. When she woke—to the sound of heavy machinery about to bring down yet another structure across the bay in East Cambridge—she retained the glow of contentment that had come over her at some point after the end of her animated hallucinations. Everything she'd done in her life had been inevitable: she'd exerted the full force of reason, deliberated extensively, almost too much, before acting on any impulse, including this most uncharacteristic one of hers. She had too much faith in the system—how it dispensed justice, how it treated people who reasoned their way into action—to worry.

It took her less than fifteen minutes to pack the Watteau, another few minutes to get ready, and then she was loading her station wagon. "Where to?" she mumbled to herself in a semblance of hysteria, the ignition key already turning. "To the highest mountains of Vermont? The humidity there would be great. *La Perspective* would live forever!" Ah, what a fool she'd been! She was ready for any punishment. In her side mirror she saw old Mildred approaching, wielding her walking stick, which she didn't really need, like a weapon for argumentation. Nancy wouldn't be surprised if it had a hidden blade, to kill a mugger or robber. But Mildred, instead of cornering her to chat, squirreled toward the building's entrance, disappearing up the stairs. All right now, today, Nancy was going to do her mother proud!

She had trouble rolling the cart up the museum's service entrance. Where was O'Brien? She wouldn't know that Pamela had given him the day off, for fear he might blurt his story to gossipers. Hardly anyone seemed to pay attention to Nancy; some sweeping directive, in the form of a terse memorandum, must have issued forth from Günter's office. The Watteau was back where it belonged, minus the covers, in a matter of minutes. Nancy started writing a letter of explanation/resignation, then decided to confess in person. It would be healthier for her soul, leave her with more of a sense of closure. Again in the hallways, having ascended to the dreaded third floor, where there was nothing but strife and pain to expect, she thought she heard laughter, the laughter of an old, old man—or rather, the echo of laughter, as if it had been emitted long ago, but was ringing still. No, she had to remain sane.

"Pamela, I..." she began, then halted, as she found Pamela weeping with her head on the desk. "I'm sorry, I can come back another—"

"No, no, wait..." There were quick moves on both sides to resume normality, Pamela wiping the obvious tears that had made a mess of her makeup, and Nancy looking out the window for the duration. "Sit, sit, I've been expecting you. I mean, you've been missed. Well, where have you been?"

"Pamela, I..." Here was the moment of truth; her confession was serenely composed in her head; she would yield to any judgment her superiors rendered. Again, the laughter in the corridors, which she'd heard for as long as she'd been at the museum, chimed in an echo, filling Pamela's office with a levity and distance it didn't have before. "I wasn't feeling well," Nancy lied. "But I'm fine now. I'm really very sorry for taking off without permission. It won't happen again." She smiled, and was pleasantly surprised to see Pamela smiling back.

"Of course...we won't say any more of that then," said Pamela.

They had a girl-to-girl talk that went on until the meeting at four, when a bustling corporate type summoned them with the eagerness of a high-school cheerleader. Nancy and Pamela talked for once about the content of some of the art in the museum's possession, not just the politics of acquisition and display and restoration. Nancy asserted the superiority of Watteau over his later frivolous imitators, and they both agreed Günter would have to be made to see the error of his ways.

PROFESSION

Their first stop was the barber shop across from his condominium at the Towers on Madison's State Street. "Here he is at last! Give the boy his first American haircut," Professor Arthur Fishbach instructed his longtime barber. "Try to even out the chopped-off style. Jeez, do they use cleavers over there to cut hair?" Then, recalling his wife Lauren's advice not to convey frustration in front of his eleven-year-old Vietnamese adoptee, Nam Loc Nguyen, Arthur assumed his steadiest Buddhist countenance, spending the duration of the haircut softly rehearsing basic Vietnamese phrases from his ambitious guidebook. The boy sat still in the chair, sorrow clouding his tiny brown eyes, never wavering his glance from the cover of Arthur's book. The barber didn't have to question where the boy had come from, since Arthur had kept him apprised of every step of the adoption process, expertly conducted by Lauren, except for the actual pickup visit to Hanoi, which Arthur had managed alone. Arthur and Lauren had spent their entire careers at this university; all these decades, the barber and Arthur had colluded in a conspiracy of innuendo against Lauren's muddled intentions, without crossing the line into outright accusation. Now the boy, unambiguous evidence of Lauren's goodness, confused the issue. "You got yourself a good one," the barber told Arthur, brushing imaginary hair from the boy's shoulders.

Back on State Street, Arthur started walking slowly toward the capitol, instead of in the other direction toward the campus. It was Saturday morning, and the Farmers Market on the edges of the state house would be in full swing. It might be a comforting sight to the boy, Arthur thought, to witness so early in his American incarnation old-style haggling and peddling, men and women in impeccable Western clothes descending to the level of primitive market barbarians over mere cents. In the early years of their marriage, Arthur and Lauren, both ardent Kennedy supporters, had held up the prolific Kennedy family as models of procreative style: the world seemed innocent enough then to populate with as many children of one's own as possible. That was before the doctors discovered, early in the Johnson years, first Lauren's, and then Arthur's, incapacity to reproduce; the ready peace they had made with their inadequacy still seemed to him testament to their total love at the time.

"We're going to the market," Arthur said to the boy, who nodded sagely. The master closest to him at the orphanage by Hoàn Kiếm Lake in Hanoi's Old Quarter had said that Nam Loc was given to the shortest melancholy spells among any of his fellows. Arthur sure hoped that was true. Lauren was not one for tolerating dejection, even for acceptable reasons.

The town's constant air of festivity—and in early October, well before the grind of exams and papers, what other mood could dominate?—had irked him for long years, until it softened into a pleasant ache. The jugglers and musicians and tricksters had vanished with the hot days of summer; every young American was again in complete charge of his own moments of distraction and leisure. The bright, shiny smiles made him think slyly of how soon their possessors would grow old beyond rescue. In her moments of compassion, Lauren explained that Arthur was finessing his way into premature acceptance of his own mortality by belittling others. He missed the panhandlers, some of whom would resort to outright insults and curses, even when he gave them money; these were necessary disruptions in a town so happy, so convinced of its perch on the pinnacle of humanism. Nam Loc's eyes were still narrow and sleepy; if he took offense at so much easy merriment, so much casual display of affluence and generosity, he didn't yet express it in any revulsion on his face.

When Arthur was growing up on the North Side of Chicago, he'd pretended that the milkman really came to pass on secret messages to his mother, her work instructions for the day; in reality, she'd been a contented Hull House worker who shunned unnecessary mystery and complexity. Now, as Nam Loc gripped his hand tighter, Arthur wondered if the boy experienced State Street's effortless traffic in similar Sherlockian terms. Did he imagine spies and double-crossers everywhere? Arthur suppressed a chuckle: over his forty years of teaching sociology, graduate students had plunged to somewhere around the level of the best high-school students of his own generation; they gave the appearance of being in class only as a hobby, while pursuing more dastardly designs as their core activity. The most radical-sounding manifesto became in the new students' hands a platitude to get by between ups and downs in private life. There were no more real wars; Vietnam was the last one. Why couldn't his charges see that? The world had reached an acceptable steady state, despite occasional conspiratorial moments; this was unlikely to change. Arthur's generation had become so efficient at managing its own guilt that future protest had become futile.

They should have driven to Ho Chi Minh City in the south first, before flying out of Vietnam; then Nam Loc could have seen that frenetic activity in the service of nothing wasn't just an American innovation. Nam Loc's father had been a schoolteacher, his mother a nurse; probably eminently middle-class Vietnamese, and nationalists too. What would they have made of the avant-garde American female professor's gesture—for it had been Lauren's idea to adopt a Vietnamese child—thirty years late in the coming?

This morning, after a long bath and a full breakfast, Nam Loc had conveyed in his rudimentary English that he wanted to forget his past, his homeland, his whole previous life, and start with a fresh slate. It had been an astounding statement. Where had he learned such a complex and mature thought? Had his master at the Hanoi orphanage, where Nam Loc had managed to thrive for two years after his parents died, trained him to say this to his new guardians? Lauren would know what to make of this near-Gothic eruption. Although nominally a professor in the English department, where in the affluent sixties she had held forth on the silences of the female-authored Victorian novel, Lauren was all over the place now: pulp fiction, Hollywood, sitcoms, billboards, and internet chat rooms. In the age of cultural studies and theory, it was what one did to maintain currency.

Lauren's newest passion was the presumed desecration of the vanishing female body in Haruki Murakami's novels. When her star graduate student, a woman with the looks of a model who Lauren said reminded her of her own impetuous youth, committed suicide last semester, Lauren went into a frenzy of output that yielded a *Times Sunday Magazine* front cover article on corpulence as a defense mechanism turned inward under late capitalism's severe regime of discipline. True, but couldn't it be as simple as some people just eating too much and getting fat? Arthur's "common sense"—as he unfashionably called it—made no headlines these days, was directly responsible for declining enrollment in his classes, while Lauren was the academic star in the family: exactly the opposite of the situation at the start of their careers. Arthur no longer felt that the institutions responsible for integrating and assimilating average people were as oppressive as the popular thinkers of the fifties and sixties had presumed. While desirable female colleagues at best only tolerated Arthur as an eccentric past his prime, so many male colleagues crowded into Lauren's personal space that Arthur had to try to stop obsessing about their evil intent toward his still petite and pretty wife. Maybe when they performed Marxist hermeneutics on the Mexican restaurant's menu, they weren't acting from romantic motivation; maybe they were as boring as he took them to be on the surface.

On Johnson Street, a music store, which sold used tapes and CDs side by side with new ones, seemed to hold Nam Loc's attention. Arthur said, "Want to go in?" and when the boy smiled with crooked teeth—the braces wouldn't have to wait long, if he knew Lauren—they found themselves immersed in a small, overheated room. A disinterested attendant with long, dirty hair waved at Nam Loc. The rap music conveyed jarring protest against women and cops. "You like this?" Arthur asked Nam Loc, and wasn't surprised when the boy broke into a rare, genuine grin. This didn't mean he couldn't yet be turned into a world-famous mathematician or physicist, under the high-powered, accelerated guidance of two of Madison's most able professors working closely with him, day and night. The lost years at the orphanage could be made up. Nam Loc folded his clothes neatly every time he discarded an outfit. He hadn't yet spilled a drop of anything. He bowed good morning and good night. He ate oatmeal and other food "good for him" without complaint. Arthur was convinced all this suggested not a naturally conformist personality but one trained to smooth out unnecessary friction. Now Nam Loc was swaying his head to the rapper's escalating lament about police brutality. The attendant seemed to have gone to sleep. "Let's go then," Arthur said, and as quickly as if he'd been in a dream, Nam Loc surrendered and stopped moving his head back and forth.

In the week he'd been in America, Nam Loc had seemed to warm up to Lauren more than he had to Arthur. Arthur tried to be mature about it. Sure, he'd been the one to make the dreary trip to Hanoi, but whereas his own demeanor was heavy and dragging, Lauren's was light and swift. How could a growing boy not respond to Lauren's aura of benign neutrality? Lauren readily admitted she wasn't exactly *motherly*, but she did perform the de facto functions of motherhood, catering to necessary needs without caving in to them, for her legions of fans and followers—so why couldn't she do the same for this innocent boy? The public school teachers in Madison were used to dealing with issues of language and cultural transition; Lauren knew, despite her critique of the devouring ways of late capitalism, when to step aside and let established institutions do their job. She would be fine. The boy would be fine.

They were waiting among a swarm of cheerful undergraduates in bright clothes at the light at State and Dayton. "Well hello, if it isn't the international man of mystery! You've been to *Hanoi*, Arthur? Oh my, what a cute boy." Gretchen Tolliver, blonde, buxom, and distinctly Southern despite having lived in the north since her college days, bent to ruffle Nam Loc's newly shorn hair, and to kiss him on his cheeks with the enthusiasm of a Victorian governess in love with her brutal master's neglected offspring. Her massive bosom rested on the poor boy's head.

"You heard then," Arthur said.

"*Everyone* has," Gretchen said, unbending. "It's awfully noble of you, Arthur."

Arthur didn't see the nobility in it; weren't all voluntary acts ultimately selfish, or at least pragmatic? Why had grown-ups who ought to know better suddenly adopted the language of romanticism and martyrdom? Gretchen was in Lauren's department, and taught Chaucer. She too was a Madison lifer. In the early seventies, when Arthur had come closer to infidelity than at any other time, Gretchen had seemed to him the very antithesis of the Connecticut old-money aloofness Lauren could easily slide into. Gretchen could consume whiskey like a World War I soldier, while uttering stern imprecations against the high culture figures around campus. He'd sat in on her class once, in the late Nixon years, and was motivated enough to reread all of Chaucer. Lately, Gretchen too wrote papers in the mystical argot of Cixous and Kristeva, poor Chaucer's invention of language but an afterthought to whatever unintentional havoc he'd wrought on women's bodies through all-too-masterful manipulation of signs and codes. That is, if Chaucer could even be said to be a discrete author in the first place, rather than merely the intertextual expression of the zeitgeist of his times. At least Lauren hadn't started off acting in the lifelong role of untouchable debutante, and jumped on the theory bandwagon only when it became professionally suicidal not to do so.

A tear seemed to roll down Gretchen's cheek; her inability to find a *real* gentleman to sire her children had long ago ceased to be a source of concern, or even amusement, among her colleagues. It was what she had chosen to do; without compromise, there was no family.

"We don't see each other enough, Arthur. Here"—she started scribbling on the back of her visiting card—"I've moved to a new place in Shorewood Hills. Come to dinner with the boy, and Lauren, any night."

"Sure. I'll ask Lauren. His name's Nam Loc, by the way."

"Nam Loc. How pretty! Oh, he's adorable!" Gretchen again smothered his head with her vast chest. She expressed a desire to visit Southeast Asia; Arthur said there was nothing to be seen there that couldn't be experienced in rural Indiana in the middle of winter: Hanoi had given him the impression of being a permanent ghost town, having fought history to a draw.

"Oh Arthur, you're ever so much the romantic!"

"No, I never was, Gretchen."

Gretchen would have started a long discussion about the difficulties of adoption in third world countries, but Arthur determinedly looked at his watch and lied that he had to meet Lauren for lunch at the University Club in about an hour, after doing some necessary shopping for the day. He'd had no intention of bothering Lauren on a busy conference day, but why not? She would be pleased to see Arthur and Nam Loc—dare he say, father and son?—extracting the maximum from a Saturday morning in the most livable city in America.

"About Lauren—Arthur, I'd like to speak to you—soon. I'm worried about her." No doubt she wanted to exercise the absurd rumors that so many in Humanities were massaging: that Lauren's unpredictable bursts of rage, her unknowably vicious putdowns of luminaries, were somehow related to a neurological disorder that had better be investigated. Lauren was fiercely resistant to modern doctors, whom she thought of as executors of a diseased gender-based separation between the utilitarian and the ideal, the Cartesian duality gone haywire. Gretchen was wrong about the state of Lauren's health, even if she was the colleague least likely to be motivated by envy. It was called growing old, entering the charmless silent zone long past menopause when approachable figures from the past bunched together into constituents of myths and fairy tales, and had to be either hated or loved. Unpredictability followed.

"Soon, Gretchen, soon."

"Okay, then. Bundle him up more next time for such a cold day." Gretchen was pointing at Nam Loc's jacket. Yes, it wasn't very thick. But Hanoi must have got cold enough. Nam Loc was supposed to have stayed inside too much. The usual way of learning English was to catch its rhythms from television shows; Nam Loc had sweated over grammar books and dictionaries for two years. He was theoretically a "boat person" who'd never seen a boat, of *that* kind, up close, which didn't make him any less a boat person. There, Arthur was indulging in essentialist categorization—or was it binary opposition?—as Lauren would have it. But then, why not, like the others, appropriate a derogatory term, and vaporize its offensiveness away?

They moved up State Street. He was glad nothing physical had ever happened with Gretchen; where would his life be now if it had? Lauren, like all educated feminists, was more possessive of the male than untrained housewives caught up in the allure of detergent and bug spray. Lauren would have been unforgiving; she would have left him. Early on, he used to congratulate himself, on days when Lauren froze him out of human consideration, that she constantly motivated him to reach for the stars, to enter realms of scholarly thought he'd have been too abashed to go near, but for her unrelenting pressure. "Why can't you be the department chair in five years?" she'd asked him in 1965, when the nightmares of bureaucracy had not yet become real. "Why can't I? Because I'm the humble son of a small-time doctor, who never so much as posted his awards on the walls." And she would playfully kick him in the back, and they would roll in lovemaking: Lauren was never so passionate as when she planned for the future.

Ah, the charming Farmers Market was at hand: out-of-season smokebush and honeysuckle, asparagus and zucchini, strawberries and cranberries, all that was primary and tropical and indispensable was to be had here, everything that in other countries at this time of the year would be unavailable, or too expensive, or simply unheard of, all at bargain prices, mere fractions of what could be had at the conglomerate grocery stores. The vendors created a civilized form of bedlam. Under clean white canopies, buyers and sellers talked about suppressed hernias and overachieving offspring. Lauren never came; neither did most university students. They preferred their organic food in the safety of modern supermarkets.

Over by the giant green grapes, bent double and propped by his equally decrepit wife, was old Charlie Wilson, once Arthur's foremost nemesis in the sociology department, twenty years his senior and argumentative like hell about every attempt of Arthur's in the sixties and seventies to introduce relevance into the classroom, some acknowledgment that a civil rights and women's movement was raging in the country. "Mark my words, Arthur. No one will read Marcuse twenty years from now—not to mention C. Wright Mills. The classics, my boy, the classics. Better stick to Weber." Charlie had been right. Arthur saw other dinosaurs from the humanities and social sciences coasting around the market; very few from the hard sciences visited the spectacle. He knew everybody so well that he had a free pass to acknowledge only when and how he wanted.

"This is like Hanoi?" Arthur probed Nam Loc, hoping to see signs of recognition in his eyes. Nam Loc nodded doubtfully, extending his small hands deeper into his pockets.

Of course, there would have to be violently disturbing smells, of discarded fish heads and shrimp shells, and rotting mangosteen and rambutan, and negotiations over prices blustery enough to equal mini-wars, for it to really feel like home. Some years from now, when Nam Loc was old enough, perhaps they could talk about how the poor boy and his parents had got along; they must have been, to use a contemporary usage Arthur derided, excellent "role models," for Nam Loc to be so studious and disciplined. Nam Loc's parents had died not on land, but on water, their pleasure boat having capsized in the South China Sea; they had been too bourgeois to be excellent swimmers. The master at the orphanage had translated every word of the newspaper article where the gory incident had been related. Arthur had tried to relay to Lauren over the phone everything of it that he remembered, but she didn't want to know. It would bias how she saw Nam Loc; the boy wasn't to be objectified as a tragic figure.

"Farm fresh fruit and vegetables," he said to Nam Loc. "Hard to get in America. Pick whatever you want. What do you like?"

Nam Loc looked uncomprehending, and Arthur started miming eating gestures, feeling silly.

"Professor *Fish*bach? Oh my God, it's you? I almost didn't recognize you outside class? It's so lively here, isn't it? So natural—so—so *pastoral*. Oh hello?" The undergraduate accosting them shook hands with Nam Loc, who'd started caressing a precarious mound of peaches, as if unnerved by their glossy smoothness.

It was Christine Marshall, from his introductory core class, which held seven hundred students, each of whom expected him to remember their name and obscure Midwestern place of origin. In Christine's case, he did remember. From St. Paul, she was the daughter of a onetime colleague, an able documentarian of the Civil War, which she thought gave her extra privileges with Arthur. She'd already proposed an independent study project for next semester on early consciousness-raising groups in the upper Midwest. She was blonde and fit and rosy and happy, like all of them now. How long would he be compelled to explain to everyone who the boy was, why he was with him? "My son, Nam Loc," said Arthur. The word was difficult to utter; at the peak of his academic career, when his journal articles were beginning to find an audience, he'd thought the wave of freshmen each year were his true children. "My son," he repeated. "Freshly arrived in America, doesn't speak much English yet, so be warned about using your poststructuralist jargon with him." He smiled weakly.

"Oh don't kid, please. He's adorable? Anyway, I just wanted to tell you I *loved* your wife's lecture the other night? Did you know two hundred people came?"

"Remind me…"

"On the unintended transgressive consequences of corporate communication manuals? Using *Madison* examples!"

Of course, using the *local* always made a pursuit more valid. The last public lecture Arthur had given was on the eve of the 1984 election, titled "The Choice Among Non-Choices: Democracy in the Age of Media." Almost no one had come.

"I'm sorry, I was in Hanoi then. Picking up my son."

Arthur still choked over the word. Even if he hadn't been out of the country, there was a good chance he'd have missed the small blip in Lauren's ever-rising chart of notoriety. Since the early eighties, Lauren had lived in her own apartment on the western side of campus, with a close view of Lake Mendota. They had weeknight dinners in their own places, and usually came together by assignation on Friday and Saturday nights. Lauren said the move to her own place had dramatically escalated her productivity; it had nothing to do with Arthur, it was her own deficiency of concentration. Certainly, she had been more productive under this setup. The predictable rumors about the oddity of the living arrangements, given Lauren's ferocious feminism, had had no staying power.

Arthur tried to describe Hanoi's dreariness to Christine: the shabby wall-sized posters of faded communist leaders, the anti-imperialist overhang which the south of the country was doing its best to forget, the ghoulish shame over corruption which was worse than its transparent acknowledgment in other third world countries. But how much could Christine understand? Already her eyes were darting back and forth, as if in search of other fresh faces her own age.

"We'll talk soon about your independent study project," Arthur said.

"Oh right, right. See you then."

She was gone. He must have bored her.

They ended up buying apples, Nam Loc's favorite fruit. "You get them all year long in America, every kind, red and green and yellow, in every store. You've made a safe choice, my boy."

He meant to sidestep the capitol and head straight to Lake Monona—there was still an hour to go before Lauren could reasonably be surprised for lunch—but changed his mind. "Heck, why not! My boy, into the big white house. This is how *we* run government." Minus sensation, he thought.

Nam Loc seemed more interested in the immobility of the speechless guards than in adoring the shiny black busts of Wisconsin visionaries and progressives, lining the halls like so many nods of affinity with the guests. Confronting the larger-than-life statue of "Fighting Bob" La Follette, dominating the rotunda, Arthur wished he had the language to explain to Nam Loc how significant the unwavering old liberal had been to his own sense of vocation. One day soon, one day. Arthur would be seventy-five when Nam Loc was twenty. He saw Nam Loc focused on a group of kids—blond and happy, half his age—and on the way the parents themselves seemed their kids' age, in innocence, lack of guile. As abruptly as he seemed to have been energized, Nam Loc lost curiosity, questioningly looking at Arthur. "You want to see Lauren? It's time, yes. I think we can safely go." The bag of apples they'd bought weighed down the pocket of Arthur's trench coat. He tried not to mind it.

In just an hour the morning's festive shopping mood on State Street seemed to have been replaced by grumpy lunchtime protest. Tromping back toward campus—he would feel stupid asking Nam Loc if it ever snowed in Hanoi, to anticipate his eventual response to Madison's true colors—he felt the aggressive extremities of underemployed graduate students and adjunct faculty members intruding into the charmed circle between would-be father and son. It was as if the hands pushing forth unfilled petitions and takeaway decals were resentful of the boy and him. "We have to rush," he said to Nam Loc's mystification.

Just before Park Street they ran into one of Arthur's former graduate students, Miles, who had dropped out a couple of years ago and never been officially heard from again. Miles had been part of a jazz band—or so he claimed—on the West Coast, not to mention having done other "dirty work," including, if you were to believe him, ditch digging. Was that even an occupation anymore? Miles had always been awkward in class, as if trying to hide his worldly knowledge from his more genteel classmates, afraid that his wised-up interpretation of theory would give away his excess of experience. Arthur had grown fond of him, but kept his disappearance secret from Lauren, whose attitude toward such loss of talent invariably was: "If they can't take the heat, let them get out of the kitchen." Miles had been spotted now and then in town; he seemed to have become part of the permanent antiwar movement. This time around, it *would* be a lifetime job. "Miles!" Arthur had decided to finally confront him, addressing his dreadlocks and grimy open collar more than his moony gray eyes. "Professor!" Miles said without a hint of recognition, as if addressing all the generic professors of the world, those who had done him in and those who were yet to. Arthur moved on.

Protest was without meaning anyway. It had none of the life-and-death value it used to have during Vietnam. It was now entirely a vicarious operation. None of these nice kids was going to suffer or die because of our policies. It meant nothing. "Don't ever get caught up in such foolishness, my boy!" he addressed Nam Loc, who dutifully nodded. Arthur had tried not to think about the inevitable ribbing that was bound to come Nam Loc's way, even in the rarefied Madison Metropolitan School District, for his odd accent, his exaggerated manners, his stiff obedience. On the street he looked physically like any other Vietnamese boy who might have been born and bred in Oshkosh or Eau Claire. But inside he was all different, his soul and mind were different. When exactly would he become an American boy? How much was it Arthur's personal job to worry about such imponderables on Nam Loc's behalf?

They were at the grand staircase of the University Club now, welcomed by the solid pillars, the walls covered with irrepressible ivy. When Arthur and Lauren first came to Madison, the club was attended only by old fogeys, fossils past their expiration date; now the most ambitious among the young aspired to hobnob here, to catch a kind word or two from colleagues with power and influence.

The warmth inside the University Club was positively blazing. "Here's where they plan the fate of the world," he whispered to Nam Loc, as Arthur was joyfully greeted by the receptionist, the manager, and one of the master chef's European deputies, as if only Arthur's presence had been missing from the serene occasion.

"Are you here for the thought or the food?" the manager repeated his old joke.

"I thought the two might go together—for once," Arthur replied as usual, and they laughed.

"Lovely boy. I heard," the manager said. "But isn't he cold?"

The one-day conference—geared toward younger faculty members at the campus, and to those at other research universities in Wisconsin—was called "Welcoming the Twenty-First Century: Rehabilitative Discourse in the Era of Diminished Expectations." Outsourcing, globalization, deindustrialization, militarization, the end of the welfare state, the evisceration of privacy, all seemed to be taken as ineluctable. The only questions, judging by the program notes, were *How do we still get along with each other, How do we talk amongst ourselves so that the least fortunate don't feel deprived and left alone?* Arthur had to remind himself that Lauren was trained as a literary critic; when was the last time she'd done any criticism?

They slipped into the back of the crowded meeting room to catch the end of Lauren's speech. There she was, holding everyone's attention, with her charisma and passion!

His Lauren, petite, indecomposable, untouched by the debilities of age, a tight bundle of warmth and energy and empathy, with a prodigious memory for every nuance of debate and scholarship, and the ability to finesse seemingly opposing points of view into a fluid conglomeration of reconcilable ideas. She looked gorgeous as always, her shiny light brown hair resting on her shoulders, the glinting gold of her earrings like tiny exclamation marks to the perfection of her symmetrical face—

blue eyes, thin nose, high cheekbones all in place, unwilling to muddy or wrinkle or jiggle or sag past the age of sixty. Why, she looked twenty years younger! He could imagine any number of younger colleagues—that smart-ass Yale deconstructionist Terry Simes, for one—lusting for her, over their younger actual mates, who probably had little to say accept assent and mumble, if they weren't in the academic profession themselves. She wore a gray suit that did nothing to hide her femininity. Arthur almost tripped over a wire as he seated himself and Nam Loc. Lauren gave him a sympathetic look from the podium.

He was glad Lauren had never been one of those feminists whose ideology seemed to intensify in correlation to the degradation of their looks. But perhaps this was the new way. To have any influence, you must look good. He thought with pride of the enviable pair they had always made: Arthur, tall and graceful, ambassadorial in presence, still with a full head of dark hair, not yet gone leathery or rubbery in his skin despite years of outdoor activity, matched with his ever-petite Lauren, smelling of precious orchids and cold spring rain. That was how they'd arrived at this campus, Lauren excited by the hothouse atmosphere of it all, which she would claim—pinned down under Arthur on warm fall nights and blissfully sanguine about the prospect of decades of harmonious sex—meant all the more because of her talented companion. Did she still think of him that way? Twice in their married life, when she was tempted to cheat, Lauren had done the honorable Madison thing, and told Arthur of her enticement, complete with the name of the offending male, before she could fall into the trap. "Gorgeous, my boy, isn't she?" he whispered to Nam Loc, and then worried that he shouldn't have passed such a remark about Nam Loc's "mother."

"In short, it isn't government that has or ever did have the power to make or break the stability or coherence of our chosen lifestyles, or shall we say, the glory of our ornery corrosion, the gestative aesthetic wherein we stew and mold and fester, like embryos in a womb, like worms—or is that too gritty a trope?—in a cocoon, sensing our eventual climax, our emergence in a world half welcoming, half suspicious, but never quite sure of the final outcome, the ultimate shape our selves will assume upon confronting the rest of creation: *Here I am, world, see me and acknowledge me and love me, if you will, but if you don't, well, I'll still find communities of affinity and solace, I'll make my way, so if it's the same to you, would you mind making room for me?* There's that little space at the head of the room I'd like to sidle up to—please. That's the attitude. Attitude is what it's going to take. Now, *how* that translates into the pedagogy of the—shall we say?—formerly imperializing gaze..." She'd left theory home; she was addressing the disaffected masses.

Arthur didn't mean to, but the room was too warm, and he dozed off. He must have snored, because he found the shriveled woman next to him violently pinching his upper arm, as he awoke to sounds of enthusiastic claps greeting the end of Lauren's talk, a young male colleague or two in the front even getting up and yelling "Bravo!" and the manager of the club appearing at the doorway to announce "Lunch!" while Nam Loc seemed embarrassed by Arthur's inability to keep awake. Arthur loudly cleared his throat, feigning that he had been meditating instead of sleeping.

"Arthur." His wife was with him, warmly kissing him on the cheeks, European style. "Oh Arthur, you look wet as a noodle, so cold, so chilled. You have any idea how pink your face is?" He was gratified that she attended to him first before Nam Loc. He could no longer deny that he'd had a severe case of child envy all the way until the final acquisition of Nam Loc. He had wondered if it was prelude to Lauren taking their separate living arrangement to its logical conclusion.

Instead, Lauren's plan was for Nam Loc to spend weekdays with Arthur and weekends with her. Because of the boy they'd see considerably more of each other. "Chào em, Nam Loc! You look wonderful, dear," Lauren said, bending to pat the boy's cheeks. "Very strong and healthy. Did you enjoy your Saturday morning walk around Madison?" Nam Loc nodded yes.

"How did you know we were walking around—"

"Oh Arthur, I've lived with you for forty years... Anyway, stay for lunch, do, I've already asked them to make a special place for you at my table. The banquet room accommodates sixty. There are more than a hundred people here today."

"That's nice of you...er, that speech you gave, it was... it was...nice, I mean..."

"Pish! That was pure bullcrap. Poppycock. Excuse me, I'm supposed to watch my language before Nam Loc, am I not? What the hey! He's starting fourth grade in two days. Sink or swim. Swim in the murkiness of American pop culture or the vultures will get you."

Another mixed metaphor. For a woman who'd read so much classic nineteenth-century literature, she sure didn't keep her tropes in line. Was it on purpose? "You're still sure we can plunge him like that into the school system, without a transition, some help..."

"The only help he needs is our confidence. Now Arthur, straighten yourself up and treat this as a challenge different in degree but not in kind...oh phooey, I'm slipping into that motivational talk again. Nam Loc will be *fine*. Didn't you read the reports from his master?" She had her hand on the boy's head. "He has fantastic learning skills!"

She squatted on the floor, squeezed the boy's hands, and talked to him in reasonably comprehensible Vietnamese phrases, infinitely better than Arthur was capable of. Nam

Loc agreed with her in surprisingly good English that he *was* very hungry and wouldn't mind meeting her friends.

"Professor Fishbach!" Arthur turned his gaze to the wide-eyed young man with the shock of blond hair plastering his forehead, but the greeting was addressed to his wife. "I loved your talk. The way you interpolated localized multivalency into politicized agency, it transformed the *idea* of insecurity into dialogic—"

"Bullcrap. Poppycock." She pivoted on her heels, still crouching on the floor, to face her admirer. "I hope you didn't take it too seriously. Pure motivational stuff, which has its place, but...by the way, there's a brilliant new theorist from Calcutta I'd like you to meet after lunch. Chakravarty is her name. She has things to teach all of us, I do believe!"

"Sure," said the young man, deflated, unable to meet Lauren's eyes.

Arthur had never been able to decide to what extent Lauren took theory seriously: were all "texts" truly worth equal time? She'd given Arthur a new digital camera and asked him to take as many pictures of the Hanoi streets as he could; no doubt she would deconstruct them, read entire histories of oppression and resistance in obvious symbols, the way he never could. To him a sign for a circumcision butcher was just that.

They had seats at President Isaiah Warren's table. He too was an old warrior, but hid his wounds well, being the most self-effacing big-time university president Arthur had ever known. It was noted with bemusement that he preferred entomology over fundraising. President Warren and Arthur had been invited to the White House in the last days of Nixon, as part of a PR mission to humanize Nixon to his academic critics; both had refused to go, and had spent the latter part of the seventies congratulating themselves for their distance.

"This man has the largest collection of butterflies in the Four Lakes area—and beyond," Arthur said to Nam Loc by way of introduction.

President Warren turned away from his even more diffident wife, a self-styled "homemaker," and feeling called upon to entertain the boy, started quizzing him about butterfly species in Vietnam.

Lauren halted that strain of conversation. "You'll have shrimp spring roll," she said to Nam Loc, "they're very light, but authentic." She ordered goat cheese and apple salad for herself. It was always salad for her.

"You had them eating out of your hands," President Warren said to Lauren. "I don't know how you retain your enthusiasm, your freshness, about the new stuff, the new... frankly, the future scares me."

President Warren's wife retreated more than ever in her capacious seat. Instead of making any wisecracks, Lauren let the President's remark go. That was an admirable ability of hers: to choose to engage or not to engage. Arthur was more controlled by emotions when it came to dialogue.

The fireplace behind them was burning hotter than it needed to; it seemed to Arthur that every place on campus exuded an excess of energy, and this in a time of supposed energy shortages. He started sweating, wiping it off his head. He could feel his wife's eyes on his plate, to make sure he finished eating; lately, Arthur had been suffering from loss of appetite, for which Lauren had so far not forced him to see his doctor.

"Nam Loc should have some time to himself, conserve his energy," Lauren said, noting how quickly the boy was eating. "Tell you what, Arthur, let him stay with me the first week of school. I've a very light workload this semester anyway. Just a couple of evening seminars. The pleasures of seniority," she winked at President Warren, who barely winked back. "No, Isaiah, the future is brilliant. Can't you see it? The doomsayers will have their day, but the juries will return a guilty verdict in the end. You'll see. The earth isn't going to toast us all. There won't be a return to feudalism. There has to be hope to keep going. Don't you see, Isaiah?"

Arthur felt the question was really addressed to him. He obediently finished his grilled chicken. There was no beef on this menu. The food tasted of nothing, it had been so deprived of anything able to kick-start you. Would physical decline suddenly arrest him? Would he be one of those who turned overnight to helpless decrepitude?

"I've met your teachers this week, Nam Loc," Lauren was saying. So she *had* had those meetings after all. Arthur thought they'd only been pious statements of intent. For a university professor to deal with teachers at a lower level, for whom pedagogy consisted of nothing but mass transference of what they considered valuable information to receptive minds, was an ordeal. Not for Lauren, apparently, because she consumed the next half hour, until the end of lunch, putting Nam Loc at ease about his school. The teachers wouldn't put pressure on him. They would be understanding about his challenges with the language, so he should never be afraid to ask for extra help. He was already a very smart boy; all he needed to do was learn the way things were accomplished in this system. He should never forget, he would have been the cream of the crop in Vietnam, and now that this was his country...

The boy had a second order of shrimp spring roll. The chicken felt like prison food to Arthur. The glass of white wine was like water. Because Lauren was sitting with President Warren, she was secure from the politest of interruptions. The President was an old fogey; if you sat with him, it must mean you required privacy. Besides, wasn't she spending quality time with her boy, converting his global insecurities into local remedies? Nam Loc was exerting his English language muscles far more vigorously than he had all morning with Arthur. "We went to music store." He mentioned his favorite rap singers, with whom Lauren was thoroughly familiar. She said Nam Loc could borrow her discs. He could have the digital camera too. Didn't Arthur still have it? An iPod for the golden boy would be next. Technology was going to smooth the way to the boy becoming American. There was Arthur's answer. The boy would become like others of his race born in Oshkosh or Eau Claire when he took his pleasures for granted, when he felt a sense of entitlement. Nobody saw the dark side of the pursuit of happiness anymore. Some day soon, when Arthur became Professor Emeritus, and scrounged to collect a handful of students interested in listening to him, Nam Loc would return home from high school, to find Arthur not yet shaved or showered, wallowing in filth, clinging to days-old newspapers. Nam Loc would be the one to finally make Lauren implement her decrees of health and well-being with real force.

Arthur felt an unconquerable sleepiness stealing over him. "Tea, I need to have some strong tea." He must have abruptly blurted it out, in the absence of any waiters, because Lauren was looking strangely at him, Nam Loc had turned red, and even President Warren had a look of concern on his face. "Excuse me, I think I need to get out of here," said Arthur. "I really must. Will you be able to take care of him the rest of the afternoon? Yes dear, please?"

Without waiting for an answer, Arthur started from the table and left, forgetting to tip the coat checker on his way out. Feeling like a cheat, someone with *abandonment issues*, as the talk shows would have it, he guiltily traced his steps toward Lake Mendota, the watery cradle of the campus, whose crisp blueness never failed to correct his vision. He was a coward. What would Nam Loc think? His better side wanted him to return, apologize, have tea with President Warren and company, stay around with Lauren for the rest of the conference, and then take his wife and child to a movie, perhaps a reprise of a forties classic at the local art house theater. Oh God, not Miles again, was he never going to get past his ghosts this most awful of days? It *was* Miles in front of him, no doubt heading to the lake himself, with a satchel of unused antiwar posters in one hand, and a soggy franchise hoagie in a disintegrating paper bag in another. *You coward*, Arthur denigrated himself, his head spinning, out of breath. He wanted to sit on the steps of one of the buildings on Park Street. He was almost in sight of the empty chairs and tables on the waterfront, he must keep going. That young man who'd come up to Lauren to compliment her and been rebuffed, that was *Terry Simes*, the famous Yale deconstructionist—Lord, why hadn't Arthur recognized him from his pictures? And she'd put him down so easily! It had to do with being a woman.

Fifteen minutes later, Arthur had lost himself enough in memories for the present moment to cease to count. Face slumped in his hands, he stared unseeingly at the far horizon cutting off the blue water. Maybe a man like Miles was better off than him: at least he thought he had something to live for. Arthur couldn't even pretend that teaching mattered. In four decades, had he been able to sway a single student to his point of view? No one could get inside another person's mind. He laughed grimly. A decade ago, it was Lauren who'd pulled out all the stops to prevent him from quitting teaching. Was it then that his resentment of her had begun? Would he have declined much faster had he been out of teaching? Was the adoption of the child a sop to Arthur's disintegration?

"Arthur." The way the soft hand was running back and forth on his right shoulder could only mean it was Lauren. Silently, she'd crept up to him, and was now looking at the water with the same unseeing eyes as his.

"What, Lauren?" he said without fully turning around. She'd known exactly where to find him. "I'm tired."

"Look who's here."

Nam Loc took the seat next to Arthur's, also facing the water, without making a fuss of the dust everywhere. "Gulf of Tonkin very blue—like this."

"I'll leave you two alone," Lauren said. "Spend the day with him. Bring him back whenever you're comfortable. School doesn't even *have* to start Monday." Then she lightly pecked Arthur on the cheek and started leaving. "I've to put in the rest of my idiot time at the club." He thought she was going to turn around to hug him tightly as if he were a child, embarrassing him before the boy, but she only waved daintily once she was a few feet away. "Cám ỏn," she thanked Nam Loc.

"So?" Arthur was going to make a genuine attempt to understand Nam Loc this time. Some odd sense of embarrassment had prevented him so far from asking Nam Loc personal questions about how his eleven years in Vietnam had really been like: if he'd felt betrayed when his parents died, if he'd suffered at the orphanage, if he'd had any friends there he missed. There was only a one-eyed girl with a limp who seemed to have been sad when Arthur came to rescue Nam Loc from the orphanage. Should Arthur talk about the time his own parents divorced when he was fourteen, which turned out to be the best thing that had happened to him because he plunged himself into study, leading straight to a full scholarship at the University of Chicago?

"In Vietnam, poor people enjoy ocean, lake, river. No cost. No worry. No police." Then Nam Loc started conjuring, as best he could, a world out of time, where people of diverse classes managed to get by on little money and much resourcefulness; where you had to be on guard all the time against theft and force, knowing however that there wasn't much to lose to begin with anyway; and where, worst come to worst, you could always count on your family to be there for you, even if you committed the most horrible act imaginable. Arthur nodded agreeably. He was willing to be educated.

GO SELL IT ON THE MOUNTAIN

I met her at lunch on opening day. Even then I had trouble holding up. Standing before me in line at the salad bar, she swung around and drilled through me with her charged eyes. "Your first time here?" she said. I nodded. "It shows," she spit out. (Of course, *she*, I would find out, had been a waiter here twice, then a scholar, and now a fellow.) She turned away to pick obsessively at the dripping wet lettuce, choosing only the smallest, greenest leaves. "Enjoy the festivities!" she advised menacingly. I choked. She was small and prim, a light-skinned Cameroonian who had been in the country all of five years, but carried herself as if she owned us, talking all the time in a swift-moving Brooklyn twang I had trouble keeping up with. Each day she wore a miraculously ballsy outfit, never with a bra. She was dangerous, even a rube like me could tell. Her name was Simone Carpentier. Projecting the most charisma among the two hundred and fifty participants, she would turn that year's edition of the Green Mountain Conference upside down. Two faculty members would be permanently barred from returning to teach. One fellowship recipient, a scruffy poet, would go missing for a month. I would suffer from nightmares, and break up with Carmen, my longtime Mexican girlfriend back home. And Simone herself—well, we'll get to that. (Did Keats say, *A thing of beauty is a joy forever*? He must not have meant live things.)

At the time of the lunch encounter, my head was swirling with the experiences I'd already had. The venerable senior editor of Random House, Chuck Lewison himself, the Grand Old Man of American letters, the discoverer of some of our most prized writers and a worthy Civil War historian himself, had helped me with my heavy green tote bag up the ancient stairs to my room on the second floor of the Inn. I'd driven up in my wasted Ford (the plan was to save money by driving instead of flying from Charleston, South Carolina), boggled at the rapid transformation of the landscape at the higher elevations of New York state, and on into Vermont: this was a corner of untouched paradise denied so far to country bumpkins like me, given to believe the Carolinas and Virginia were beautiful. Cutting through the picturesque town of Ripton (for two weeks I would feel like I was living inside a postcard), my clunky car speared higher and higher along Route 125 in the dissipating early August fog, the stately rows of sugar maples bestowing paradisial shade on my bohemian carriage. I passed idyllic waterfalls bordering shady groves, white trickling streams spreading over ancient rocks: this would all be around long after mankind ceased to exist. Passing the roadside sign for the Robert Frost Trail, leading to his cabin, I wanted then and there to hike toward it, even though the last time I had hiked I was still a virgin. Green rolling hills rose to my right, the soft morning sun spreading rippling circles of golden light over them. A Vermont Country Store stood weather-beaten and proud, intact as if from Sinclair Lewis's thirties, a few miles down Route 125 from the Inn at the Conference. At my destination, I parked on the side of the road behind a long row of new cars with mostly New England license plates.

This was it! I was finally here, after fifteen years of solitary struggle, writing away to my heart's content, without fear of judgment or censorship, in my bare studio in one of the most literary of Southern towns. Forevermore now I would have some kind of an audience, I would be part of a network of writers, and my work wouldn't suffer from the deadly mark of isolation. Was it now I'd finally make the connection with some influential person in the New York publishing industry, someone who could alter my life at one stroke of his will? I had chosen not to join a graduate writing program, since I believed, like my dead carpenter father who had a taste for good poetry, that real writers, real artists, didn't join academic programs: they were naturally forged from the flux and flow of normal stressful life. I'd spent three thousand dollars, all told, for the right to be at the Conference. Would my idiosyncratic path finally pay off?

When Chuck Lewison said, at the bottom of the stairs inside the Inn, once I'd registered at the office and slapped on my nametag, "Can I help you? Seems like a big load you're carrying," at first I was shy to bother the mighty personage, but then couldn't resist the chance to be in close proximity to him, even if for a few moments. "It's my thirtieth year straight, coming to the Conference. Never get tired of it. There's always some great new writer to be discovered," he said as he trailed the stairs behind me with the other end of the bag, as if explaining his early presence, this being only the first day. He wasn't huffing and puffing as I was, remaining exquisite in his khakis and polo shirt, his gray-haired classical Roman profile impervious to strain. "I'm Paul Madsen," I said, extending my sweaty hand when we'd reached my room at the end of the second floor. The door was open; there were no locks to any rooms at the Conference. My window overlooked Route 125; the green mountain on the other side of it lifted into a swirl of smoky clouds. A horse-drawn hay wagon stood unattended, as if part of the eternal natural landscape. "Paul," Chuck Lewison acknowledged with a godly nod, "I'll look forward to hearing about you." You can't imagine the discipline I exercised not to immediately unzip my tote bag and plunge my hand inside it to retrieve one of the beautifully bound copies of my finished novel, *Sandiman in Paradise*, and make Chuck Lewison sit on my bare bed to start reading it right then. "Yes, sir! Pleasure, sir! Thank you, sir!" I said instead, revealing my hick origins; excessive formality and respect in casual interactions are dead giveaways of those belonging outside the Boston-Manhattan-D.C. power corridor.

Then began a whirlwind of activities that would give none of us any breathing room for a fortnight. All that time I would think I was so bland as to be unnoticeable, but in fact my very lack of polish was making a definite impression on some of the Conference heavies. My roommate Darren, one of the few overt Southerners there besides me, sporting a shabby beard and never dressed but in a lumberman's plaid shirt, was a poet who wrote at his farm near Roanoke, Virginia. The minute I met him, he started showing me pictures of his beautiful Scottish wife and three young blond children. "Poetry is like farming," Darren said. "You plant, you plow, you dig, you hoe—and the harvest may never get better than the previous years'. But you're always grateful to get anything out of the ground." During the worst cataclysms of the Conference, even when people started fainting right and left, Darren's calm would never be disturbed, although he and I would consume enormous amounts of alcohol at the Barn most nights to maintain our sanity.

By the time Simone shattered my calculated peace at the salad bar, I'd also met Sally Lombardi, memoirist of alcoholism, the graying but always gracious administrator of the conference; her fat novelist husband Al flirted with everything in sight, from the pubescent to the matronly, apparently without offending Sally; Celia Perkins, the freckled, curly-haired, dreamy Maine fisherman's daughter, an occasional journalist and the Conference's longtime administrative assistant, on whom I developed an immediate brotherly crush; and my workshop leader, Adriana Bishop, arguably the most famous teacher at the Conference that year, with two Pulitzers already in the bag at forty-five, her novels about the relentless unraveling of quiet Midwestern marriages said to be the last president's wife's favorite reading.

That afternoon, at the introductory workshop meeting, at the Inn's Purple Parlor—I was one of only two males among ten participants—Adriana made it clear she would run a tight ship. The rules were, before we said anything negative about a fellow workshopper's story, we'd have to detail what we liked about it. Adriana turned out to be a firm taskmaster; the minute one of us started grandstanding, spouting half-baked theories of "what literature is all about" and "the function of the writer in modern society," she chopped off that person's balls without any mercy: "Time out!" she'd interject. "We were talking about the narrative arc of Emily's story. How does it square with Aristotle's paradigm?" I always felt for some reason Adriana didn't like me—perhaps my gentlemanly Southern reticence was mistaken for lack of passion? Darren thought I shouldn't be too eager to make an impression. "Let your story speak for itself," he advised. "Don't try too hard."

But the person that year—other than Simone, of course—who provoked the most emotion for and against was the Conference director himself, Peter Mandelson, winner of the Yale Series of Younger Poets at a tender twenty-five, and since then bent on the mission of cleaning up the filth and decadence in American writing, of which tidying up the Conference was a necessary though minor component. Professionalization, standardization, systematization, these were his obsessions, from the administering of contests to the editing of manuscripts, and his aim was no lower than rigorous enforcement of the rule of law to the three hundred and fifty writing programs in the country, to the extent his influence had any meaning. "The quirky personal element has been too romanticized. I want to establish the *business* of writing," he'd famously said in his inaugural year as director a decade ago, as reported in *Poets & Writers*. On the one hand, this cold attitude scared me; on the other hand, meritocracy, even as an outsider, was my only chance.

To the recipients of the coveted waiterships, Peter was a cult figure. Intricate cheers, reminding me of frat house friends my freshman year in college, went up among them, as the headwaiter clinked his glass at the conclusion of dinner the first night, proclaiming, "The one, the only, Peter Mandelson." *Peter! Peter!* went up the chant, even among grizzled octogenarian poets, masticating the last of the dry roast beef. A hush, as in a medieval church, fell over, silencing even the sleek, badmouthing New York blonde sitting next to me. As Peter surveyed his empire, I was dumbstruck to find Simone, two tables away from me, staring me down: Was I drooling? Did I have my elbows on the table? My fly was invisible.

I don't remember what Peter said. He probably congratulated everyone for having made it to this exclusive club, and asked us to treat it as a privilege of the highest order. Oh, I'm sure he said something about the need to pace ourselves, and not to participate in everything on the schedule, otherwise we'd be dead of exhaustion in forty-eight hours: the standard warning at these high-intensity conferences, where every hour, from seven in the morning to midnight, is packed with heavily publicized events that make you feel like a moron if you choose to skip any. I was beginning to doze off. I wished I'd had a couple more months to revise the ending of *Sandiman in Paradise*. Carmen, always practical, had wanted me to wrap things up in time for the Conference.

Simone's deep voice woke me. She had taken the floor, and her head was threateningly leaning to one side. "Excuse me, Peter, I realize this is your show, and my speaking up now is definitely against protocol—but then, everything we take for protocol today was some madwoman's impulse before it became protocol, was it not? Anyway, it strikes me that this year's Conference has already managed to be an exact replica of how last year's began. The same tinkling of the glass by the headwaiter, the same gladiatorial cheers. 'Hip, hip, Peter! Rock the Mountain, Peter!' Et cetera. I see five Indians here—East Indians, I mean—and ten Asians, and twenty blacks, half of whom are waiters. Oh, and maybe fifty gays. A third of the faculty." The first groans escaped the veterans; Peter's cold red lips had parted to show his sharp yellow teeth, and his blue eyes were pure ice. Simone hit her stride: "We'll find no formalists among the versifiers. Everyone will think the short story is the art form par excellence. Experimentalism will be in vogue. There will be declamations of the unfortunate current tendency to introduce politics into art. Novelists will talk of the unavoidability of rewriting drafts fifty to a hundred times. Writing will be compared to hard labor—concentration camp labor? Brilliant first successes will be dismissed as illusionary, unrepeatable serendipities. We'll be told it's not a tragedy if the *Atlantic* and the *New Yorker* don't buy much first fiction from newcomers. Agents will try to convince us that publication is not the important thing, perfecting our craft is. The merits of low-residency writing programs will be articulated by recent graduates. There'll be humorous Homeland Security and Sexual Transgression readings. The *Daily Crust* will greet us every morning with news of the arrival of celebrities who run Simon & Schuster and Penguin, whom we'll sometimes actually spot at mealtimes. Veteran faculty will hang out only with their kind, as will younger faculty. Fellows will try to exclude waiters from their parties, waiters will try to exclude scholars, and scholars will try to exclude paying contributors. Someone will be caught fucking in the laundry room after a week. Two minority girls will faint in the Frost Theater during the first days, only to be rescued by white male doctors in the audience. A middle-aged housewife will break down at a reading by a poet of color. The bookstore will run out of books to be signed by novelists. Most people will get drunk, but almost no one will really make a fool of themselves." Simone abruptly halted.

I could have sworn she was swaying on her feet. This was magic, this was electricity, this was pure confounded challenge! Three hundred people held their breath to see how Peter would respond. I thought I heard a collective undervoiced "Oh fuck" animate the audience.

"Thank you, Simone, for summarizing the Conference—as you see it. Now, allow me to invite each of you to discover the Conference for yourself, to violate each and every one of—shall we call them Simone's Rules?—just as you wish!"

Ear-shattering cheers of *Peter! Peter!* exploded among the younger waiters. The faculty broke into prolonged clapping and table-thumping. I was unclear what we were celebrating. In the days to come, I would find out that most of the participants were intent on pretending that Simone never existed: this was their precious time to recharge their batteries, to get hyped and motivated and befriended, and they weren't going to let the Cameroonian's personal problems, whatever they might be, interfere with their determination to leave the Mountain elevated in all senses of the word.

What had happened was impossible; it wasn't supposed to happen. Simone had spoken like filibustering James Stewart in one of those forties Capra movies. "I kinda agree with what she said," I said to my foulmouthed blonde neighbor. She turned up her nose: "Humph. Some people have manners, and others—others are into showmanship."

At the cocktail reception that followed at the Barn, a massive structure sheltering huge leather chairs and sofas that allowed for groups to assemble in isolated corners, most of the cliques continued to act as if Simone didn't exist. She herself wasn't to be seen. I was desperate to change her first opinion of me. Even if she had won the AWP fiction award two years ago, for her novel about Cameroonian immigrants, *Les Statues de Liberté*, while I had yet to get a story published in an august venue like the *Kenyon Review* or the *Southern Review*, wasn't the whole point of coming to the Conference to inspire myself to join the upper ranks of today's writers? I thought of Jean, my idol in tenth grade, who'd publicly humiliated our epileptic English teacher for "undressing" women with his eyes; I'd always lamented not getting to know Jean better.

Peter Mandelson was having a drink with poet Stu Delacruz, who would soon don a reindeer head while he spoke at the Frost Theater of his surrealist influences, Apollinaire and Ernst, Breton and Magritte. Infected by Simone's daring, I chose this moment to politely join their conversation. "Would you say that surrealism is the necessary counterforce to fascism, to authoritarian politics of any kind, and as such it needs to acquire an overt political tone these days?" I asked Stu after introducing myself. Peter seemed to mind having been interrupted, but Stu launched into a scathing denunciation of my suggestion: "Politics corrupts art, period. I don't think writers should approach their work with any kind of an agenda." As Stu nervously denounced the straw man I hadn't really set up, Peter excused himself and left.

I soon found myself alone, unable to plug into any of the vibrant cliques, which seemed to have been formed *ex nihilo*, perfected and ready to perform, going back to hip schools and clubs in the Back Bay and on the Main Line. Everyone already seemed to know each other. "Oh right, Grace Flook, she taught me Advanced Pedagogical Methods at Sarah Wilson." "No kidding, me too! Five years before she taught you though." The agents and editors present at the Barn were already known to the hipster kids, who weren't going to make any impolite advances. I would find that the youths from the MFA programs were invariably polite to me, but I would also always feel an air of condescension. I had no choice but to start gravitating toward the older people, the "nontraditional" writers with families and jobs, and spotty publication credits for years or decades of struggle. People like my roommate Darren.

"Come join us, man," Darren invited me to his twelve-foot-long green sofa. "Did you already meet Lisa? And Christie? How's your back?" I'd slipped that morning on the Inn steps, wet with morning mist. While my own instinct was to try to get to meet as many as possible of the kinds of people I normally wouldn't encounter, Darren, more typical of the Conference attendees, was content with hanging out for the fortnight with no more than the five or ten people he visually trusted immediately, like Lisa Loos, a folk singer with screenwriting credits, and Christie Cunningham, a thumping hearty Midwestern girl whose husband used to be a miner—people not threateningly beautiful. Of course, I had a novel ready to take the world by storm, while Darren was happy to produce a couple of good poems a year. I showed as much enthusiasm as I could when I was with Darren's friends, but something always tugged at my heart, making me wonder if all the action was somewhere else: in late-night parties at the far-flung cottages up the road, assigned to the scholars and fellows, where drunken rituals made for mystical bonding? In serious discussions in some nearby parallel universe, where everyone fretted over the vitality of art in a culture of consumerism, instead of the "Do you know so-and-so?" exchange usually to be heard?

At ten that night was the first of the readings in the Frost Theater, where, in the sliver of spotlight at the podium, novelist Jack Johnson read his virile prose about hunting and fishing in Idaho as a boy on the verge of manhood might have experienced it. The doors were firmly shut to prevent their slamming in the blustery wind. The half-lit shadowy faces of the listeners held heads dreaming of their own presence some day at the platform. Every once in a while, Jack would stop reading altogether and stare goggle-eyed and open-mouthed at the packed theater, as if challenging someone to rise and disabuse him of the veracity of his narrative. (I would discover that Jack was in the minority in creating straight fiction out of such mundane stuff; most others were turning to memoir.) Where was Simone's ghost?

Darren turned out to be the ideal roommate, quiet and considerate, who didn't even snore. I woke up at five-thirty, as I would for the duration of the Conference, so I would have privacy in the communal bathroom. My bathing and shaving rituals were perhaps too excessive for public knowledge. At nine there was a lecture in the Frost Theater, Cuban poet Cristina Alvarado talking about structure in the novel, which turned out to be mostly about memories of growing up on her grandmother's lap in old Havana before the Fidelistas took over. At ten there was a craft class with gay novelist Justin Kramer, who praised the demands made on the reader to keep up with the rapid time shifts enacted by his idols, James Salter and Denis Johnson. "Writing is a multiple course feast. You are the host king and the guest lord, but also the humble waiter, and the unseen baker and butcher." *What?* Hello, Simone!

Things unraveled quickly in Adriana's workshop. We were to have read Felicia Hunter's story beforehand, and I had, on the toilet seat at two-thirty in the morning in the common bathroom. Felicia was an anorexic, from some MFA program in Michigan, and she'd written about an anorexic hiding her problems. I was eager to get a lively discussion going, and as soon as Megan Wiley had recited the story's strengths, the impressive faithfulness of the physical descriptions of sadistic nuns and indifferent teachers, I said: "I don't know where the narrative arc of the story is. Yesterday," I gestured knowingly at Adriana, "you were talking about the Aristotelian paradigm, the rising arc, the climax, the resting point. Well, where is it? This is only a series of random incidents with the thinnest narrative connection. And besides, what is the narrator's moral stand toward the lead character's afflictions? Does she have a moral opinion? Or is she neutral to her ups and downs? I don't see the author present behind the scenes." A girl named Hannah Wasserstein said, "Actually, I liked the story. I liked it a lot. Precisely because it *doesn't* impose on us the author's attitude, whatever it might be. I like being allowed to decide for myself." Hannah had asked before workshop where I'd got my MFA from, and when I said, "I've always just written on my own," she'd asked: "But how do you make a living without an MFA? You must tell me after workshop. Really, I'm curious." To my surprise, Adriana took Felicia's side, never saying a word about Aristotle: "I appreciated what you did with dreams, Felicia, but I would have liked to see more of the dark underside. What fears and compulsions truly motivate your heroine? Be more explicit. Ratchet up the tension." Throughout, Felicia listened distantly as if there weren't a bunch of critics in the room taking apart her work. When invited to respond at the end, Felicia said, "I wouldn't mind having a private word with Adriana later, but I really don't have much to say at this point."

Trekking back from the Barn after a craft class—the enigmatic line breaks of Robert Creeley were spoken of rhapsodically—I was struck by the beauty of the scene. As the late morning mist dissipated, and the peaceful sun shed warm golden light on the mountain, treading on the soft grass it seemed to me that this whole tableau was suspended from the lower reaches of heaven. I stopped on the path winding down toward the Inn. There was absolute silence. After a while, I heard a bird chirp from far out on the meadow to the left. There was usually someone chattering away in the lone phone box on campus, a contraption left over from the fifties, but the box stood empty now. Part of me never wanted to leave this enchantment. Part of me felt this attraction was a dishonorable betrayal of the real world.

Simone was at lunch! She looked grim and forlorn, as she sat near an elderly woman—a Middlebury resident whose husband had performed free legal favors for the Conference in the seventies. I didn't hesitate as I plunked my tray, loaded with mangled cheesy pasta and other institutional fare, on the table. "May I?"

Simone looked disappointed. "Oh it's you. Still the new kid on the block, aye?" I blushed a deep red. Simone smiled. I thought I perceived friendliness. "Let me guess. You've brought with you a novel—about a shy Southern teacher who has a fatal crush on an underage girl, inviting reprobation from the moral community. Something along those lines." She had come surprisingly close—actually, it was a doctor, not a teacher—but I ascribed it to sheer volume of familiarity with the writings of people of my background. But how did she know my background so well? "You have high expectations. Sky-high! Take it from me, these people are not who you think they are. This Conference is not what you think it's all about." Her eyes seemed to water as they panned the busily chattering participants, firmly settled into their various in-groups. A short Jewish poet with woolly hair, the idol of all the black writers at the Conference, cracked some joke to make a roar go up by the salad bar.

"Oh yeah," I said challengingly, "what is it about?"

"It's about breaking down your ego. Taking a hammer to it. Splitting it apart, bit by bit, so that when you leave you're no more than a flatulent, deconstructed zombie—with airs, because you've been to the Mountain, and welcomed into the club. Of course, the zombieness tends to wear off after a while, so you need to keep returning, on scholarships if you can, year after year. Human beings weren't meant to be zombies, were they?" Simone asked the Middlebury woman, who shook her head uncomprehendingly.

Before I could contribute to the zombie question, Al Lombardi planted his yard-wide ass on the chair next to Simone's. "I wanted to compliment you," he said, looking Simone's body up and down with his frog vision.

"On my eyes?" Simone asked coquettishly. She was one-upping the flirtatious plump fictionist.

"On your stand yesterday," he lowered his voice conspiratorially. "Between you and me..." he looked over his shoulders as if Peter's minions might be listening in, "Peter's a jerk. All the fun has gone out of the Conference. No one does anything crazy anymore. They're all closet fascists. And half of them are gay." He leaned back in the chair, entirely inadequate to hold him, then drained his mug of black coffee in two huge swallows. "Not that your eyes aren't to be complimented." As he smiled conqueringly, I felt Al would as soon I weren't present at the instigation. But I wasn't going to give him the satisfaction, even if his ignoring me was irritating. Al started criticizing the militarism of the current administration; he liked to think of himself as a fearsome critic of the Nixonians. Simone was in another world. Her beautiful brown skin, even and luxuriant everywhere, invited long afternoon caresses. Carmen seemed coarse, rude, vulgar by comparison—unmade and unmakeable. For financing this trip, she'd expect me to marry her. Simone's unattainability was a challenge.

Her writing was curiously glassy on the surface: it gave you no entry point, no means to project your living, breathing mass of flesh onto the consciousness of the author. This kind of writing was in vogue now, while I wrote in the old-fashioned raconteur's spiraling manner, leisurely getting to the core of the story. My models were the forgotten story writers of the thirties, forties, and fifties, like Roderick Lull and Morley Callaghan, who killed you with their explosive revelations of your own culpability in injustice. I didn't think Simone was capable of this type of slowly building lacerative effect: her convictions were too subterranean in *Les Statues de Liberté*. But at least she'd wanted to deal with elements of the real world, where labor was exploited and the revelation was that labor wanted to be exploited, as opposed to dissecting solitary individual egos as their marriages and adulteries unraveled to no point.

"Race is never a distinct presence in your work," Al said, still on his flirtative horse. "Why, my dear Simone? Your characters could be anyone, white or black. And yet, with your advantages, your colonial heritage, oppression French and British and American and—"

"You're disgusting!" Simone hissed, getting up. "Do you know how much you hurt your wife? Have you ever looked into her eyes? She looks—completely shattered! You want the Conference to be all about screwing and drinking? You want this to be a brothel? Are there no choices besides Vegas and Yale? What happened to the enlightenment? What did you do with it? Did you eat it? Hunh?"

I swallowed the lump in my throat, over and over. Al was equally taken aback. The old woman from Middlebury had left.

"Excuse me, I have to go kill myself," Simone said to Al, and to me, "You're cute. But I bet you lack the fire in the belly to really anger people with your writing. However, if you want to leave a few pages of your manuscript...under the door of my cottage, up the road...I can't promise, but I might be able to, you know..." She shrugged her shoulders.

I barely had the presence of mind to thank her.

Al looked scathingly at me. "So, Paul! In with the big guns already, are you? I always wonder what it is about you Southern boys, with your humble act and all, that gets to our women. You know, women trained and educated in the Puritan ethic. It's the old exotic game." Al was talking more to himself now than to me. "The Northern woman always falls for the Southern man. Biology screams, or something. I hope Adriana isn't giving you too hard a time, Paul?" So he knew whose workshop I was in. "She's supposed to be a manslayer. I wouldn't be surprised if she were a dyke. Is she, do you think? I know she's married, but what does that mean when both husband and wife teach in the same writing program?"

Al's hapless wife Sally came up at that moment, witness from afar of his latest move on Simone. "Paul." She placed her pale small hand over mine. "Are you enjoying the Conference so far?" Al snorted derisively, making it plain he wanted to be away from her.

I would see Al mortally struggling to score with girls the rest of the Conference. He became more and more shameless about it, but Simone seemed to have jinxed his strategy. She seemed to have put a hex on the rest of the Conference too. Everyone's vital spirit toward the confab— the ceaseless hip-hip camaraderie, the highflying rumors of self-annihilation, the frenzied nose-to-the-grindstone with winging-it-on-the-fly combination—seemed to have been dealt a death blow with Simone's Cassandra act. I believe the moment of Al's failed coddling of Simone's presumed race instinct was the point of no return. The Conference would never really recover.

There were packed Frost Theater readings morning, afternoon, and evening, each of the faculty readers matched with a fellow, the Conference administrators having been careful to pair the lugubrious or the dramatic with their own kind. Peter seemed to get up after dinner every night to make gratuitous announcements, which we already knew of from the *Daily Crust*, and to repeat the inescapable buzz about the comings and goings; he seemed to be inviting Simone to challenge him again, as if ashamed of his mute response the first night. I stopped often outside the Conference office, where Celia, the fisherman's daughter I wanted to squeeze in an affectionate bear hug, seemed ready to pass out from exhaustion at handling the complaints and inquiries of housewives buried in the avalanche of flyers and handouts. "Can I help you?" I asked Celia once, almost spilling the coffee on her desk with my nervous wave. "No, thank you, Paul." But several times she let me buy her a beer late at night at the Barn, while the youngsters courted agents and editors.

When Simone abruptly left the Conference well before its scheduled end, the Amish poet David King would disappear too, not to be found until a month later in a North Carolina trailer park, drunk, disheveled, and picked up by the cops for rowdiness. David set the standard for country-style cheerfulness. He had the hirsute mien of a person raised by wolves in a forest, and he seemed to write the most self-delightedly obscure verse since John Ashbery. He was a fellow now, and had been a waiter and a scholar in previous years, like Simone. I adored him. I wished I could ask him to read my manuscript, and tell me if it was any good. He had a Ph.D. in American history from Yale, but you'd never know it by his homespun clothes and lavishly curling Hasidic-like beard. David had had an unrequited crush on Simone since their first meeting.

I read from *Sandiman in Paradise* at the Purple Parlor. I'd decided to go early, to get the nerves out of the way. Two fat girls who spun loud verse exclusively about the intake and expulsion of food preceded me. Chuck Lewison, the Random House god, was standing by the door, his head bowed, thumb twirling in his blazer buttonhole. Just before I took the lectern, someone called him from the corridor and he had to leave. I read slowly. Carmen had been the first to convince me that the languid pace suited my prose well. Mostly I read the description of a summer sunset at Charleston Harbor. My characters are always thoroughly integrated into the landscape. At times, I've tried to get away from this tendency, to make the setting and the people disparate, but it doesn't work. As I read, the nerves left me, and I felt I was making an impression. But afterward, no one complimented me. I resolved to go easier on the remaining stories in Adriana's workshop, afraid of my own turn at the end.

Next morning I had my first scheduled meeting with an agent, Dylan Marcus, who liked to publicize his five-year-long stay at a Buddhist monastery in northern India, at a formative stage of his career. "Max was awesome this morning, don't you think? What a zany reader, I don't know where the inspiration comes from," Dylan said, when it was my turn for the precious twenty minutes with him on the front porch of the Inn. Darren's friend Christie had gone before me. Sitting at a respectful distance on the porch, I could hear her speak ninety percent of the time, with Dylan occasionally nodding—not asking her at the conclusion to give him the manuscript of her memoir (about her miner husband's insane family) but to mail it to him. If Dylan were to ask me to hand him my manuscript on the spot, I'd consider it a success. Max, the subject of Dylan's accolade, was a person of indefinite gender identity. At times, he/she appeared merely a very effeminate homosexual. At other times, I felt the sexual ambiguities extended much farther. At the Conference Max always came with partner Sam, another person of immense gender confusion, with a face that looked male or female, depending on the mood and time. Max had read exclusively from other poets' work, people who weren't afraid to break the rigid genre boundaries that straitjacketed the bourgeois imagination; besides, Max was experiencing a much-needed spell of silence, which had gone on for some seven years. Most of Max's workshop participants were older females. "Yeah, Max was great," I said, wanting to use my priceless twenty minutes to plug my work. Dylan talked for a few more minutes about the metaphysical intensities of listening to some of the greatest writers of the time in the history-drenched Frost Theater. "So, about my novel—can I tell you what it's about?" I finally interjected. "Oh, sure...we have plenty of time still, but...of course, go ahead. I'm all ears." Dylan cocked his head. I entered into a robotic recital of the main plot points, feeling every moment as if I were losing a race I was never meant to win.

I bumped into Simone's ghostly form at the mailboxes; mine was stuffed with leaflets as usual. "Hey," she said. "It's not going to work. The agent stuff. It's only for show. To make the Conference more saleable to the naïve, I suppose. But you're not naïve. You're worldly-wise. I could tell from the beginning. So don't fall for it. I bet if you go to his cottage after he flies back to New York, you'll find all the manuscripts given to him dumped on the floor." He had asked for my manuscript at the end, but was it because I'd already implied I was a stickler for form? I was desperate to find out how Simone had been part of the system, and yet was so outside it, such a critic. How had she sold her novel? As if reading my mind, Simone said, "Tomorrow is my last night to drink at the Lodge. Come at seven? You'll be my guest." The Lodge was where faculty and fellows got together to drink, as opposed to the plebeian Barn; only published writers could come, or guests of such. To crash into the Lodge was considered the height of bad manners. "Sure," I said with trepidation. To be Simone's guest! I hadn't yet had the nerve to show her my manuscript. Maybe now? I wondered what I'd wear; my clothes, I'd discovered, were utterly out of sync, in their fifties staidness, from the trendy, bright fashions of the depressed free verse poets and experimental story writers.

Imagine my disappointment when I turned up at the Lodge on time that evening, only to be rudely turned away. A half-Japanese, half-black girl, who'd written a well-received novel about the West Coast internment camps from the point of view of a sadistic guard, explained: "Simone's already left the Conference, in case you didn't know."

"But I only met her a few hours ago."

"Yeah well, a few hours can be an eternity on the Mountain. You're gonna have to leave." As if I were so desperate to enter the sacred precinct of the Lodge that I would have lied about Simone's invitation, which was clearly this girl's implication!

A group of levitating waiters and scholars could be heard inside, making fun of Peter's earnestness. A shrill female voice imitated Peter's: "At this Conference, we do not believe in art for commerce's sake. So if you don't already have a job lined up after getting your MFA, you might as well start on a Ph.D. At this Conference, Prohibition-era rules are occasionally in force. Guys and gals make out at their own risk. Homemade liquor is the most potent, and better not forget to pay off the spies, the agents provocateurs, the bullying cops." A male voice, doing Al Lombardi, asked: "And who might the agents provocateurs be?" The female voice replied, "Certainly not the literary agents!" To which a roomful of drunk-sounding scholars responded with hooting laughter. The Japanese-black girl firmly closed the Lodge door in my face.

It would turn out to be true that Simone had left the Conference, perhaps even the country. For some months afterward, her publisher, a small Midwestern outfit, wouldn't be able to track her down. The book she'd promised, to follow up on her first big success, didn't come through. There were rumors immigration had nabbed her on some technical visa violation and deported her back to Cameroon. Others on the grapevine, within my reach for the first time, claimed she was so disgusted with writing she'd become a nun, or an investment banker. I liked to think that Simone was studying privately with some great Irish playwright in Dublin, while exploring the last hidden dimensions of her sexuality. We all know now what Simone has produced as an encore, the heartless denunciation of multiculturalism masked as a novel that has left so many scratching their heads; but where she was and what she was doing when she wrote it, no one yet knows for sure.

David King went missing a couple of days later. He failed to show up at the Conference office, after lunch, and Celia hit the panic button. It was the middle of a reading by nature writer Gideon Spivey, and I was feeling guilty for not yet having been able to visit the Robert Frost cabin, or even participate in any of a number of goofy made-for-the-nonathlete sporting events on the vast greens of the Mountain. Celia passed Gordon a note, and he read off: "If anyone knows where David King is, please contact the office. The Middlebury police are waiting." Gideon wasn't supposed to read out loud the last sentence. The nerves of two hundred and fifty of the nation's most ambitious writers collapsed at the same time. The older woman next to me, with a long face and a beak nose, started wheezing loudly, and her skin seemed to break into red splotches; her companion, a woman remarkably similar in appearance, rubbed the afflicted one's cheeks hard as if that would resuscitate her. Back in the higher rows, a scream went up. The second of the Indian girls, Rupali, had fainted. (When the first of the faintings had struck a tiny Indian girl a few days ago, everyone had pointed out Peter's wisdom in advising us to "pace ourselves"; I, on the other hand, was proud not to have missed a single nonconflicting event so far.) Following Simone's script, two inhumanly calm white doctors cleared out the crowd and fanned the Indian girl back to life.

All day long, the Middlebury police interviewed Conference participants who confessed to be friends with David; David was the kind of welcoming guy everyone instantly claimed as their own, so the police had their work cut out. Had David killed himself? This was everyone's unspoken thought. My instinct was mute on David's fate. It wasn't until months later that I found out, from the few friends from the Conference I maintained touch with, about

Simone's alleged cruel treatment of David, which was said to have brought on the disappearance. Apparently, Simone had been relentlessly browbeating David that his Amish reticence was merely a convenient persona, a shell David's inner self would break free of given half the chance. I had a difficult time imagining the unshakably peaceful David getting riled up over Simone's provocations.

And yet, hadn't Peter Mandelson been shaken up enough by Simone's challenge to go out of his way to be exuberant? At the first Barn dance the night before, Peter had not only stood on a table to gyrate his hips like an Elvis off his painkillers, but stripped off his shirt, revealing his structured bony frame, and seemed about ready to take off his pants too, when his dance partner, the blondest and youngest Middlebury undergraduate at the Conference, restrained him. Later, I found out that Peter always let loose at the Barn dances, although not to the extent of going nude! How naturally rhythmic Carmen was, compared to the awkwardly hustling sets of pale limbs I'd seen at the Barn dance! (Disco and new wave at least evoked general enthusiasm, while hip-hop brought groans.) And yet, I felt a sudden stab of conviction that Carmen and I were doomed: as goodhearted as she was, she didn't have the judgment or resources to give my writing career a big enough boost—and was that too unfair to expect? From time immemorial, writers had leeched onto rich patrons, lovers when possible, to feed their habit. Was I such a criminal?

A pair of lesbians from the Iowa writing program fell out of the hayride wagon the next afternoon, one on top of the other, but they were unhurt—although clearly drunk. Chuck Lewison of Random House, looking more glamorous than ever in a navy blazer and yellow ascot, was the first to the rescue. The girls laughed so hard, I thought the Mountain would get sick of their demanding echoes. How did one fall out of an enclosed hay wagon? Darren, at my side, said: "My little girls would've been embarrassed. These folks apparently never get to let off steam." The ruddy, wild-bearded farmer—who'd been maneuvering the mechanized wagon through hair-raising turns, the wagon twisting up and down the green hill on the other side of the Inn—barely broke stride.

Meanwhile, in sight of the hayride, at the edge of the lawn, right along Route 125, a cocktail party was in progress; drinks were free, and everyone seemed determined to lose it before dinner, which today was going to be a picnic outside the Frost Theater. Faculty members were balancing drinks with books presented to them for signature. The writer was compelled to make up intimate-sounding notes for bare acquaintances on the spot ("For Sheila, whose writing kicks, and who's never afraid to make us think harder"). There were some who seemed to buy many hundreds of dollars worth of books, lining up after every reading to grab the precious autograph and note; I, on the other hand, marveling at the ritual, was determined not to buy a single book at the Conference. Dylan Marcus, the agent I'd been assigned, went by, clearly not recognizing me. He was making a beeline for a slim redhead in my workshop; Sadie wrote exclusively about Central American refugees. Dylan kept volubly hitting on Sadie, still praising Max the gender-smashing silent poet, well after most people had headed over to the picnic. Even at the picnic, in their drunken state, people started gunning for the most hopeless targets. "Jerry," the eighty-three-year-old editor of the greatest Southern literary journal, whose forebears had kept the progressive-agrarian flame alive during fascism's bleakest years in the thirties and forties, was going after the Irish editor of Thornapple, the independent Wisconsin press, at least forty years his junior. I saw *Sandiman in Paradise* go up in flames; nobody cared for my writing.

My second agent meeting was more discouraging than the first because the svelte Manhattan blonde assigned to me feigned unnatural exuberance; I didn't believe her faked enthusiasm for a second. The subject of Carmen came up, which brought on more effusion about the dynamism of Mexico City. I was out of the loop, and I knew it. I had thought I could plug into the literary circuit at a high point of elevation, at a time of my choosing, but this was not to be. My novel excerpt left everyone in Adriana's workshop mystified. "You mean to say," Hannah Wasserstein exclaimed, "that in this day and age, a *dirty old man* wouldn't be hauled up and prosecuted by neighbors, teachers, responsible community members, the minute they got wind of his insidious attempts to lure this—this innocent—fourteen-year-old girl? I mean, I know progressive laws lag behind in some regions of the country, but come on!" Felicia Hunter, the anorexic, who seemed to have forgiven my harsh critique of her story a week ago, excused me with, "You could have made the girl more vulnerable. You know, given her some bigger trauma to deal with. I could see how visits to the therapist might help flesh out her character more convincingly." No one wanted to talk about the "dirty old man," my hero, the aristocratic Sandiman, who was an expert in Egyptian hieroglyphics, and whose great-aunt had married into the extended Vanderbilt clan. Later, Adriana, in our private follow-up meeting at the Barn, would say, "Paul, have you considered joining a low-residency MFA program? It might be just the thing to hone your craft. You already have tremendous narrative skill—I like how you move along seamlessly from Point A to Point B—but your characterization could do with more texture, more thickness. Regular feedback from readers might force you to face up to challenges you might now be stepping back from." When I walked outside, the warm early afternoon sun hit me in the face, made my body tingle with a sense of lost perfection. I thought how sad it was that writers missed out on the ability to experience reality without filtering censors. Darren, climbing the path the other way, clapped me on the shoulders and said, "They love me in workshop. They think I oughta send out my poems to much better magazines than I've been shooting for so far. How about that?"

Three days before the end of the Conference, in their own cottage, Sally Lombardi caught her husband screwing Delphina Sommers, the silver-haired poet with pencil-thin lips, who preferred gnomic non-utterances to actual conversation. Reportedly, Delphina had a penchant for prolonged anal sex. Al, instead of apologizing and begging Sally to keep things quiet, became so angry that Sally started shouting and crying, bringing neighboring faculty to their cottage, only to find Al still naked and enraged, pronouncing, "I have put up with you for thirty-two years. You still don't get me, Sally. This might be the time to think of divorce." Whether Al and Sally will ever get divorced is something we on the fringes of the established writing circles don't know yet, but Peter did fire Al from the Conference that very day, canceling his contract for the following year as well. Delphina was gone too, but not before she threw a hissy fit in the Conference office, complaining about the incompetence of the staff who hadn't been forwarding her phone messages.

Yet who could have been prepared for the greatest surprise of all? It happened at the final bonfire, in the woods behind the farthest cottages. Several of these secretive events were supposed to have occurred already, late at night after the official parties were over. Only the initiates—that is, the youngest and most vivacious among the waiters and scholars— were invited at first. But as the Conference went on, older and older people started finding their way to the bonfires, including the hard-edged among the faculty members, and any paying contributors who were so inclined. The Conference wasn't far from closing day when the blonde Middlebury student who'd been Peter's partner at the first Barn dance asked me to walk with her to the bonfire one night. By this time I'd all but forgotten any hankering sense of loyalty I might have had toward Carmen. We passed the parking lot, where my old Ford had lain unused for almost two weeks now. I'd never once driven into Middlebury, worried I might miss out on something at the Conference, some sudden opportunity for a breakthrough. Only inane come-ons, like "the stars are sure out in full force tonight, aren't they?" occurred to me, as the Middlebury girl casually slipped her arm into mine.

Reaching the site of the bonfire, she left me as nonchalantly as if she didn't know me. In the discernible chill, women in revealing short dresses squatted awkwardly around the fire, watching the licking flames as if mesmerized, while helpful young men roasted marshmallows and occasionally burst into songs which I assumed were part of the Conference lore. I felt utterly excluded from this group of writers overtly courted and rewarded by the prestigious magazines and residencies. A mediocre poet like Peter had established himself as the guardian of the Conference, so that no one he didn't approve of could get through to the next stages. Peter was untouchable. Simone was gone, but Peter would always be here, year after year, long after I had acquired gray hair and collected many unpublished novels in my drawers. I hated Peter. I hated him with my guts. I wanted to take one of the sharp marshmallow sticks and poke it into his belly, to see some emotion from icy Peter.

"People, I have something important to tell you." Standing up in the shadowy light of the bonfire was Peter himself, dressed in a gray sweatshirt with the Conference logo on it, and tight jeans that showed off his trim hips. "This, I'm afraid to tell you, will be my last year at the Conference." Thirty or so men and women moaned in unison. Max, the gender-defying poet, the silent voice of his generation, sneezed violently—I thought he had tears in his eyes. "My decision is irrevocable," Peter went on. "I've done this long enough. There's a time for everything, and I feel like my time is past. We need fresh blood here. Some day, maybe one of you will stand in my footprints. All of you are immensely qualified, and worthy of however far you end up going." He paused. "But now, let's let loose, and one more time..." And here Peter launched the most popular of the Conference cheers. All around me I felt an emotional surge, which contained sorrow and gladness, anger and calm, retreat and advance, blended together in an indecipherable concoction only the young and healthy could fully imbibe. Before long, I slipped away from the bonfire, as the others started converting the yet-to-be-concluded Conference into instant nuggets of nostalgia, snapshots for the perpetual memory banks that would outlast even Peter's sturdy helmsmanship.

I was indescribably sad the final couple of days. Provisional goodbyes were being expressed all the time, excited promises made by one and all to keep in touch. Everyone—minus Simone and David, and Al and Sally and Delphina, of course—praised how strongly their work ethic had been revived, including those who'd grumbled earlier about the relentless pace of events. "You see the logic of this thing play out over two weeks," Jerry, the philandering editor of the venerable Southern magazine, was heard pronouncing at the sign-out desk the morning of departure. "I don't see how you get to a substantially different point from where you started, except in conditions of total immersion." Peter had become invisible. The farewell dinner, formal in a thirties

Lost Generation kind of way, had been addressed by a young black poet on the faculty, who evoked the necessary ghosts to end on the right note of elusiveness.

"Well, young man, I never did see you after that first day. Are you off soon?"

Chuck Lewison had collared me as I sat on my favorite chair on the Inn porch, my tote bag before my feet, its contents as heavy as when I arrived, failing as I had to distribute copies of my manuscript. Darren had just left in a van for Burlington airport, making me promise to spend a day in Roanoke on my drive back to Charleston. A young man with a Stegner fellowship had slipped on the wet Inn steps, and like me escaped unhurt. I had been waving to group after group of departing participants. Across the road was the forsaken lawn, favored for cocktail parties, and the hill where the hayride had brought out the country bumpkin in tenured writing teachers. Soon, everyone would be gone, and the warm Vermont August sun would reign over the desolation on the mountain.

"Mr. Lewison, sir, it's good to see you again." I stood up to shake the great man's hand. "I'm driving, so I can leave when I choose."

"That's good, that's very good, because I'd really like to talk to you. I asked Adriana about you. She says you have great promise. Now would I be remiss in thinking you just might have a manuscript you'd be interested in showing me?"

The most ecstatic half-hour of my life followed, as I happily plucked the manuscript from its coffin-darkness in the tote bag, and at Chuck Lewison's request, hit on the narrative's key plot turnings.

"It sounds really intriguing. Now, I'm going to take this with me, and I promise I'll read the whole thing on the flight back home to Orlando. I live in Florida most of the year, you know. And I'll be in touch with you soon—you do have your email here? Good, good. So then!"

We shook hands almost like equals. I felt elevated, enthralled, distinguished. All my life's bad memories escaped me for that moment. My carpenter father would have been proud.

I'd heard, of course, over the duration of the Conference that Chuck Lewison hardly ever acquired manuscripts anymore, that he was more of a venerated figurehead than an active editor, except to the few gray eminences who remained loyal to his literary judgment. But I didn't care. If I wasn't yet on my way, I had at least had a glimpse of what lay beyond obscurity. Simone never had to force her way in. Couldn't I do the same?

ANATOLIA

Evening was falling with its usual rapidity on the coastal Mediterranean town of Alanya, wiping out the smoky mirages of the summer day. Giant galleons with red and green sails, overloaded with goods, made a strict beeline for the port.

Lately, it seemed to Kadi Ahmed Efendi, the reâyâ had become insatiable about goods, the more inconsequential the better. All of Anatolia's precious mohair and silk and cotton were being shipped to Europe, and in return more expensive wool and silk and cotton were being imported. Where was the sense in that? In the twenty-five years of Padişah Ahmed III's rule, the houses in provincial Alanya had grown far sturdier than their occupants' needs, the quality of wood and glass far superior than from when he was a child. If you could spend, why save? On every street, no matter how removed from the leading jamis, çarşis, bedestans, and hans, some hustler jostled your arms: "Paşa, Paşa! I have the most precious silks from Venice. Your eyes have never fallen on such beauty, I assure you. Would you stop and look?" How could he refuse, if he didn't want to acquire a worse reputation for being against ordinary human traffic than he already had?

Kadi Efendi sat on the rocky abutment of a lonely portion of the coast, where he liked to come in the evenings to be with his opinions. His wife and sons thought his desire to be by himself was an illness of a kind. Why couldn't he join a tekke? Even membership of the dreaded Bektaşis—heaven knew what illicit practices they really approved—would be preferable to isolation. Not that isolation was possible anywhere in the empire these days. Soon, some subaşi, with nothing better to do than bother innocent citizens, would come his way, rhythmically tapping his night stick, occasionally raising it as if ready to use it if an argument got out of hand. Recognizing the kadi, the subaşi would fail to issue orders to leave before darkness; but Kadi Efendi would perceive another mental notch go up against his weirdness.

With the luck of the draw, he could have been a kadi in Izmir, or Bursa, or even Edirne. As it was, he had to seize the first suitable opening. He had married early: fatherless and motherless since late childhood, he'd had no choice. And his wife was relentless about wanting children; they'd had five sons so far, without break. She was a beautiful woman, who never had any illusions about kadis to begin with. But her beauty was all on the surface; when you tried to talk to her, she didn't want to get serious.

In the tenth year of his marriage, on his first visit back to Istanbul, he'd exchanged a few words with the Şeyhülislam, in a public audience. Kadi Efendi had plucked the nerve to refute an answer by a leading provincial mufti, deciding to speak in favor of a softer punishment, which wouldn't have been acceptable at face value to shari'a. In the capital, such softness was admired; it was what made Istanbul the powerful administrative machine it was, omnipotent because of its flexibility. But the citizens of Alanya expected him to betray a touch of arrogance, nay, demanded it of him. To display weakness was lethal.

In court tomorrow, for instance, Kadi Efendi would have no choice but to rule against Noah ibn Nehmias in the case of tax evasion brought against him by Alanya's muhtar, Iskander Halilbey. To rule against Halilbey would be to invite chaos in the administration of justice in this town. Kadi Efendi had no choice but to go through the motions; the rules of justice required no less. It was common talk among the reâyâ that kadis could be bought for a few miserable akçe. What lies! What calumny! Never in seventeen years of administering his court had Kadi Efendi failed to grasp the relevant portions of shari'a, kanün, and 'örf before passing judgment. Yet the brevity of his hükms often gave rise to rumors: he had his mind made up before he ever heard the witnesses, he had it in for the defendant or the plaintiff, he was in league with the askeri class or the landlord class, he had little respect for custom or precedent. The problem with the Osmanli mind was that even when it understood the logic of a decision, it had to put up a valiant defense to preserve the honor of all parties concerned, and that came by way of universal absolution. No one was ever at actual fault!

Take Noah ibn Nehmias's patrons, for example. How deluded they surely were about their client's impending fate, how impossibly sanguine!

Twice a year, when Noah sailed back from Venice on ships loaded with luxury goods, he stayed at the house of his friend Mustafa Çelebi, who had his hands full with both farming and trading. When Kadi Efendi first settled in Alanya, Mustafa owned but a small plot of land. One of the kadi's first cases was about an encroachment Mustafa was supposed to have made on neighboring land. In the end, Mustafa bought out all the farming plots next to his. He was too enterprising to be held back. Now with a stable of sons as strong as the mightiest gazis must have been in Osman and Orhan's time, no one quite knew the extent of Mustafa's holdings of land. Mustafa hadn't abandoned his original family compound in the center of Alanya; he'd simply incorporated more and more houses surrounding it, so that its outer walls now touched the central jami. A widower, Mustafa was said to be about to endow a major veqif in his daughter's name.

Mustafa's daughter, of course, was what really set him apart from other provincial upstarts. Neslihan Hanim was perhaps a little over twenty-one; yet no prospect of marriage was on the horizon, since she was said to look down on anyone without a foreign education, or at least extensive exposure to the newest ideas. She was rumored to be as beautiful as the Padişah's most alluring Georgian concubines, her skin and hair as fair and golden as the beauties one saw illustrated in rare books possessed by Istanbul's powerful. Kadi Efendi had heard that it was not impossible to talk to Neslihan for a young man with pretensions to possession of new knowledge—herself behind a screen, and both safely under the watch of Mustafa, of course—and that she always came away the winner in these disputations. All in all, Neslihan was a terrible, terrible example to the young women of Alanya, and beyond. It wasn't a surprise that in Padişah Ahmed's soft reign—when everything outside Anatolia was considered superior and worthy of emulation—Neslihan would be the standard against which other girls would be measured.

Noah ibn Nehmias had this going against him: his patrons were too different from the leading local lights, too prone to march to their own drummer. They were already at the limits of tolerable eccentricity. No case could ever be decided strictly on its own merits; the practicality of human affairs dictated otherwise. Everything must fit in its whole context.

"Kadi Efendi! Kadi Efendi!" Here came the interfering subaşi! "Fancy seeing you here. May the Padişah be praised. I thought it was a skeleton of you, a mere shadow. You have lost weight."

"What is it, Murat subaşi?"

"Just that at home you have unexpected guests. You'd better head back right away. The muhtar is there, with the muhtesib." Murat subaşi had a victorious gleam in his eyes, belying his calm words. "There is such a commotion at your home. I had to calm your wife down."

Ignoring this insult at the expense of his wife, Kadi Efendi said, "You have lost your head, Murat subaşi. Go away!" The town's ehl-i 'örf were not known to pay him social visits.

But as it turned out, there was even more than met the eye in the subaşi's accurate first-hand report. When the muhtar showed up with the muhtesib at the lowly kadi's home, the poor soul had to take notice.

Neslihan Hanim despised her brothers, each of whom she felt in turn was a bigger idiot than the others. They only had to open their mouths to depress her with their dullness.

The several younger ones were content with teasing her for her lonely ways; the last of them was now permanently out of the women's haremlik, thank God, and asserting his dubious credentials in the men's selamlik. The oldest brother, Selim, had married a cow, and was actually content with her. The woman kept growing out of all her clothes every six months. The family compound had thankfully swollen big enough that Neslihan didn't have to see her smug sisters-in-law too often. Selim, when he was a boy, loved to hide Neslihan's books, echoing one of the stupid local mufti's fetvas that printed books were a heretical innovation, bid'at against the practice of the Prophet. "But did they have printing presses in the time of the Prophet?" she would ask, only for Selim, at a hefty twelve, to retort: "No man will keep you his wife if you have that attitude."

The second oldest brother, Süleiman, had allowed as to how the Osmanlis had something to learn from Europe about science and industry, particularly the acquisition of new weapons and arms, ships and cannon, only to fight the infidel better. And perhaps there was something to be said for the ruthless efficiency with which the Frenks seemed to discipline their fighting men, whereas the Osmanli Janissaries were out of control, putting a damper on the free movements and actions of farmers and manufacturers and traders. But beyond that? Europe was a cesspool. Hadn't Neslihan read the accounts of the Padişah's newest emissaries to London and Paris and Vienna? Women there acted like whores—yes, there was no other word for it— openly seducing their men in public, acting for all the world as if they were no different in body and mind from men. This, in the end, would be the downfall of Europe, even if Europe's star shone bright for the moment. And there Süleiman wanted to stop all discussion.

The newspapers—another recent innovation about which the local mufti was up in arms—published for the first time in Istanbul, and brought over two weeks after publication to Alanya, were full of opinions the likes of which Selim and Süleiman could gladly endorse. Even resilient Neslihan would have grown dejected had it not been for the cheerfulness of some of the people in her life—like Noah ibn Nehmias, the stellar character whom her father was blessed to have as his friend. Noah was to appear before the kadi the next morning, with the village elders ganged up against him, but all one would hear from him today would be cheerful songs in French and quotations from the great European essayists. For Noah the eve of the millennium, when the secrets of the world would be broken open, and the messiah would reside in each of us, was now, today and every day.

As Neslihan put away the last of her notebooks in their safe compartment in the wall, and shuttered the windows against the afternoon sun, she thought she could actually hear Noah's booming voice singing in some part of the house. But that was impossible, even if he had arrived; the house was too big. She'd let her maid go at noon (rarely did she keep her even that long) to look after her sons.

Neslihan had been told she was one of those women who looked beautiful despite—or perhaps because of—making no effort to do so; it was her one vanity, to smile at this flattering compliment. Soon, her father would be asking again if she was ready to give herself in marriage to some suitable prospect. He would list, without obvious passion, some new young men that had come into his field of vision. So and so, the handsome son of a spice merchant, aspired to live and prosper in Istanbul. So and so, the educated son of a defterdâr, was praised heartily by the kethüda of the scribes' guild. Mercifully, her father never brought up soldiers as potential husbands. Some merchants weren't so scrupulous; even the corrupt Janissaries were grist for the mill, when it came to lending reality to their ambitions by means of their daughters. She would deflect easily: "Father, I've told you, it would interrupt my studies." Her father never protested. Neslihan liked to think that Noah's biannual visits were encouraged by her father at least in part to please her. For she had grown terribly fond of him, even if thinking of him as a possible husband had occurred only once or twice to her, early in their friendship, when she was still but a girl.

"Neslihan Hanim," she heard the greeting, "it's your old friend Noah ibn Nehmias. I'm settled in my quarters, and would like, if you have time, to continue our discussion of Spinoza's ethics." He was speaking outside the door of the girl's room, from the mabeyn, the common area where the haremlik ended. No doubt he was settled already on the divan, bowls of cashews and almonds by his side, ready to continue the debate they'd last had six months ago as if it had happened yesterday.

"I'm always ready, Lâla," she said, getting up and pacing. "I've been reading. The question is, are you ready?"

"The moving sights and sounds I've seen and heard on my latest journey have made me more than eager for prolonged discourse with a serious mind. You see, Neslihan Hanim, the great universities at Padua and Seville can do no good for a dull mind. It's God's gift."

As far as she knew, Noah had never seen Neslihan. Neslihan had had glimpses of him from windows. He was chubby and pink-faced, and lacked any facial hair, but carried his weight and childlike looks well. He seemed to be the happiest man alive, laughing uproariously at stupid jokes by servants—to honor them, she felt—and always talking about the beneficial aspects of even the worst situation. How could anyone not like him? But her brothers, especially Selim, loathed Noah. They thought he was introducing too many heretical ideas to the settled ways of trade in peaceful Alanya.

Last year, for instance, Noah had said in a gathering of guild heads, among them those responsible for approving the substance and quality of his latest woolen imports from Venice, that one of the reasons for Europe's maritime success was comprehensive "insurance" for loss of goods and men at sea. Such a scheme would be managed not by the Padişah and his able administrators, but by voluntary organizations of private men, who pooled large amounts of money to eliminate risk for individual merchants. He'd spoken about it in great detail and left a huge impression. Wasn't it enough that Noah's people lent money at interest? Why did they act as if they more than any others were the truest Osmanli subjects, with the selfless interest of the reâyâ always at heart? Noah, Selim complained, was never seen at one of Alanya's synagogues, not even at one of their many festivals and feasts: wasn't that where he belonged? Why did he set such a poor example for Muslims? If nobody believed in God, the entire social order would collapse overnight. Blood would run in the streets, no woman's dignity would be safe, and property would be looted by desperate men.

They had covered Spinoza well the last time. Not much remained to be said. Neslihan heard a touch of sadness in Noah's voice. Had he grown fatter than last time? He always joked about not being able to grow a proper beard; this hadn't at last made him look less of a man, had it? Was his face completely devoid of hair? She wished she could see now.

"Noah ibn Nehmias, let's not talk about Spinoza. Tell me about Venice. Tell me about Europe, Lâla."

"Ah yes, Neslihan Hanim, for this you don't need my services anymore. The Padişah has more spies and infiltrators than ever before—they call themselves travelers, seyyahs, sightseers"—and here Noah indulged in a fit of laughter that wouldn't stop—"creeping around in every salon and church in the West."

"They're stupid."

"Indeed they are. The only thing they've brought back with them is tulips."

They both had to laugh now.

But really, tulips had for so long been such a mania they were no longer cause for mirth. The thing about the successful West Ahmed III had decided to imitate, twenty-five years ago when he came to the throne, was the sense of luxury and ease and beautiful surroundings, something on the scale of the boulevards in Paris and the palazzos in Venice. All across the length and breadth of Anatolia—the coastal outpost of Alanya being no exception—large plots of land had been given up to the growth of tulips. Entirely unforeseen Anatolian varieties of the flower had come into being, so that now Europe had replaced its stock of dainty white tulips with the hardy, upright, frighteningly pink Anatolian version. According to Noah, you couldn't walk anywhere in Istanbul now without bursting into sneezing among the fields of flowers—that is, if you were near the palace, not the workers' communities, for there the stench of overcrowding and illness still overcame any competing odor.

"Tell me about the time you stepped on the turtle, Lâla," said Neslihan.

Another fit of laughter. Some years ago, in an Istanbul gathering of leading merchants and guild kethüdas, Noah had trampled on one of the little turtles with fragrant candles on their backs that were let loose in the tulip gardens, and had been thrown out for laughing uncontrollably at his blunder. "I laughed until I had tears in my eyes, until I bent over. Oh, the poor turtle. I hope I didn't kill it." But there was a harsh side to this. People said you could tell the taxes were about to go up when new fields of tulips appeared. It was general consensus in Alanya that the frivolity introduced by the Padişah was a bad sign that once and for all Europe was going to slaughter the Osmanlis on the battlefield, and that the sensuous decay, while it kept the Janissaries and government officials entertained in Istanbul, was causing a fatal weakening of the martial spirit all over Anatolia. Noah didn't take such a dark view of it; a little fun never hurt—as long as you didn't step on turtles and murder them, ha ha!

"You're not worried about tomorrow, Noah ibn Nehmias?"

"What? Worry? Of course not. The kadi is an honest man."

"A kadi is never an honest man. You don't even know this one."

"True, but—look, you have to have faith, otherwise ill-will is returned in kind. I can't help what's going to happen tomorrow. I do have—real faith."

"Is the case against you entirely false?"

"Of course, Neslihan Hanim." He didn't sound offended. "Why would I cheat? I make enough as it is. There's no reason to deprive the state's coffers of a few akçe here and there. The charge is absurd. I take pride in meticulous recordkeeping. My documents will settle the matter in minutes."

"I hope for your sake you're right, Noah ibn Nehmias."

"Don't worry. I won't be the turtle they step on."

It wasn't an auspicious sign that for the first time ever, Selim's fat wife interrupted their discourse on some trivial excuse: "Sister, I just wanted to see what you preferred for dinner tonight. Will it be the usual zerdé-pilaf?" Then she giggled helplessly, as if Noah, on the other side of the screen, couldn't hear. No doubt Selim's wife had a thing for Noah herself. How could anyone not?

∽∝

"Paşa, your horse is ready for tomorrow." Mustafa Çelebi's youngest stable attendant bowed deeply at the waist, then kept moving his head up and down.

Such a low opinion of oneself, such a pathetic need to be loved! The vast compound, with stables and pens for animals, servants' quarters at the edges and the three-storied whitewashed house in the middle, seemed deserted except for this slave at heart. Mustafa was reminded of the wandering group of Bektaşi dervishes he'd run into in the street just now; they'd shown exaggerated politeness to him, and Mustafa couldn't get rid of the impression that they were mocking him. Their şeyh, a man whose thick eyebrows were white, had grabbed a stray chicken from the street, and held it up high, close to Mustafa's face: "You see this? This is how helpless we appear to Allah. Like this chicken. And how many eggs it lays month after month, thinking it's life everlasting. This chicken! Hmm. So let's cluck like chickens. Let's laugh and dance. It's the only way to be."

"Get up, man!" Mustafa barked at the groom, distracted. "Tomorrow, what's tomorrow?"

"Ağa, the hunt. With the kethüda of the tanner's guild and the kethüda of the—"

"We're not going tomorrow. Tomorrow is court day. Has no one told the kethüdas yet?"

The stable boy, a local from Alanya, all but spread himself prostrate on the ground. Was he going to recite the kalima now? He seemed ready for a whipping. It was said that slaves from Habeş had inherent dignity; never would they bend so low before a lord. But look at the pride of Anatolia! A boy educated through the hâric medrese. Mustafa could understand why so many of them took to men instead of women. He slipped a few akçe in the boy's hand.

The hunt. It would be fat local tradesmen pursuing poor bustards as if butchering the infidel within the gates of Vienna. They slobbered at the mouth and let out heathenish whoops at every kill. The real world was unimpressed by these antics. In Rumelia, the âyâns had put the self-satisfied traders and government officers on notice; these warlords, claiming direct descent from the great Turkish nomad tribes, were to take over Osmanli Europe, introducing a reign of terror. The budding derebeys in Anatolia would follow the path the âyâns had laid out; warlords demolishing law and order were inevitable. All Mustafa's friends wanted to do was hunt and play, and laugh like girls at the latest intrigue in the Padişah's harem, by yet another cunning Circassian or

Georgian woman. There was little one could do though; it was the price of prosperity. How did one prepare for insecurity?

He'd come home early, for dinner with his guest Noah ibn Nehmias. As usual, Noah would wax poetic about the exemplary commercial practices of the Venetians and other Europeans. Noah would want to know why the Anatolians weren't building more roads and bridges and ports throughout the land, why the palace continued to rely so heavily on berâts granting special favors to European merchants instead of educating Anatolians themselves to do the necessary tasks, why the local notables weren't more upset about the steep rise in taxes to support the lavish lifestyles of the Janissaries, the timar-holders, and other useless vassals of the Padişah? *These things don't matter*, Mustafa wanted to tell him; *nothing changes*. One could only care for one's own soul, and even then, did it ever pay off?

Mustafa wouldn't even let his dear children know, but lately he'd been feeling a weariness that wouldn't dissipate. Earlier and earlier in the day, he found himself wanting to make for the Mevlevi tekke, to be overwhelmed by the purity of the fair young men working hard for their respective guilds. Compared to them, Mustafa's every thought was transparently sinful. The muezzin's call left him cold. He couldn't summon the requisite anger at the Janissaries' corruption—the sight of one of them, overgrown and awkward, loafing around the gates of a bedestan or han, looking for an opportunity to make a few unearned akçe by throwing his weight around, no longer inspired real revulsion in him. The more land and property Mustafa acquired, and the more his children told him what a great man he was, the more he wanted to turn away from the world.

The necessary corollary to loving anything or anyone was the capacity to hate; if hate lagged, so did love. Last Şeker

Bayrami, he distributed bakşiş to all the keepers of order hanging around him, without so much as a feinted good wish for their families. Mustafa was only fifty-three, but convinced his heart was dead already. If there were a firman from the Padişah ordering all able-bodied men to fight a new gazâ on his behalf, venturing into the deepest heart of Europe, where the Osmanlis hadn't gone before, he would gladly sign up. But the days of gazâs were over; those born Muslim hadn't themselves fought a war since the days of Mehmet Fatih. The Janissaries—converted Christians, slaves personally beholden to the Padişah—didn't want to fight; they did everything possible to avoid war, and when war happened, they hired others, less capable, to go on their behalf.

It might be—as Neslihan said—that there came a time when every person felt like turning away from the life meant for him. Neslihan said that reading great works of the imagination was the only rescue for the soul at such moments. She talked all the time about this great English book that had just been translated, *Robinson Crusoe*, about a sailor who gets shipwrecked on a forlorn island and builds a secure life for himself, and another one, *Gulliver's Travels*, that was the talk of Europe and was soon to be translated, about another sailor who gets shipwrecked on many islands. For her, such characters of fantasy were more real than her brothers and their wives and children and Mustafa himself. He wished he possessed the mind to read such stuff, but he didn't. It had been tough enough to get through the first five years of reading the Kur'an at the hâric medrese. All he remembered of that was having to stand on one leg for hours, or squat with his head squeezed between his knees like a rooster, or being smacked on the wrist with a stick by the grumpy ustad. In this respect—his ignorance of the intricacies of his faith—he was like his old friend Noah.

Neslihan had come to believe that Mustafa encouraged Noah's friendship in part for her sake. That might be true, but the real reason was Noah's innocence, his faith in the dignity and benevolence of the world, his sheer joy at the smallest of delights, which others took for granted. Noah helped restore Mustafa's soul twice a year. The business Mustafa did with Noah was so minute a fraction of Mustafa's total sales that it wasn't worth mentioning; but it was Noah's apostate spirit—apostate against the stable view of the world, where one played one's assigned role, and the authorities either laughed or frowned at you—that struck Mustafa's rawest nerve.

With any luck, despite Mustafa's being bound to be called as a witness for or against Noah tomorrow in court—did Noah even realize Mustafa was to be one of the crucial witnesses?—his old friend wouldn't think unkindly of Mustafa. The memory of Noah's father—as religious a man, besotted by the scent of the synagogue and the dress of the martyr, as Noah was irreligious—was too painful to warrant any thought of replication in his son. Noah's father, despite being greatly respected by Alanya's notables, had chosen to exile himself to Venice, where he'd died only a few years later, alone in a ghetto, without the good medical care he'd have received in Alanya. It would be a shame if Noah turned away from the world; no, he couldn't be allowed to.

Mustafa felt confident he could finesse the issue: on the one hand, he had to satisfy muhtar Iskander Halilbey—who'd visited Mustafa at his offices yesterday—that Mustafa was firmly on the side of the local traders. On the other hand, Mustafa must not chastise Noah so severely that soon Mustafa himself might become a target of the rapacious tax-farmers and their even more corrupt contractors.

The charge being brought against Noah was flimsy—ridiculous, even. It was the symbolic importance that counted.

A respected Jew would be brought in front of a kadi of Alanya. He would be put on notice. He would be asked to account for the exact quantity and value of goods he'd loaded on his ships on his last few visits to the port, because the kethüdas in Alanya were supposed to have submitted records to the tax collectors that suggested more had been loaded on the ships than the Jew had paid taxes for. This against an almost unworldly subject who railed against the Osmanli rulers for not finding ways to charge everyone *more* taxes, to improve the physical layout of the empire! Mustafa would play it down the middle, not make enemies of either side. The real danger, Noah would have said, was from European citizens obtaining undue advantage from the capitulations granted by the Padişah. The real action was in Istanbul. Yet the worthies of Alanya wanted to make an example of Noah, one of their own, most faithful, citizens!

If only Neslihan had shown some interest in marrying Noah! Noah could have nominally converted to Islam. Nobody would have dared bring trumped-up charges against him then. But the girl had a mind of her own. Oh well, it was how Mustafa had brought her up. Besides, it was difficult to think of the self-sufficient Noah as a son-in-law, having to consult with him day after day. Perhaps the Jew was good only in small biannual doses.

All morning, Kadi Ahmed Efendi had had to go easy on shameless thieves and pickpockets, lying letter-writers and vanishing storytellers, and above all, prostitutes. Minimal fines, a few akçe, nothing to put the prostitutes out of pocket, and a stern admonition: "For decency's sake, can't you find an honest living?" But who would marry a prostitute? Even the detested Yörüks, the original Turks, nomads to the bone and pagan in custom, had acquired too much civilization to feel pity for those forced into unsavory occupations.

The last case was of a man guarding a han who'd been found stealing the guests' clothes for a number of years; he hadn't sold any, his little house being chockful of other men's worn jubbés and salvârs. Now this was sickness of a new kind. The kadi didn't even stoop low enough to fine him; he couldn't muster the imagination to come up with an appropriate humiliation for this man before his fellow guards at the han. "Return the clothes!" Kadi Efendi ordered. The guard replied, "Should I travel to Rumelia and Russia and Persia and India in search of each of the men, Ağa?"

Actually, the kadi was being evasive, squeezing in as many small-time cases as possible in the morning, having hoped against hope that the muhtar and the muhtesib, with whom he'd pleaded the night before at his home not to proceed against Noah ibn Nehmias, would have come to a settlement outside court.

But here they were, sitting in a corner of the one-room building. Nothing distinguished the kadi's seat from a commercial building. In the summer it was too hot, in the winter too cold—in the north, in a place like Kars, when it snowed almost all official business came to a stop because no one had figured out how to secure the buildings against the severe cold. The muhtar and the muhtesib, the pair of kethüdas who'd been brought in gratuitously, all sat without expression, keeping their eyes away from each others' faces. Mustafa Çelebi, as decent a man as any in Alanya, was not a direct party to the case, but present as a witness—both sides had probably asked this man of reputation to testify on their behalf.

Only the defendant, Noah ibn Nehmias, had eyes full of curiosity, his expression rising and falling with the fate of the other defendants in court today. Every time the kadi let go a prostitute without punishment, Noah seemed to breathe easier, searching the kadi's eyes to bestow a stamp of approval. Noah was wearing too much silk for an adult man, and it looked like he'd just finished eating a hefty meal at a roadside cookshop, his face and lips shone so. The kadi's scribe, whose immaculate sicills were beautiful enough to be works of calligraphy in demand in Istanbul, adjusted his ankles more comfortably under his spreading rump; his face, drained of all blood, pale as a cow's offal, always frightened the kadi.

"The case of the muhtar of Alanya, Iskander Halilbey, against Noah ibn Nehmias," Kadi Efendi said at last, noting that Mustafa's face darkened and strained visibly. "Have the parties come to sulh, any resolution between themselves?" the kadi asked hopelessly. Meeting with shakes of the head all around, and a wry smile from Noah, the kadi asked, "Does the defendant accept or deny the charges?"

"I deny everything," Noah said. "Everything."

"Then the case must go forward. The accusing party will choose a representative to lay out the beyyine."

The riffraff loitering in the room vanished as if recognizing that heftier matters than stolen pockets and undeliverable letters were at stake. The subaşi, on alert all morning at the wide door to the building, plunked his plump self on the bare divan by the doorway, searching through his pockets.

Kadi Efendi's wife had lectured him until well after dark the previous night, admonishing him, for the sake of the children, to do the right thing, judge as the muhtar and the muhtesib wished him to. *For the sake of the children?*— whom his wife protected and kept away from the kadi as if he were the most ill-meaning of the djinn the storytellers were always going on about. Like all women, she could become immensely practical at the slightest external push. For their short but disconcerting visit, the muhtar and the muhtesib seemed to have conspired to say as little as possible, nothing to incriminate them in a plot; they kept asking so keenly about the kadi's welfare—what was the future of the older child after he finished the dahîl medrese? Was enrollment at Istanbul's Süleymaniyye medrese in the offing?—that the kadi had to stop reading them as signals of bribes. It couldn't be done openly, anyway; it could only come in the form of gifts from unknown parties. Suddenly, one morning, a white Arabian horse would show up at one's door. Or a trunk of rare silks. And a note: "From the unworthy giver to the most worthy receiver: Know that your unstinting service to the best standards of the sultanate is much appreciated." Without staying long, his two official visitors had left him feeling more dejected about his chosen line of business than ever before.

"Ağa, I'll present the evidence." Muhtar Iskander Halilbey spread his sheaves of documents on the floor before the kadi's feet. "You see, here's a clear trail of the accused, the Jew Noah ibn Nehmias, always cheating by underdeclaring the quality of the wools he buys in the local markets. Our merchants here record nothing but the actual value of the goods and pay taxes accordingly. But the buyer who spends most of his time in foreign lands—this ibn Nehmias—well, he's had no shame about cheating the Padişah. I demand the severest punishment in light of the evidence. Lifetime banishment from conducting trade in any part of the sultanate. Immediate restitution of the amount lost to the state coffers, barring which appropriate jail time to be decided by your lordship."

Muhtar Halilbey, a nondescript man except for his exaggerated moustache, had made a name for himself in two decades of service in Alanya on only a couple of occasions: once when he prosecuted an illiterate Christian for blaspheming the Prophet on the streets—yet another case when the kadi wouldn't bend to popular passion to punish the offender, because clearly the man was insane—and another time when the muhtar had it in for one of the Bektaşi tekkes for consuming large quantities of alcohol. Didn't everyone know that was what the Bektaşis did? Nothing said you had to violate someone's space behind four walls to find out what they were up to. That wasn't the police's job; the kadi had refused to hear the case. And now the muhtar hoped to nail a popular Jew. Many a time the kadi had been cornered by the muhtar on the street, with bad news of yet another series of Osmanli losses on the battlefield, to the vile Europeans or Russians or Persians: "The best way to push them back is to organize a new gazâ, something so huge it catches all our enemies by surprise," the muhtar would assert. "We're taking things too easy."

"What do the others supporting the accusation have to say?" asked Kadi Efendi. The muhtesib, who stammered, made an inappropriate joke about the rarity of precious wool in Andalus, clearly an underhanded reference to the exile of the Jews from one of their chosen lands, where so much good had come to them before they were kicked out by the fanatic Christian rulers. This undertone of violence couldn't be allowed to persist. "Would you stick to the facts in the case?" the kadi pleaded, his throat dry. "Kethüda Ibrahimoğlu?" The head of the wool spinners guild testified to the accuracy of the muhtar's records, but there was a desultoriness about his testimony. The same lack of passion went for the kethüda of the wool weavers. Muhtar Halilbey kept stealing glances at Mustafa Çelebi; the muhtar probably expected Mustafa to testify on his behalf. But Mustafa only looked on wearily.

"If there's no further testimony from the plaintiff's side, I'll call the defendant."

With a flourish, Noah got up to speak. There was
no need for that. Perhaps they did that in European courts,
all the unnecessary pomp and ceremony, to go with cases
that dragged on for years and years, often to no resolution.
The Osmanli way was swift and sure justice, based on local
custom, immediate witness, irrefutable evidence; no excessive
glorification, speculation, abstraction, stretching of analogies
and reasoning. The Padişah's kanünnâmes covered every
contingency in specifics. Further, Noah had a hectoring,
schoolmasterish tone about him today that the kadi didn't
like one bit. But the kadi resolved to do justice anyway.

"What you have here is a pure case of—envy! I'll
explain." The merits of the case Noah expertly demolished in
a few minutes. Noah bought goods in very large volume; so a
minute discrepancy in valuation could explain large deficits
in taxes paid. The judging of the precise grade of wool was an
art, not a science. It was difficult to get wool merchants with
decades of experience to speak with one voice on the subject.
Noah had accepted the assessments of the wools in good
faith; he'd been patronizing the same kethüdas year after year,
so if anyone was to be blamed for miscalculation, wasn't it the
guild heads, not him? Noah hadn't been on notice that such a
case would be brought against him on this trip immediately
on arrival, but if the kadi were to give him six months, until
his next visit, Noah would bring documents from Venice to
prove his side of the case. The browbeating tone went away by
the end of Noah's plea. Muhtar Halilbey was agitated, his face
red and splotchy, his fists clenching and unclenching; the man
needed a good holiday, to some distant spot on the Black Sea.

"Good, very good. Any witnesses for or against?"

Kadi Efendi hoped Mustafa Çelebi would say
something definitively in favor of the Jew and take the
decision out of his hands. Indeed, Mustafa got up too,

copying the declamatory style of his old friend. "Kadi Efendi, I vouch for Noah ibn Nehmias's honor. I undertake personal guarantee that he'll return six months from now to present the documents he says he has in his possession to prove his case. Further, I believe that under no circumstances would this man cheat the Padişah of revenues. He's incapable of doing that. I'm willing to submit any other guarantees." Mustafa might have been expected to finesse the issue so he wouldn't come out so openly against the muhtar and his allies, but apparently he'd thrown caution to the winds.

Still, Kadi Efendi knew he couldn't create for himself a hostile enemy in Muhtar Halilbey. The muhtar could make life unbearable for the kadi, tying up the court with frivolous cases, speaking against him at every opportunity he got with his superiors, the illiterate representatives of the beylerbeyi and sançakbeyi. Some slight slap on the wrist was called for. "With the arguments and testimony concluded, I rule that henceforth Noah ibn Nehmias will *personally* present his shipping documents to the muhtesib's inspection right after arrival and before departure each time in the port of Alanya." For regular traders, the inspection of documents was a formality that could be conducted in due course of time, so as not to hold up arrival or departure. Furthermore, nothing had been said about his *arrival* with goods; the kadi thought it sounded right, for the sake of symmetry and balance.

"Kadi Efendi, this is an outrage!" Noah was up again.

Kadi Efendi was stunned. He'd thought the Jew wouldn't resent the imposition too much. After all, the news was that in Europe the inspection of documents and goods and persons had reached a far more advanced stage than anything seen so far in Anatolia. Why should his reasonable demand become an issue? The muhtesib wouldn't personally inspect and deal with Noah ibn Nehmias. It would be some lowly naip of his.

But Noah was unpacifiable. "I won't put up with this. This is a mark on my honor. There's no need to subject me to extra inspection compared to other shippers. My record is without blemish. I dare the muhtar to explain the causes of his envy. The man is a wreck, can't you see? He's sick, he hates me, and he doesn't even know why." Noah was shouting.

"I will not have this outburst in my court. My ruling is final."

In the end, Noah had to be controlled by the subaşi, the first physical workout the officer had managed to get in many years. It had been a sad day; contrary to what Kadi Efendi had hoped for, everyone had gone away unhappy. The muhtar was livid at the kadi, because Kadi Efendi didn't order any punishment for Noah's violation of court etiquette. Mustafa Çelebi had put a hand on the kadi's shoulder, as though to commiserate: "We did our best, my friend. But it's hopeless, once things get this far."

Noah walked out of the courthouse alone, spurning Mustafa Çelebi's offer to accompany him, but not in a rude way.

Noah was chastened by his first direct experience with Osmanli justice. He understood that the kadi had been as lenient with him as possible given the need to stay on good terms with the ehl-i 'örf. A similar case in Venice, if brought by a powerful enough personage, might have resulted in immediate disbarment. Here the tone was friendly. Still, it was confusing. Why, for instance, had the kethüdas—whom he'd always thought of as a shade otherworldly, for all their ability to drive a hard bargain—distorted the reality? If the test of a man's courage was a time of tribulation, then every single person in that courthouse had failed. Himself too, for had he not whined and groaned, instead of facing up to the strength of his enemies? Envy? Who was envying whom?

The kadi was a decent man; according to the philosophical treatises Noah talked about with Neslihan, Noah should quickly forget and forgive. To hold a grudge against the pettiness of the local merchants—why, that would be to fall right into their trap! One of the great men of Noah's race had been Sabbatai Sevi, who, pushed to the wall, converted to Islam as a guest of Mehmet IV, abandoning his messianic claims. That was a worthy act of sacrifice in the name of sanity. Half the Jews in Venice hated Sabbatai, the other half were in love with him. But Sabbatai was only a man, who hadn't succeeded in surviving to old age.

Without knowing it, Noah had walked to the coffeehouse where he'd first met Mustafa years ago. Noah ordered tea and helva, no heavy food, thank you, even though it was early afternoon, and long past time for a real meal. His appetite hadn't returned. Most locals assumed Noah was from Alanya itself, a Jew who spoke their language in every sense of the word. In fact, most places he visited in the Osmanli empire assumed this: whether he was in Erzurum or Kayseri or Aydin, the residents assumed he was one of them, extensive travel having diluted the singularity of his accent. He was good with languages; in only a few days he would start adopting the tones and rhythms of wherever he happened to be staying.

It was warm, a good day to appreciate the stark blueness of the Mediterranean. Unlike Europeans, Turks didn't seem obsessed with the loveliness of the ocean; only the residents of Istanbul had a love affair with the water, and wasn't that because of their proximity to European notions of beauty? For the average resident of Alanya, the ocean was the ocean; it wasn't as though you needed to make special excursions to witness it of an evening, alone or with family.

Here was a swarm of Bektaşis now, heading his way; their wandering troupes had vastly increased in number over the last few years—they, and the companies following the âyâns and derebeys, the warlords beginning to take advantage of Osmanli generosity by seizing control of timars held by weak sipahis who no longer had the courage and strength to protect their lands. Well, what was to be done about it? One could say all the right things about the durability of the empire, but Europe was progressing by lightning speed. A rudimentary steam engine had been invented. The Osmanlis didn't seem to know anything about it.

To Noah's surprise, the şeyh of the Bektaşis approached him. "Paşa, are you from around here?" The şeyh was an emaciated man, of indeterminate age, with a paleness of face meant to suggest spiritual advancement.

"What of it, haçi?" Noah spoke harshly, spitting to the side a piece of helva stuck in his teeth. "What if I am or am not from around here? Does it matter? To you Bektaşis, of all people?"

"No offence. I'm just asking, Paşa, because I haven't seen you in any of the bedestans, and you look like a merchant, a rich one, at that. We like to do special favors for our visitors from outside Alanya."

"Favors?" Noah smirked. "Like what?" Did the şeyh mean rare stimulants, drugs?

"Why not come to the tekke tonight and find out?"

"Sorry. I'm a Jew." Noah laughed scornfully. "Am I expected to do these things?"

"My apologies. A thousand apologies, Paşa. It's just that I didn't see any visible signs. You're not wearing the kipot."

Well, who did anyway? How many Jews avoided wearing green, the Muslim color, or took care to wear black shoes? A dark look began to cross Noah's face. Meanwhile, a lift of the şeyh's eyebrow dispersed the congregation. The şeyh himself bowed and left.

The lunch eaters around him murmured in low voices. Why didn't they complain vocally about rising taxes, shoddy goods, corrupt officials? Europeans were under the illusion that Turks treated eating purely functionally—potential armies of fearless soldiers feeding only for necessary fuel to spur the fighting machine, the human cannon. How false an impression! Mealtimes were precious here, as anywhere else. But it did look like the artisans at the kehfené were aiming to finish eating at the same time. Ah, there was the ubiquitous fat storyteller— you could tell by his comical turban, emblem of his trade—in the far corner. Soon, those who had knocked off work for the day would assemble outside the coffeehouse for a couple of hours before the practiced raconteur. If only the storytellers understood the art of satire: then they would tell thinly disguised tales about the vâlidé sultan's latest conspiracies in the harem, the chief Black Eunuch's double-crossing of the Greek Orthodox Patriarch, the Grand Vêzir's ignorance of his own hanging until the last moment. In all likelihood, a shadow puppet theater would also be spontaneously set up to entertain the crowd, the illiterate Karagöz predictably getting the better of the genteel Haçivat in the play.

Noah was forced to return to reality. A judgment had been passed against him today. How real had his anger been?

He probed in his pockets to retrieve a crumpled letter written to him by his aunt in Selânik. "Dear Noah, I'm not getting any younger. Gray mists, swarms of mosquitoes, get thicker in my eyes. My legs hurt and sometimes I can't sleep the entire night. Every Jew in blessed Selânik feels charmed and content. They write love poetry and sing happy songs. They seek miracles proving their own happiness. But my dear nephew, I'm unhappy and wish nothing better before I die than to see you married to Rebekah. She will make you a good wife. She cooks, she cleans, she sews, she has a good knowledge of Torah..." It went on for a couple of pages—for a dying woman his aunt certainly had a steady hand—singing the praises of the daughter.

Rebekah was a fair enough girl, eager to please, and undoubtedly capable of producing many children. Her knowledge of Torah would have pleased Noah's father, a needless martyr to his forefathers' only understanding of the meaning of life. But there was nothing exceptional about Rebekah. For weeks now, Noah had put off writing a delicate refusal. In the past, the aunt, his father's favorite sister, had only hinted; her coming out in the open meant that Noah probably wouldn't visit Selânik now, even for business. Rebekah was the kind of girl who, if she were his wife, would remind him that the judgment rendered against him today was because he'd lost touch with his faith. "Head right to the synagogue! Worship the way our forefathers have, for five thousand years, and your troubles will melt away! Talk to the rabbi! Let nothing weigh on your heart!"

Noah's other pocket held, in an exquisite ivory box, the ring he'd bought for Neslihan in Venice's cutthroat jewelry row.

The ring was a European custom Neslihan would surely appreciate, he'd thought when he bought it. He and Neslihan had of late been running out of things to say about the muddles in Maimonides's and Spinoza's thought. Their pattern of conversation had become too fixed. It was time to secure their alliance, make it permanent. No girl more able, more aspiring of the higher feelings, could be found in the realm. True, years ago Neslihan had hinted that she wasn't interested in marriage. But why couldn't inklings of love be revived? Was he mistaken in detecting more openness on

Neslihan's part on his last two visits? She probably felt the pressure of age. And her father? Mustafa wouldn't make more of a fuss than Noah's nominal conversion to Islam.

Still, wasn't Noah supposed to feel engrossing passion toward the woman of his choice? Wasn't he to think all the time of ravishing her? He felt no such emotion. He'd seen too much, traveled too widely, to let his emotions run wild like a nomad's. Noah tried to visualize Neslihan—he'd never caught a glimpse of her, although everyone did say her beauty was miraculous—but only the dour faces of the muhtar and the muhtesib, and the two kethüdas, all joined together in conspiracy, visited him.

He gave up trying to feel better about himself. He pushed the undercooked helva away. Perhaps Europe did make things easier for the battered self. Though the stringent rules and customs were more rigidly enforced, there were enough beautiful things with only a decorative purpose around to compensate for it. A coffeehouse in such a good neighborhood in Europe would have proper chairs and tables, flower vases and wall decorations, an air of pride and possession and prestige. Here he sat on a stone "bench" and ate at a stone "table," while the sights and sounds of the cooks at work with their grills and pans were out in the open. Instructions to cook and serve and discard were issued within earshot of customers; none of the processes of making and disposing were kept hidden. Just because it was a provincial kehfené frequented mostly by artisans didn't mean that the most prosperous merchant, or the Ağa of the Janissaries, or the sançakbeyi himself, couldn't drop in at any moment. Perhaps there was beauty after all in keeping things separate, not letting odd combinations mix and match at will. There must be some transcendent definition of order eluding even the orderly Osmanlis.

Noah got up to leave—but where would he go? To head back to Mustafa's home would be torture!—when he was stopped by a commotion in the street. A chase was on, headed his way. A motley gang of starving thieves, perhaps six or seven, was on the run, the healthy subaşis close on their heels. They chose the coffeehouse for the place of capture. The trinkets stolen by the thieves—probably from some sleepy merchant at the nearby bedestan—were unceremoniously extracted from their pockets. The muhtar and the muhtesib, last seen trying to nail Noah, were right behind the pursued and the pursuers, maintaining a dignified pace.

"In the name of the Padişah," Muhtar Halilbey proclaimed, "I arrest you for theft. Let this be an example to your fellow criminals..." It was embarrassing to listen to the muhtar's self-righteous speech. Noah had never seen a low-level Osmanli official grandstand so indecently. It made a shiver run through his body. The muhtar concluded: "Padişahim chok yasher!" Long live our Padişah.

"Show them mercy, Ağa," Noah said, meeting the muhtar's cold eyes. Noah quoted an apt example from the last Şheyülislam's famous fetva about the injustices of the social order compelling most petty crimes. "So be merciful, Ağa." Muhtar Halilbey's lips were pinched blue, his eyes narrowed to small points. Before the muhtar could come up with a response, Noah put his arm on the official's shoulder. "I won't be bothering you again."

Had the subaşis not been hard on their case, Noah would have slipped the ring to one of the thieves. But no, that would be throwing coals on fire. The recipient would be charged with a further crime.

A calming sense of practicality began to overcome him. He had to see to his cargo. His ships. The sailors would be getting restless. The goods to take back to Venice were already on the docks. Let them be loaded and let him be on his way. Noah ibn Nehmias was a merchant above all. He must carry on. The unpredictable acts of a couple of paltry officials didn't necessarily describe a pattern. What had happened to him was an individual incident with no universal meaning.

One of Noah's assistants—an amiable young Jew for whom he couldn't help feeling helpless sympathy—was getting married on their return to Venice. The man's wife, whoever she was, would love the ring.

INDEPENDENCE

Three times already that day, Saleem had shunned the advances of his older brother Yaqub's wife Saira. The first was in the kitchen in the early morning, when he was fixing himself a cup of tea—he wasn't one to call on servants for every little thing—and she followed him in there. The second was during the afternoon conversation in the garden, when she took his side against her husband's on some obscure political issue, embarrassing and flustering Saleem. And the last was after dinner, when he was hiding in the library and she found him there. Yaqub must know what his wife was up to; no doubt he used the knowledge to rib her at boring times, perhaps cajole her into better sex. Over the course of the day, Saira's appearance became progressively wilder: whereas only her thick, wavy hair was disheveled in the morning, by evening her sari was a mere scrap of indulgence, exposing without shame all her generous middle section. Saira seemed to have picked up the notion that Saleem went in for Kipling's war-mindedness: whatever gave her that idea? Tennyson's inconsolable sadness would be closer to the mark. "Do we need any more storms in a teacup?" he'd said to her in the library, to which, instead of taking the hint—for the exact reason the three brothers had been summoned by their father from the east, west, and north of India in that burning August of 1953 remained as always difficult to divine—she seemed to stick her scantily hid breasts out further, and said, "A real storm would clean out all the blockage, don't you think?"

Saleem's own wife Zuleikha, Julie to the world, was too delicate and graceful a woman to remark publicly on Saira's wantonness. She pretended to be busy at all times with their only child, five-year-old Sadiq, who, as it happened, was fiercely independent. On the train from Bombay to Madras, and from there to Pondicherry, to his father's antiquated French quarter estate which he'd owned since 1918, Julie had made a loud fuss over each of Sadiq's needs: they should have brought the tutor along, after all (no, Saleem believed a child should be left to his own devices as much as possible), and would Sadiq develop respiratory problems from the heavy air of the Deccan plateau if Saleem insisted on keeping the compartment window open. Sadiq was too hot or too cold, not eating well enough or gorging himself, his eyes were glazed over or he seemed feverishly excited: *for God's sakes, leave the kid alone,* Saleem wanted to scream, but of course he never raised his voice against Julie who, for all he knew, might collapse at such a development. Julie, who must look less like a married woman than any woman in India, brittle on the surface like expensive china, how had she given birth to a big, healthy baby, wonder of wonders! Not even when they were granted the unexpected visit in their train compartment by one of Saleem's friendly rivals in the Bombay textile industry—a fat man by the name of Ishtiaq, who was with his one-time movie actress wife Leila, herself running to fat but putting on moves as if she remained the sultry siren she was supposed to have been in the forties— and Julie veered every political or business discussion toward little Sadiq's daily physical and psychological odysseys, not even then did Saleem acknowledge how upset he was.

He'd played the good father, the good husband, in Madras too, where they stopped for three days—they'd left Bombay with plenty of time to spare to meet his father's biyearly summons—and at Fort St. George, a monumental building that always gave Saleem the creeps, Julie insisted on familiarizing Sadiq with every little memento (pen or sword) of the Clives and Wellesleys and other viceroys who'd made Madras the beachhead of the Raj, as if the dead viceroys had been family friends. "They were damned colonizers, Julie," he wanted to say to rouse her from her torpor. They never walked along the beach promenade, never came in sight of the Bay of Bengal during their entire stay in Madras, because the ocean air wasn't supposed to be good for Sadiq. She saw dangers where there were none, and ignored real ones. Had Julie ever been alert to the ruthlessness of the world? After seven years of marriage—Saleem had married late at thirty-three, when Julie was only twenty-one—Julie still treated Yaqub, and Saleem's younger brother Mushtaq, as if they too were family friends. She treated Saleem's crusty old father—a diabolic man who thought all relationships in life, including ones with immediate family members, were silent chess games to the death—with genuine affection and respect; luckily, the old man didn't have the usual symptoms that develop with age, frigid bones and unreliable digestion, for Julie to recommend this or that elite French doctor in the sacred Pondicherry confines east of the canal.

What kind of a city was this anyway? He'd gotten away at last, on the early morning of his third day in Pondicherry, glad to have escaped Saira's notice. You didn't need sturdy shoes to walk in this city. The street lamps dazzled well into daylight, a rarity in India. Everyone with money and power seemed bent on preserving Pondicherry as it had been for two centuries. There was to be a formal dinner at Saleem's father's home next week, to which were invited the city's leading European and Indian philanthropists, who generously endowed the Romain Rolland library, the Sacred Heart church, and other monuments of French rule. The wives of the great industrialist's three sons would be expected to display the graciousness of the new India. Everyone would pretend that the canal that divided the city's eastern, European section from the western, Indian section, was an actual, flowing canal, not the static, rising garbage dump it had become since independence. Everyone would assume that the local Indians subscribed to the progressive teachings of the churches patronized by the Europeans. Everyone would channel anger at the recent desecration of the Mahatma Gandhi statue on Beach Road toward the federal, never the municipal, authorities: "It's the work of outsiders," the daintiest among the guests would declaim. In fact, Pondicherry was *three* cities in one: the third being the zone without physical space inhabited by Indians lucky enough to move back and forth between the two worlds in some employed capacity, somewhat like the workers at his factory who in their first years liked to believe that home wasn't anarchic Bombay, but whatever orderly place they'd come from.

On Thollandal Street, where his father's estate lay, he headed toward the canal, encountering on his way composed domestic servants crossing over to the European side for a hard day's work, the women's silver jewelry and colorful slippers illusively suggesting holidaymaking. Thollandal Street became Koil Street at the dividing line; that was where he took a seat on a stone bench, and observed on the other side of the street, on an identical bench, a pretty, young Indian girl with some obvious European blood sell her body to a middle-aged papadum seller. Fifty rupees. The openness of the transaction, loud and unashamed, this early in the morning, shattered his emerging daydream of his mother—who would die the morning the world economy collapsed in 1929, gathering her family around for a breakfast of parathas and omelets—and returned him to the force of present reality: When was he going to have it out with his father? He heard from Yaqub and Mushtaq that their factories, in Calcutta and Delhi, ran as if on automatic pilot; his brothers were keen to expand into new lines of manufactures, and scale up their production of existing lines. He had to warn his father of overreach; he foresaw lowered demand in the years ahead, the need for contraction. All Saleem could manage to do was hold things together, daily walking the tightrope between fiscal soundness and worker concessions. Julie was reconciled to Saleem's established role in the business empire. Not once since Sadiq had been born had Julie brought up the idea of Saleem quitting the family business to start an independent venture of his own, or perhaps doing something different on the side: they once used to talk about starting a foundation for poor people, drawing on the wealth of Saleem's rich business friends.

When he got back, the house was stirring. Servants in clean uniforms saluted him right and left, as if he were his father's true avatar. His father was in fine form early; normally he wasn't himself until the lunch hour: "Wonderful, wonderful news! Did you hear?" The old man's bony frame belied preternatural muscular strength; in his youth he'd wrestled to the ground many a petty verbal challenger. His face looked as if a fat-sucking machine had explored every crevice, leaving only bare bone and flesh. Yet he didn't look unhandsome; his thin moustache didn't have any gray in it, and at seventy-five he looked like he could continue as paterfamilias for another couple of decades, perhaps establish the seven (and counting) grandchildren, all boys, in the family inheritance. By that time, India would have moved into the space age; the year would be 1973; everywhere on the planet the fruits of industrialization would be evident: more leisure, more money, more goods, more happiness. "You didn't answer!" his father went on. "I said Pondicherry is definitely to be turned over to Indians. We're to be an independent territory— the Union Territories, I think they'll call it—to preserve the unique cultural atmosphere around here. The French will stay on, in an advisory capacity, but Indians will rule."

"Independence within independence, then," Saleem said cynically, as one of Mushtaq's boys, about Sadiq's age, tried to crawl onto Saleem's lap, chattering in a false, staccato, cowboy movie English. "Haven't these liberations been happening without stop since 1947, with the princely states, and what-have-you? Will the Indians be cleaning up the canal, once they take charge?" Saleem thought of the beautiful young woman who'd sold herself at the bench to the repulsive papadum-wallah. In his youth, at university in Bombay, nearly all his rich friends would boast of having made it with prostitutes—not streetwalkers, of course, but specially protected women, soundly maintained for men of their means, free of disease and depression, not unlike mentally gouged versions of their own wives later on. "I think too the Indians should be allowed to move into the French quarter. What do you think, father?" His abrasive attitude wouldn't get him anywhere when later he broached the subject of retrenchment; he was engendering needless hostility. Yet it also couldn't be denied that if at times his father broke into sympathetic gestures toward any of his progeny, it was toward Saleem, probably because he'd been his mother's favorite. Mushtaq his father seemed to have the least affection for, perhaps because his mother had died soon after giving birth to him, and Yaqub tended to talk down to his father, throw around his acquired profundity. Their father's sympathy consisted of not more than listening, but it was something.

"Now, now, I won't have this kind of morbidity around the house at a time like this." His father refused to take the bait, breaking into a broad smile. "Come, Yasin, jump on grandfather's lap," he said to Mushtaq's boy, who'd started clawing at Saleem's gray trousers with sharp nails. "We're on the verge of, what shall I call it, victory almost. Yes, victory. Things couldn't be going better. The country at peace, prosperity everywhere. True, we have poverty. More than just pockets of it, there's a lot of poverty. But over time—oh, I can't imagine free India's future, as long as we don't make any rash mistakes, as long as we keep the peace and order. The rest will take care of itself." His father looked at the antsy grandchild now trying to pull on the patriarch's chest hair, underneath his starched white kurta. Unlike other Indian men of his generation who had held similar degrees of power, Saleem's memory of his father was of someone who had counted on British rule to elapse through sheer passage of time; it hadn't to be forced to vacate, per se; it would happen on its own, given enough Indian maturity. As late as the late thirties, when young men of Saleem's age took pride in going to jail on charges of sedition, his father made him keep all his energies focused on the business; the good graces of the British were needed to get anywhere. When World War II rolled around, his father had said, "I told you so," and then cranked up production. And now, Indian maturity had reached the point where it was about to take charge of Pondicherry. Would there be fierce local elections, with candidates promising to turn the city into a bigger tourist attraction? Would there be sectional squabbling? Would a theosophist unite Muslims, Hindus, Buddhists, Christians, Parsees, Sikhs?

Why had he thought that breakfast was about to be eaten? In fact, it was over, the plates having already been removed. He realized this when a servant informed him, "An omelet can still be made, sahib. Would you like one?"

He shook his head, and leaving his father to the clawing joys of Yasin, went into the kitchen to look for a chiku or sitaphal. His father's must be the largest kitchen in free India. It was more like a chamber of open secrets, with multiple points of entry and stopping stations: chopping boards with entire counters dedicated to them, arrays of pots and pans dancing on hooks and strings as if parodying the headhunting ways of barbarous tribes, shiny knives that ought to slice off the heads of sturdy mountain goats in a single strike should one of the khansamas be so inclined at 'Eid time, or to offer a petty sacrifice for the health of one of the seven boy-princes of the clan. But there was no rest for him in the kitchen. The servants were all absent, which meant that the memsahibs would be there. Saira, whose pale yellow sari seemed designed to engender confusion about where skin ended and cloth began, shone as if her whole body had been dipped in some exotic massage oil, and she had no intention to wash off the glossy accretion. She immediately stopped chewing the apple in her hand, settled her hips more comfortably against the edge of the counter, and turning away from Mushtaq's young wife Zeenat, who gave every indication of following the older Saira into the ways of permanent low-key seduction, said to Saleem: "Look who's here! Where have *you* been hiding? Did you know I've been looking for you all morning? You weren't at breakfast. Your father was most unhappy. *Saleem must be wandering the city, as usual.* You think we aren't on to your habits? So who is it? It must be some girl, no? Some little European patakha? Blonde hair and blue eyes? Too bad we can't go blonde. It'd look pathetic with our dark skins. Even

171

when we call ourselves fair, we're no more than darkies." Her monologue went on in this train for some time; Saleem was helpless to leave. He found his sitaphal and started stripping off the green skin to bite into the delectable white flesh of the fruit, spitting out the big black seeds in his left hand. He wanted to be uncouth around these two delicate ladies, who were always so expert at maneuvering their kids away from their immediate presence. No doubt individual servants— at least six of them—had been given charge of the boys, to play with them on the vast grounds of the mansion, to take them to the beach if they should feel like it; in short, to do anything but let them bother their mothers. The only person who'd be more beholden to a child than any of the servants would be Julie, who wouldn't even let precious Sadiq listen to too much of the servants' conversation, for fear he might pick up their bad grammar and pronunciation.

"What is it that you *want* from me?" Saleem said abruptly, spitting out a large black seed so hard that it missed his open palm and went rolling toward the feet of Zeenat, who looked at it as if it were an unexploded bomb.

"I think I'll go back to my room. Mushtaq needs his shirts ironed," Zeenat said, abandoning her sister-in-law to Saleem's rage. On her way out, from the arched doorway without a door, Zeenat squinted hard at her renegade brother-in-law suffering loss of control.

"What *is it* that you want from me?" Saleem repeated, conscious that he hadn't spoken so incautiously in years. In business circles, his politeness was legendary; when had he ever been heard raising his voice against incompetent suppliers or marketers, not to mention machinists and technicians who fouled up everything they touched? He spoke in perfect Urdu, in ghazal-like cadences, giving no excuse for young Sadiq to have later elocution difficulties. These biennial family get-togethers, where his father built up anticipation to the breaking point, as if he was going to announce something that would radically change their lives, but then left them deflated, with mere trumpet calls and rallying cries, were getting on his nerves. He couldn't handle one more of these visits; at the business, at least he wasn't forced to look at himself from a distance. Here, he had no choice. Was this, in fact, the point of these retreats, to have to pull back any tendencies toward self-glorification, and subsume them all over again to their father's will? Sighing, he said to Saira, who had a fire burning in her dark eyes, "I'm sorry, I don't know what's wrong with me."

"Good, I'm glad you're sorry," Saira said, jumping on his tenderness, "because I was just about to say, you don't have to take out on me whatever frustration you have with your pretty little wife. She does leave you high and dry, does she not?" And without waiting for an answer, she clicked her high heels and walked out.

What had he done? Created another antagonist, to make his life more difficult? Were Saira's come-ons that repulsive, after all? You had to admit, she had far more sex appeal than dainty, correct, cohesive Julie ever would have. He was a fool. There had been no need for his outburst. He would apologize to Saira.

In their bedroom, Julie was dozing peacefully with Sadiq's head on her small chest. What was it about his boy that made him so dejected with himself? Was it that he faced his mortality in the mirror the innocent boy held up to him? Was it that he saw in the boy's mindless questions and motiveless harmony some challenge to the ordinary man Saleem himself had become? Saleem had never been a rebel; he'd never gone through the wild phase his university classmates had, putting their fathers through the ropes, driving their poor mothers to distraction. He'd been obedient from the word go; when Julie stopped talking about doing something for the poor, he too had put the idea on the back burner. But a young boy was the quintessence of not knowing what and whom to listen to; he was all receptiveness and all inventiveness. As the middle child, Saleem had experienced neither the force of his father's authority that Yaqub must have had to confront, in many cases giving up his right to childhood, nor had he undergone the prolonged childhood Mushtaq, as the youngest, would have known. He was caught squarely in the middle; ordinariness was the cause of his dejection. He'd never thought of being anything but a businessman; why not? But what else was there to do? Poetry, the arts, painting, writing, these seemed like frivolities, in a world that needed to have people fed, kept alive, by whatever means necessary. Politics was for fools. Philanthropy probably a distraction. Then what was left? At least he was *doing*, as opposed to thinking about doing, or talking about doing, which seemed to be the only other options.

Julie woke up. "Please don't give your father such a hard time," she said without greeting him. "He was upset you went missing for breakfast. We're only here for a couple of weeks."

"I'll try not to irritate my father more than necessary," he said, half in apology. His son kept sleeping. Even at five, he seemed to sleep an inordinate amount. Wasn't he supposed to be up and about, wild and hysterical, playing thieves and policemen, or emperors and slaves, or whatever boys played these days, bloodying his nose and those of Mushtaq's and Yaqub's sons too? He shook Sadiq's leg, then tickled him in the belly, but the child kept sleeping. They never played sports together, like father and son were supposed to; he hadn't even bought a cricket bat for him, his own interest in the slow-moving sport having entirely dissipated over the years.

"I don't want you missing the big dinner—the ambassadors, the municipal chiefs, everyone invited." Julie almost never wondered what he ate during the day, how he kept body and soul together, unlike the typical Indian wife's preoccupation. She herself only nibbled at food, as if eating entire chunks of it would turn her into a monster.

"Why would I ever miss it? Pondicherry's semi-official pre-independence kickoff. Freedom at last!" He sighed, and went slack on the bed. "Look, Julie, let's never come to one of these get-togethers again. They drive me crazy. My brothers hardly speak to me; they think I'm stupid, that they're the only ones with a good mind for business. I don't like their attitude."

"You might learn something from your brothers, if you gave them a chance. At Yaqub's factory, they've started a Hindu-Muslim dialogue. Less superstition all the way around. And Mushtaq says he's good friends with a government minister who won't forget the Muslim industrialists in Delhi when it comes to awarding the big new contracts to supply the Indian military. I think your brothers have good ideas."

Julie never talked like this at home; it was Sadiq, Sadiq, all the time, worries about the air, the food, the water, the language. Now she was talking as if she were his father's faithful secretary; everyone was abandoning Saleem. He wished desperately he knew some alternative to the life he led now, but he didn't. His only consolation was that this ordeal would be over next week, and they could take the train back to Bombay. This time they would perhaps catch sight of the Nilgiri Hills, where peasants were said to still harbor outsized dreams. This time he'd also like to stop in Hyderabad, the hot, baked city on the plateau that the prosperous Muslims of India liked to leave alone, because it provoked too many uncomfortable memories of their greatness at one time, their unbridled nationalism, even more than did Delhi and

Agra. In Hyderabad, almost successful wars of sedition and rebellion had started, only to be put down. It was a city of burnt, hollowed out, eternally fresh memories; it was too much to handle, if you believed in progress.

"In any case," Saleem said meaninglessly, "by the time our son is grown up, these communal prejudices, these needless hassles, will be a thing of the past." None of the three brothers had gone abroad for education; it was because their father, anomalous as always, believed that it would have been a slap in the face of India to be sent into exile to learn to speak proper English. Was it a loss? Saleem had never been able to decide. He was free from the insecurities his British-educated friends exhibited all the time, but was this because of ignorance? If he had gone abroad to study, he probably wouldn't have married Julie; then, upon return to the desh, his demand would have been for a more activist bride, someone who set in motion pledge drives and consciousness seminars, not just attended them at others' instigation. Had he gone abroad to study, he might have remained a bachelor until an unseasonably rumor-producing age.

"Our son is very happy here," Julie said. "Have you noticed?"

"That's because you don't let him deal with the big boys, Yaqub's and Mushtaq's insensitive rascals, on their terms. You keep him sheltered. He'll resent that when he grows up."

After a moment, Julie said, "You're right. I should let him mingle. But I hate to let him out of sight. Look at him now, so cute. What a pretty little button nose he has!" She pinched his cheeks and ruffled his hair; still, he didn't wake up.

The good thing about Julie was that she didn't jump into defending her mothering skills when Saleem accused her of shortfalls in that area. She listened seriously, like a good pupil. Julie's education was also indigenous. Perhaps both of them were too obedient; perhaps that was why everyone on the outside thought they had an ideal marriage. Everyone, that is, except Saira, with antennae sharper than his dull brothers', who talked as if they, not unruly local panchayats and corruptible civil servants, decided what was good for India and what wasn't. Seven growing boys in the house at one time. Why couldn't there be a bloody fight, where the boys all got their noses broken and their heads split open?

A wife could be a liability, he speculated over the next couple of days. He'd proffered his apology to Saira at last, when she lingered at the end of afternoon tea, the day following the incident in the kitchen. She'd gone missing from breakfast that morning. Yaqub said she had a headache, and then launched into a recital of her latest initiative: bringing together Hindu and Muslim parents who had adopted children of the opposite faith. Saleem thought he'd already heard this account, of Saira's bravery in broaching the potentially explosive subject. With each telling, Yaqub's view of Saira seemed to become more rationalizing, coloring his interpretation of the progressive interfaith developments taking place in his own factory. Saleem's father listened politely, playing with the buttons on his kurta, indicating he was processing the news for higher synthesis at a moment of his own choosing. Zeenat tried to draw Julie into a discussion of growing children's recalcitrant eating habits, but Julie wouldn't fall for it: it was to be left to the children's choice. Mushtaq wanted to sound excited like his father about the impending liberation of Pondicherry, but all he could manage was false assumption of his own maturity during the real independence struggle; in fact, he'd been too young then to have been a participant. The breakfast dragged on in this vein for two hours, until almost lunch time; soon they'd be gathered to eat again. Perhaps Saira's presence tended to provide more of a spark than Saleem had realized, even if a bit shady, a bit on the suspicious side.

So when later that day everyone wanted to disperse to their cool rooms, out of the heat of the lawn, Saleem accosted Saira to apologize. She listened regally, without offering any words of remorse on her own part, and afterward Saleem felt worse than ever, and a fool to boot, perceiving that forever after he'd be degraded in Saira's eyes. Real men didn't say sorry. Even Julie, who hardly took her cues from the Bombay movies, understood that principle.

It came to the midpoint of their visit, time for Saleem's father to turn serious. He was the only one who understood how all the parts of the business fit together. Every day now, from midmorning to early afternoon, he wanted to hear every detail of how the businesses were being run; he pressed to know plans for expansion: always expansion, swallowing up smaller, competing entities, growing vertically and horizontally, spreading the tentacles of their model business, known for its fairness to employees and generosity to customers, into the dark, labyrinthine, haphazard Indian business soil, where independent proprietors who knew no better than to overcharge and undermanage had to be put out of their misery. At these sessions, where children—thank heavens—and wives weren't allowed, his father offered almost no editorial commentary, but simply listened, like the sage old man he'd never given anyone reason to believe he wasn't.

In the third or fourth of these exhausting sessions, Yaqub gave up the notion of impressing their father, and directed his energies to educating Saleem instead: "You have no social presence whatsoever. I never hear from my Bombay friends about your company. Out of sight, out of mind.

Visibility, in every way you can achieve it, is of the highest importance. My dear brother, without people esteeming you outside the strict confines of the business transaction, how will your standing in society rise enough for you to be thought of when new opportunities arise? Opportunities for investment and profit we haven't begun to dream of."

"I like to keep to myself," said Saleem, involuntarily smirking. Their father only nodded and hummed. Saleem detested being put on the defensive by the older Yaqub. He suspected among the three brothers Yaqub had the dullest mind, although as the eldest he was supposed to be the brightest. Yaqub had never stopped trying to please their father in the most shameless ways possible.

"Keeping to yourself," Mushtaq echoed. "Like a poet? If I don't get around, Zeenat makes me do it." This was a barb at the quiescent Julie, who everyone knew was afraid to expose Sadiq to the clamorous lives of boys and girls of his own background. Mushtaq leaned back in the garden chair, stretched his arms behind himself, like a bird extending its wings before flight, and smiled self-contentedly at Saleem. It was a surprise they hadn't yet started talking celebratorily about the Pondicherry freedom movement.

"What I do in my business is my own affair," Saleem said. "What do the figures tell you? Productivity? Profit? Then what do we have to complain about? Anyway, I don't believe in excessive socializing. It's a drain of energy. If your product is good enough, and you keep your customers happy, more business will come your way than you can handle."

"That's true," Yaqub jumped in, without letting their father pause for a moment to appreciate Saleem's noble sentiment; "but how do we know what we're missing? Existing product lines, existing business, that's all helped by perfecting old methods of making and delivering, but what about—"

"New stuff," interrupted Saleem, "yes, I know, new stuff."

"Well, so then..." said Yaqub.

"I've said what I had to say."

Their father pinched and rolled his chin, in an expression of concern. At the clap of his hands, a servant brought a fresh helping of pineapple slices.

"I don't know if I'm getting much out of these discussions," continued Saleem, recklessly. He thought he saw Saira prancing around, in a state of half undress, in her bedroom window upstairs. His chair was the only one facing the house; everyone else's faced east, the better to feel the ocean breeze from a couple of miles away. Saira hardly talked to him now; when Saleem issued an open invitation for everyone to see a new French movie at the Colonial theatre, Saira was the first to refuse him vocally, which inclined everyone else to follow suit. "These talks consume effort. We might as well write each other letters once every couple of years, update progress, and be done with it." He rose, stretching his limber body. He was in much better shape than the others, even the younger Mushtaq, whom Zeenat seemed to be feeding laddoo and jalebi with her own hands every time he saw them together. "Anyone for the beach? I haven't gone once. Has anyone? It's a golden beach, so much more pristine than Bombay's crud."

His two brothers and his father had their hands cradled helplessly in their bellies, like itinerant bodhisattvas caught by surprise at the inhospitality of the local tyrant ruler. Brahmins, and others fanatically driven by rules of purity and impurity, they were the ones who were going to make the rules in the future, and his two shapeless brothers, and his ageless father, would have to reconcile with that. In this home, no one ever prayed. His father didn't make a show of sacrificing animals on the brutal 'Eid-al-Adha. The money was donated to some slaughterhouse, so the business could be done out of sight, the meat distributed to the poor on the other side of the canal. His father used to walk a lot when they lived in Bombay, Saleem remembered from his childhood. But never in Pondicherry. Saleem, the ignoble one, left the group.

He couldn't compel himself to go to the beach. Nor to the cinema by himself. He couldn't venture into the forbidden zone of the city, the western part. He could only go so far as the canal, as if that were an uncrossable barrier. He thought he'd see the girl who'd sold herself for paisas the other morning, but he never did, even when he went early in the mornings to the same place. At mealtimes, Saira was now beginning to issue cutting remarks about Saleem—still small in magnitude, but real nevertheless; any other wife but Julie would have noticed and leaped to her husband's defense. So then, this sad, miserable trip, where he felt more than ever a stranger to his wife, and where he hardly ever talked to his growing son, let alone played with him or took him on an excursion, was drawing to a close, and life would go on as before, and the misery in his heart would be hid by the frenetic activity of Bombay, where there were too many actors putting on diversionary roles for anyone to be taken seriously. This period of enforced seriousness was almost over.

Then one afternoon, after a sprinkle of cooling rain, the French consul dropped in. Monsieur Lafargue was all but hunchbacked, sported a bloated face and unkempt moustache, but dressed as if he were auditioning for cultural representative of the shadow government of France, with yellow ascot and suspenders, sparkling brown shoes, and a newsboy cap he liked to switch from hand to hand. When he talked to you, his eyes stared into the far distance, but when he wasn't addressing you, his eyes bored into you as if during interrogation at the local thana. He seemed to treat Saleem with undisguised contempt from the very beginning, although this was the first time they had met.

"Mr. Sultan," Monsieur Lafargue addressed Saleem's father, "my compliments on getting every little squabbling faction to agree to come to your dinner. It'll be an interesting prelude." Prelude to what, Monsieur Lafargue wasn't going to clarify.

"Ah, Jacques," Saleem's father said, "old men past their prime can do no better than try to ease the lines of communication."

They both laughed uproariously, as if at a private joke, perhaps anticipating some overdue humiliation of the British consul or some officer associated with maritime trade or cultural affairs.

"My middle son, Saleem," the old man interrupted one of his grotesque laughing spells to introduce the visitor to the bystander.

The Frenchman nodded briskly and dismissively. "My, but how the begonias are growing, so lush, like in a tropical paradise. My, my! Mr. Sultan, your gardens must be the most fabulous in all of Pondicherry." Saleem recalled what a tremendous expenditure it was to keep the gardens in such undefiled shape: armies of gardeners, seriously going about their business all the time, like archeologists salvaging the finest points of an empire for future generations. "And the house—oh my, you could fit in generation upon generation of a family, and the right hand wouldn't know what the left was doing. It's beautiful."

The women of the house now started to appear before the European visitor—as if all day they had been preparing for his arrival—with understated flamboyance, concentrated attention. First came Saira—of course—dressed in a tulle gown, floating as if on air, looking twenty years younger than her age. For this occasion she had decided to deploy all her debutante charms, offering her hand for the Frenchman to kiss before he had a chance to ask for it.

Saleem's father rose from his chair—what a strong old man he was, without any trace of disease, any sign of atrophy or rust: he walked straight, with a sportsman's gait, and looked like he could go on living for another few decades. His secret of longevity was relentless delegation: never do yourself what someone else could do half as well on your behalf. Back in the days when he was one of the rare Muslims with sufficient capital to start large industry, it was easy to do so because the British favored old-line Muslims as more reliable subjects than the upstart Brahmin Hindus. Where the family's original capital had come from was shrouded half in mystery: some said lands, some said a special British concession to distribute indigenous products in this very region of South India, long before the Mutiny. Saleem's father walked toward the little dance of flirtation going on between Saira and Jacques, rejoining the two younger persons' hands, his big, bony hand caught in between. "It'll be a wonderful year; the central government couldn't be playing it smarter," he said. "Staying in the background, letting the factions work it out smoothly on their own. Tremendous common sense all around." The Frenchman, with his sibilant assents, couldn't agree more.

The other wives came, Zeenat first, a bit more demure than Saira, but not by much, dressed in exquisite turquoise, wearing a young girl's paper-thin slippers. She let the Frenchman hold her hand as long as he wanted, speaking intelligently of local municipal affairs: where had she picked up this argot? Probably from the newspapers, which Saleem never glanced at. Water, electricity, infrastructure, construction, these were the loci around which the wheels of flirtation were spinning. Then Julie arrived, talking almost like an adult; they'd all grown up dramatically for the Frenchman's benefit.

But it wasn't some unique charm of the Frenchman's, and Saleem's father and Monsieur Lafargue had nothing ulterior planned against the British or any other alien faction, as Saleem learned soon when the British consul himself dropped in next. By now the servants were in full-blown catering mode, easily shifting from the family's preferred lemonade to the Europeans' gin and tonic, and bringing forth the kind of hors d'oeuvres that had only emerged into reality after centuries of Indian and European culinary cohabitation. The boys were on their best behavior, acting like midget businessmen, including Saleem's own, Sadiq wearing a blue blazer with gold buttons and not complaining about having his hair wet and brushed back, like a Bombay movie star's. The Englishman had also come to compliment Mr. Sultan, and hoped that neighborliness in the future would assume new meaning, when the best of all traditions would harmoniously merge, et cetera, et cetera: "And we don't mean in some vague, fuzzy way, like the Aurobindo people outside town, but based on harmonious reconciliation of material interests..." The women listened, enchanted, to this prattle, as did the old patriarch, smiling beneficently, as if his personal largesse had put these Europeans through school, to enable them to show off their cultural acquisition in front of their benefactor. The boys were having civilized conversations with each other.

Other Europeans were called on the phone, and they came: the Portuguese, the Germans, the Dutch, the Scandinavians. It was like a dress rehearsal for the real dinner next week; good, everyone got along already, there would be no surprises. Before long, his brothers—who'd driven a few miles north of Pondicherry to scout a vacant plot of land for possible purchase, before real estate prices escalated when the French officially decamped—entered the fray, assuming the role of bighearted diplomats from the get-go. European politics were discussed intelligently; M. Laniel came in for gentle ribbing, as did Mr. Churchill. No one dared make a joke at Nehru's expense. Or at Mr. Sultan's. Everyone praised the gardens, the house, the efficiency of the servants, the beauty of the wives, the manners of the children. Everything was in good order, and seemed meant to last that way eternally.

It seemed to Saleem that there was deep collaboration between the three wives, that they were three heads to the same person. Julie looked more like them today than she ever had before; he'd always thought there was an irreducible crust of refinement about his petite wife that the older brothers' brassy consorts lacked, but he might have been off in his estimation. Did he feel any affection toward his father, who'd been such a good provider, who'd hardly ever let him feel the absence of his mother, who'd tried to treat the three brothers fairly? He couldn't say he did; he'd feel little sorrow if the old man were to die tomorrow. The rage within him that had been bursting to get out ever since they left Bombay almost pushed him to make a fool of himself. He wanted to seize someone by the throat—perhaps the pompous, fat Englishman, who spoke in a clipped Oxford accent as if he were at a gathering of neutered BBC reporters, not a household of former colonials who internally rejoiced at every setback of the empire, now benevolently known as the Commonwealth—and ask: "Isn't this the wrong party, at the wrong time? Shouldn't we be consorting with the Chinese? What about the canal? Who's going to clean that up? Are you going to invite any Indians from the wrong side to the celebration? Will there be a party for them? Will you share the spoils amongst yourselves? What about that girl who sold herself for fifty rupees? Fifty bloody rupees, for that ugly merchant to grab and poke her—fifty rupees, the price of one of these bottles of gin, one of the packets of seeds for these orchids and tulips, imported from Marseilles or wherever." To which interrogation, one of the Europeans might well have turned around, if he had any sense at all, and asked Saleem in turn: "Well, what are *you* doing about it? It's your country, after all. Hunh? What about the canal? What about the girl?"

Something in him seemed to break that afternoon. When later that night he was haunting the library—long after everyone had gone to sleep—hoping that perhaps Dickens would soothe him, and Saira came, dressed not in one of the diaphanous gowns she liked to wear at night, but in a sober, concealing outfit, he gently closed *Our Mutual Friend* shut.

"I'm sorry—" he began to apologize yet again.

"No need for that," Saira interrupted. "I understand how much you hate to come to these affairs. So do I. I think my husband does too. But we have to make do somehow. We owe a lot to the old man and must humor him. It's not too much to ask, is it? Look how fortunate we all are." Usually, he would have been irritated by yet another reminder of their collective good fortune. But this time he wasn't. "Look, let's be friends. That's what I've always hoped we'd be."

"Always?" Saleem laughed.

"All right, almost always. But you have a lovely wife. She feels ignored."

"I try to—"

"No need to explain to me," Saira interrupted again. "I'm just saying. And most of all, your son needs you."

"I've been meaning to ask you—or someone—how *do* you manage with three boys?"

"If I gave as little time as you do to your son, I could manage with a dozen." This was said without rancor, accusation.

Again, he should have been severely annoyed, but he wasn't. He tried to look at himself as Saira might. "Do you think I'm a cold fish? Do I shun normal human interaction?"

Saira started laughing loudly at this, good-humoredly, he thought, and he joined in the laughter. "If you have to ask, then you aren't. And look, I know you worry about this city going to hell in a handbasket, but it won't. There's too much solid physical basis for it to degenerate. Is it too bad if it becomes a tourist haven? They'll clean up the canal, you'll see, because who'll the Indians blame if the French leave?"

He didn't mention that Indians hadn't cleaned up the rest of India once the British had left. Be that as it may. He felt a calm enveloping him, a peace with the world. It could well be that this feeling wouldn't last long; perhaps the last time he'd felt so restful was when he'd decided once and for all that he wouldn't pursue a science degree as an undergraduate. He'd visited his mother's grave outside Bombay in the early hours of the night then, for the first time not feeling depressed in the cemetery.

Some late-night bird was squawking outside the library window. An army of servants was asleep. India slept, most of it, hundreds of millions of people, most of them content with their lot in life: why did he have to take on more than he could bear? The calm Bay of Bengal would be gently crashing on the shore; perhaps on the beach right this moment some couple was whisperingly planning their elopement to Bombay. Wasn't the Frenchman's, the Englishman's equanimity explained by Christianity imposing a limit on how much they felt personally responsible for? He would take his son to the beach in the morning. There were only a couple of days left, before the frantic preparations for the big formal dinner would exhaust any possibilities for love.

"I think I'll turn in early," he said, pushing the book away from his reach. It had been a long time since he'd felt passionate toward Julie. She didn't exactly invite ravishment, although he'd tried in the early years. But he could try again. All in all, she'd been a good wife.

"I will too," Saira said. Then she did something unusual. From her purse she brought out a box of cigarettes, and matches. "Do you want one?"

He hadn't known that she smoked. He hadn't smoked in years, for fear of irritating Sadiq's lungs. "I think I will."

When he took the cigarette from Saira's hand, her touch was electric, her fingers as if on fire.

He never made it to Julie that night, but he did look at her with more compassion in the morning, as she lay helplessly in her bed, and he fulfilled his promise to take young Sadiq to the beach. The boy turned out to be an intelligent companion.

REPATRIATION

September 2. The rule has long been, no pregnancy, no childbirth. Grass turns to food, turns to humans, turns to death, a losing equation, with or without intervention. O planters! O bold solicitors of the sun's first rays, lay off! Lay off and surrender! She wouldn't understand. Crowded among the women in my section of the lower deck, a little prematurely Diana's water breaks, and she starts moaning. My sleepmate, who calls himself Billy, to the rescue: "Fuckin' step aside, y'all. I was a nurse's aide in Memphis. Nothin' to do with maternity, but is there anyone here knows better?" Billy's too white to be on the ship, but his last name is Salvador. The damning birth certificate, leading the holder quietly to the noose! I watch a live birth for the first time. So do thirty others, in our crowded compartment. Only one flickering bulb works. Plenty enough to see the hemorrhage. The overturned mound of the woman, marooned to the help of strangers. Blood flowing like a river. The child lives. As soon as it's been slapped and starts breathing, one of the ship's officers comes down the stairs to seize it. Diana is only half-conscious. Miracle she's still alive. The baby will be thrown overboard with much hooting and jeering by the captain's mates. The captain himself gets to do the honors. I saw that, a baby being thrown overboard, once—two days ago (there isn't excessive restriction on mobility around the ship). Then it'll be Diana's turn. But first she must regain consciousness. No one can be processed for death unless they're conscious. That's the rule of law.

September 3. When we talk, we claim gratitude at not being on a container ship. Most people on those ships, not meant for human habitation, die. Or we could be on our way to Latin America or East Asia. The news is, angry militias greet the arrivals at those continents, shepherd them to special camps, where those who've survived quickly expire. Regardless of the destination, a ship—or a plane or train, when that's possible—is never outright turned back. The arrivals are always accepted, processed, the paperwork matched against all sorts of lists of unwanteds, as if these were still the old days and we were only asylum seekers, refugees. We're going to the West Coast of Africa, not the violent, inhospitable Southern part of the continent. An Asian man who calls himself Wu, a university writing teacher from Minneapolis, draws elaborate word pictures of the openness and free spirit likely to be found in West Africa—plenty of game birds, animals amenable to hunting, golden sun and well-watered fields, clusters of huts where ideal communes just might flourish. We will survive, he begins and ends each peroration. I'm reputed to be a great listener, among all here. Wu's mother killed herself when news of the repatriation was announced. I remember the blonde CNN announcer spelling out the details with pronounced relief. I never watched television after that morning.

September 5. It's been raining hard, for a change. I'd always pictured the Atlantic as relentlessly gray, choppy, dangerous. Most days it looks like a paradise in search of inhabitants. My mother-in-law wanted me and Anna, before

Anna's first bout with leukemia, to accompany her on a cruise ship to Europe. "Cruise ships!" Anna snorted. "So bourgeois! So end-times." Five years later, Anna died at Beth Israel, under the most expensive medical care in the Western world.

September 6. All that you're reading is in my head. I'm not actually writing. I memorize a certain number of words a day. Everyday I repeat all that I've memorized so far. Books—let alone writing materials—are strictly forbidden, discovery punishable by instant death. We're famous for being overread. This was part of the indictment the president read in his address, to universal applause. We're overread. We overthink. So our loyalty can never be trusted, because we aren't prompted by our hearts, only by our minds. The basis is claimed to be heredity. Shifting, contingent loyalties are unacceptable now. Standards must be constant, invulnerable to new thought.

September 7. Onions and garlic are a big part of our diet. The American heartland was mostly unaffected by the contamination on the coasts. It keeps producing massive quantities of food, enough still for all the white people in the world. I expect Europe to soon give up sovereignty. They'll need American force to repatriate their own nonwhite populations, proportionally so high in countries like France, Germany, Britain. Some say the contamination has already happened in France, but no one knows for sure. News develops in impenetrable bubbles now. If enough consensus holds, it becomes accepted fact. I find I have absolute revulsion for anyone who narrates events realistically, sequentially, without interjecting massive doses of heart-feeling—the way history might have unfolded if the world had been run by naughty imps, dreadlocked fairies.

September 8. I think the ship is moving too slowly, and it's intentional.

September 8. My whole left side has developed cramps. My skin is caked. Too much exposure to salt? Wu says a friend of his at Harvard Medical School experimented with designer viruses. He says the entire population experienced low-grade symptoms of perpetual fatigue, listlessness, depression—why was that?

September 9. In my corner of the deck, theft of bedding is common. Where does it go? The ubiquitous onion and garlic prevails, in great quantities, no matter the dish. We stink. We take communal showers at six every morning. Afterward we spend a few hours in the semidark, until the sun really comes out. We're to go to bed when the sun goes down. The ship is going so slow it might as well be stalled. Memory is precious. Even the essentials must be pruned. Memory lingers on great musical events. Symphonies one attended in youth. Young love, and trading in poetry. Empty highways.

September 10. Most of us don't give out our names, unless we really know who we're talking to. I've already noticed strict segregation by color—not race so much, but color. I tried to talk to some very dark-skinned blacks, from Baltimore, and they were offended. "You're half-Indonesian? You were born in Jakarta?" they'd asked me when I'd reported at the Nashua registration office. "Yes, but my mother only gave birth to me there. I was a week old when I was brought to Brooklyn—and never left." They smiled at the explanation, and the silver-haired Puritan woman in charge said, "Well, you gave us great cuisine—while it lasted." Wu sleepwalks now, stepping on sleeping women's faces. I don't think he'll make it in Africa—not as an adventurer.

September 11. "Folks, we're turnin' around," is the cheerful announcement on the loudspeaker after the showers. But after an excruciating pause, "Sorry, just kiddin'." Was that the captain's voice? I've seen him. He threw that baby overboard. (No abortions allowed, under any circumstances.) He likes to make the rounds, mingle with the passengers. "How's the human rights situation in the lower deck today, my fellow citizens?" he asked once. "Well, how is it?" He has trouble growing facial hair, I can tell, but he tries. I've never trusted men with that problem. Around his neck is a string holding a cracked monocle.

September 12. The man named Billy, who helped Diana give birth, has told me yet another version of his life story. He was an engineer fixing broken levees in Michigan. Diana's cousin, a wizened woman in her fifties, says she'd rather have gone to Mexico City—at least, she'd have spoken the language there. None of us talks about cars and homes and jobs and friends and property we've left behind. We only talk about the future. Groups of particularly sociable men rouse those of us who feel like sleeping in the afternoons. "Hey, man, what's bothering you? You so quiet. Are you some sort of a misanthrope?" one of them, an Indian called Ram, says in a marked Chicago accent, kicking people around. Truth has gone up in a mushroom cloud. It's a mental lapse that I still dream so prolifically, mostly about Anna and I when we were young, so desperately in love. We should have had the baby when it was still possible. Leukemia has a slightly higher rate of occurrence among Asians. Only slightly higher.

September 13. The officers laugh and scream and party. We can hear them. Most of them look homosexual. But they brag about raping women. I think when they take one of the women, they kill her instantly, without raping her. Mostly they leave us alone. I suspect some of the younger officers— the stocky blond guys from places like Minnesota and Iowa— are reluctant law-enforcers. They're caught up in the whole thing, like everyone else. They must be forgiven. They know not what they do. The president's policy of repatriation of fifty to sixty million people of definite foreign origin was welcomed by the national and world press as the most humane and reasonable one under the circumstances. Under the circumstances. Both coasts littered with corpses. So many sentenced to death for the mere act of breathing. Domestic camps, no matter how long-term, would have been inadequate. Let the foreigners be repatriated for now; later, we'll see. Keep your papers on you. Were you born in America? We'll treat you differently than if you were born elsewhere. Later, we'll see. I was given the choice of donating my book collection to the public library or to the children's shelter.

September 14. Overnight Billy and Wu disappeared, as did the voluble Indian Ram. No one knows where they are. I promise myself I won't speak a word to anyone all day long. It isn't difficult. An optimistic blue flyer is passed around. It says the "reception committees" at our port of arrival will give each of us the essential commodities, canned food, bedding, light clothes appropriate for the climate, housing vouchers, lists of contacts in the local government, and some currency, not to exceed twenty American dollars; the rest will be up to us. This is said to be a sign of wonderful international cooperation under conditions of extreme crisis. The bullet points in the flyer are prefaced by a quotation from Adam Smith's *Wealth of Nations* which I either don't recall or find it too painful to do so. Later that evening, the flyers are assiduously collected by young officers, as if not a trace of them must remain. "Sorry, sorry—they should never have been distributed." What was the purpose of this whole game?

September 15. Anna said to me, when we visited the innards of the New York Stock Exchange for the first time, that even the greatest minds, like Shakespeare's and

Beethoven's, are no more than derivatives, mere glosses over their era's collective mindset. No one is really original. The stock market hit an all-time peak that afternoon. Oil prices were their lowest in years. On the streets of New York, the grim police presence was barely detectable. We leaned over the barriers at the Battery, breathing in the oily water, staring hard at the past, at masses of people in search of home. Oh Anna, Anna! How lucky you are to be spared this! This return!

September 16. Women don't mind exposing their breasts. Most of them are veiny, saggy, blueish and cracked, the nipples either too large or too small. They snore loudly, their hands under their heads, sprawled loosely, as if the siesta will soon be over, and the store's customers should not have to greet exhausted keepers. I used to be proud of so many of my physical attributes.

September 17. This is a day of mourning. They tell us in America there have been more "incidents." No details are offered. We'll find out in Africa.

September 18. For years I used to patronize an Iranian cab driver. It had been a random meeting at Boston's South Station. We kept up a correspondence. He loved education. I had some ideas about where his daughter might go to college. Such friendships used to develop. He might not have been so open with a white patron.

September 19. For the last few days, the quantity of food we're being allowed has increased greatly. We eat and eat, endlessly, until lethargy overcomes us. But still the garlic and onion are pervasive.

September 20. Just as suddenly as they'd disappeared, Wu and Billy reappear. "Hey man, what about them chicks?" Billy says. "You don't show any interest in women. This isn't right." I still don't know what happened to them. They act as if they never went away. Now when Wu imagines conditions in Africa, he tends to speak of the distant future, as if we were years away from arrival.

September 21. I half wake up, hearing church bells— or think I do. Yes, it's not imagination, there's a fly skipping around on my nose. "Billy, will you get that fly?" I utter squeamishly. He likes to sleep close to me. Anna used to let me be a slob around the house, papers everywhere, unread newspapers and magazines piled high. I reach down to my limp penis. It's an offense, an affront to my human state, its very existence. I wish someone would crack my skull open and let me bleed to death. "Wake up, shower time!" an officer seems to be shouting right in my ear. "There's some awful pretty women down here," the same voice continues. "All them Chinese and Mexicans and Arabs. Real pretty skin tone. Like fresh Russet potatoes…"

TEXAS

The baby either ate too much or threw up. No in-between state of mind. If it could be said to have a state of mind. Eight months old. Round. Thick. Thick-headed. A female bundle of agony. Girls Amy Beederman's age were supposed to go gaga over babies like this, want one of their own instantly, with a Hispanic guy, a black guy, a white guy if he were masochistic enough, with anyone!

Amy tried to make some inventive gurgling, cooing noises. The baby lay in its cot, looking on the verge of throwing up again. Oh please, not on the fresh covers. But if she lifted it out of the cot, and hugged it, and patted it on the back, it would do it on Amy's new pink dress. The dress was a gift of the baby's mother, Adila, who loved shopping almost as much as she loved the baby. "I want to get pregnant again next June," she'd confided to Amy in her Lexus SUV, returning from the Galleria after spending six hundred dollars on a useless suit Adila was unlikely to ever wear. Why June? The most miserable month in Houston, which Amy still thought of, after three months here, as not a proper city, but an agglomeration of runaway suburbs in centrifugal thrust away from multiple non-centers, like black holes in a constantly expanding universe. She'd heard L.A. and Phoenix and all the new Southwestern cities were similar, but this being her first trip outside the settled Northeast it was difficult to imagine any city more resistant to focusing in on itself than Houston.

"Baby, do you feel like sleeping, huh?" Amy said. "Sleep?"

The baby opened its fiery black eyes wider, refuting Amy as usual. Oh, she felt so helpless with it. After weeks of working for the Zainul-Abidins, in Houston's exclusive River Oaks area, where Dato Sri Abdul Razak had been gifted a home by Enron, the hottest employer in the region, Amy still had a hard time signifying the baby by anything other than the gender-neutral pronoun. In the Middle Ages, she remembered from her only semester at junior college in Bristol, Connecticut, in the survey course in Western Civ. taught by the shaggy-haired professor, babies weren't even named, in case they died, which they did more often than not. It was hard to form an attachment to an "it." Amy's mother had had three children besides her, and they weren't even Catholics—well-defined Congregationalists—and yet, the lure of the smelly diaper, irresistible!

The baby was squirming. Stomach blues. There was no choice now but to pick it up. Sometimes, if you showed it genuine affection before acute distress set in, it didn't begin crying. Once a crying spell began, there was no end to it. You had to prevent it. If Adila came back from the baby shower, for a Malaysian woman in the Memorial West neighborhood, and saw the baby crying so helplessly, she would conclude Amy hadn't fed it all afternoon. Eight months old. Too early for real solids. Adila had stopped breastfeeding at six months. Amy had had glimpses of her near-naked body. She looked like she'd never been pregnant—except for the slight sag in her breasts, which was unavoidable. Extremely pale, with red nipples, and reddish pubic hair—pale white all over, like any of Amy's friends back in Connecticut. Adila went about with a hijab hiding her lustrous red-black hair. Only her husband saw all her charms. What a shame! But it was only a cultural thing with Adila.

Amy wished Adila would start an affair, if only to puncture Dato Sri Razak's balloon of self-satisfaction. Every evening at six Dato Sri Razak would return home in the other Lexus SUV, wanting to know every detail of how the day had transpired among "the three women of my family," as he liked to group them. "Go ahead, Amy," Adila would say, "tell him how Nurhaliza almost walked, he won't believe me if I tell him." This imputation of early prowess was a stretch, at best. Dato Sri Razak treated Amy as if there was absolutely nothing sexual about her. This hadn't been Amy's experience babysitting in her neighborhood in Bristol. All the middle-aged men there were discombobulated by her conjectured sexuality, either tongue-tied or unable to stop talking. Dato Sri Razak treated her like what she was: hired help.

"Come on, baby, let me take you out to the garden, okay?" As usual the baby's weightlessness surprised Amy. Such fragile creatures. How did they survive the first year? And they were ill all the time. Not this particular one, so much, but Adila was always talking about runaway ear infections and night-shattering colic among her friends' babies. Was there any married Malaysian woman here without a child? Such arrogant infertility was inconceivable. Sperm was precious in this worldview, as were eggs and ovaries and the womb and uterus and the whole equipment for reproduction. If it was there, it must be there for a reason.

Amy patted the baby on its back. Oops! Was it going to throw up? No, not yet. Maybe not at all. Let's hope for the best, and distract it with the blooming flowers in the garden, the roses and lilies, smelling like—like nothing, really, despite the absurdly bright colors, for you could make them grow in this city, but you couldn't make them smell of anything, good or bad. Let's distract it with the red tricycle it would ride one day and the bouncing balloons dotting the garden that made every day feel like the baby's birthday. Amy had often yearned to give away the tricycle and the balloons and the warehouse of toys, past, present, and future, to one of the three Mexicans who worked in the garden, one in the morning, one in the afternoon, one in the evening, all named José—or at least, Dato Sri Razak preferred to call them all José. Here was the evening José now— well, there really wasn't an evening proper in Houston, it was only a blinding, steaming, groaning afternoon, that eventually became less hot, and then the weak stars would come out, swaying in the eternal smog.

"Hello, José—how's work today? Getting a lot of— gardening done?"

"Señorita, my wife, Adriana, she very sick. Maybe— maybe she have appendicitis."

Amy kept stroking the baby's back, and listened to the gory tale. Adriana was also fertile, four kids so far. Every Hispanic servant decided to spill his guts to Amy without warning. She must give off the pliant guidance counselor vibes, a helpless energy in need of being vacuumed up by diffuse emotional desperation. "Yes, yes," she said, as José slipped more and more into Spanglish, and then eventually almost entirely into Spanish, of which she knew nothing. The baby, if attention was deflected from it for so long, would usually scream and claw and choke, but it was placid today, almost treating Amy like a real mother. Was that a slight caress with a pudgy little hand on her bare shoulder? It felt like it.

"Well, José, I'm sorry about your wife, but if your nurse friend says she must go to the hospital, she must go. Appendicitis can be fatal, you know. Fatal—like she could die?"

"Sí, sí, señorita," José said, smiling at his petite, clean- cut interlocutor, as if she'd just given him a brilliant taco recipe.

She would walk the neighborhood. It wasn't meant to be walked in, this neighborhood, even though all day long armies of Mexican workers blew leaves and picked up real or imagined trash and kept the streets looking untouched and unvisited—except for their own momentary presence. Adila thought the baby couldn't handle the heat outside. A timed spin in the heavily shaded stroller was okay, if the sun had already gone down or hadn't yet come up to full strength, but not if the baby was only being carried in one's arms. Well, Amy felt like breaking the rules today.

The first house next to the Zainul-Abidins' was bigger than theirs. It had the same faux pillars and gables and pediments, only more super-sized, more assertive. It was inhabited by the daughter of a former Republican congressman who'd resigned from office after being accused of taking bribes from Saudi oilmen. Amy had seen her a couple of times, fat and with a completely expressionless face. The house that came after that was—well, they were all variations on the same theme, the Colonial Revival look, imposing façades, houses set far back from the street, and never any human presence in the front yards or the garages or any of the windows that were open and visible from the street. If there were other caretakers of children, and human beings who had business being in these houses in the daytime, children themselves, their mothers, Amy never saw them. Maybe this was what they meant by Texas privacy. Amy had known the essential facts about every single family on her Bristol street, where she had lived all her nineteen years of life until now.

Amy walked to the end of the street, and then took a right, walking into uncharted territory. The baby seemed very happy. If the Zainul-Abidins stayed in this country long enough, it would have an indistinguishable accent from any other American girl's. If she spoke to you on the phone, you'd never know her parents had immigrated—not that they were anything but the most accomplished immigrants. Only three years in the country, and the Zainul-Abidins understood infinitely more about the levers of power than Amy or anyone she'd grown up with could understand in a thousand years. Amy had never quite comprehended what Dato Sri Razak did at Enron; at first she'd assumed he was an oil engineer of some sort, but she was soon enlightened by her employer that Enron was about much more than energy exploration—Oh yes, it was the fastest-growing company in Texas, if not the whole country, with its hands in everything, its global financial investments already dwarfing its physical American presence. She didn't want to admit to herself that Dato Sri Razak might be no more than a glorified paper pusher; he did have multiple degrees in engineering from Kuala Lumpur, after all.

The end of the street, and the beginning of another, and still no humans, but a happy baby on her hands. It laughed. Yes, it was unmistakable. Perhaps it resented being cooped up in the big house all the time. Adila never did. She loved the bigness of the house. You could play the syrupy nasyid, the hip religious music, which verged at times on ersatz New Wave, in one corner of the house, and the rest of it never know. The Zainul-Abidins, as they had informed Amy during their first meal together, were "secular" Muslims, meaning, none of the stupid radicalism for them—no, not in this household. They were up-to-date, modern, moderate, moving toward ever-greater enlightenment. They loved America. Here it was possible to discover your *real self*. Dato Sri Razak had actually said that. He'd also said, "I love how you people are so mobile, never settling down in one place, the place of your birth. I love it." Amy felt second-class, in her own country. These people were smart. They knew how to get ahead. Amy hadn't yet picked up the admissions application at the University of Houston. She felt at a loss filling out financial aid paperwork, even though her mother hardly made enough to keep their shabby house together, and Amy's three younger siblings in check. Yes, she was definitely second-class; but if America was all about encouraging true talent, no matter where it came from, then this was all right, wasn't it?

The baby pulled her head back from Amy, as if to look directly into Amy's eyes. It had never looked so happy. The baby's cheeks were flushed, and she made articulate goo-gooing sounds, raising her little arms, then clenching and unclenching her fists. "Oh, you're a cute one," Amy said. What was that, an actual pang of baby-lust, a signal of imminent womanhood? No, no, Amy didn't want to grow up yet. This—suspension in limbo, this paralysis of analysis— this was good enough for her. Growing up was for adults, with responsibilities and mortgages and leases and real jobs. If she wanted to, she could read all day long, she could learn languages, she could do anything to improve—or discover?— her real self, and no one would mind. She had a savings account, which was growing fast, because Amy had no real expenses, staying as she did with the Zainul-Abidins, and she felt like sending it all to her mother. "Texas has been good to me—so far," she told herself.

The trees planted on the street were all of short stature, dwarf redbuds and hawthorns; the planters probably didn't want them to grow to absurd heights. You could tell which were the oldest homes on the blocks by the height of some of the trees inside the perimeter of the houses, probably grown long before uniformity of appearance must have become the paramount concern in this neighborhood.

"I wish I could let you walk," she said to the baby. "You will, in another few months, you know."

Suddenly, Amy was bored. Yes, it was nice to feel at one with the baby-spirit of the world, innocent and guileless, being ready for the next adventure, the unanticipated walk into the blue, but—what else was there? Should she be satisfied with her second-class status? Dato Sri Razak—was he being offensive in treating Amy's family, when the subject came up, as no more worthy of serious consideration than one of the three gardeners? How should Amy feel about herself? Not to mention the not irrelevant fact that her sexual experience was highly limited, compared to the average for her age and background. The smartest boy in her high school had aspired to be an astronaut. An astronaut? This baby in her arms, she would never think a stupid thought like that, if she grew up in America. She would be an investment banker. A secular first-generation Malaysian-American, proud of her identity, fixed in her lodestar and origin and destiny. Was it possible to feel jealous of an eight-month-old baby who couldn't yet walk and talk?

The baby was gurgling happily, tapping her little hands rhythmically against Amy's shoulder. "Oh, you like my smell, do you? Well, I like yours." It wasn't even pooping in the diaper. Just pure contentment. But it was time to turn around. How long could a baby shower go on? They were all beautiful Malaysian women, Adila's friends, with no indication that any of them had ever been depressed, or felt left out, or had unmet higher spiritual or material aspirations. Some of them went to school part-time, usually for something appropriately esoteric and technical. Most of them lived in apparent bliss, flying from place to place in their BMWs and Volvos. They were happy. America had been good to them, on a very large scale.

It was possible to return to the Zainul-Abidins' house by way of a circle, which you usually couldn't do in a modern subdivision, because you would only meet a dead-end and have to turn around.

Both Dato Sri Razak's and Adila's SUVs were parked in the driveway.

"Oh, Amy, there you are, there you are-lah!" Adila came running out the front door, her feet bare, her hair uncovered for once—flying all over the place, wild and wet. "Oh, Amy, I was so worried-lah, I didn't know what had happened-lah! I was about to—about to—you know." Adila shrugged. No, Amy didn't know. What was there to be so worried about?

Adila almost rudely took the baby away from Amy. "There you are, Nurhaliza, my baby. Did you eat-lah? Did you play-lah? Was the sun too hot for you-lah?" Adila looked at Amy, as if for clarification about the heat of the sun.

"The sun's always hot in this city." This evil city, Amy wanted to add, where no human beings talked to one another, where people loaded up their giant SUVs with things they didn't need at Wal-Mart and Home Depot, and felt good about being able to do so. She hated this place. She missed home—Connecticut. She would send all her savings to her mother, tomorrow. She would get to know a decent guy back home in Bristol—a white guy, not someone black or brown or yellow, that you fucked or even married to make a statement.

"Oh hello, there you are, lah!" Dato Sri Razak, also in bare feet, and with his belt undone, came jogging out of the house too, joining the baby-greeting fiesta occurring at the edge of their property. He took the baby from his wife. "The police, they said..." He stopped abruptly. "You know..." he shrugged.

Amy didn't know. They'd already called the police? She must have been gone, what, forty-five minutes, at most? Hadn't the gardener, José, seen her walk out with the baby, openly, with nothing to hide? There he was, huddled over, trying to disappear into the background. They thought she was a baby-stealer? They'd seen too many scary American movies where the babysitter is never anything less than a child abductor, where you must ward off your entire proprietarial setup against constant intruders willing to take advantage of your generosity. She must speak up now, or be forever silenced. "I only took her for a walk…it was a…nice day. I think it's a nice day, relatively speaking…"

"We'll talk later about when to and when not to—go out in the sun-lah!" Adila said.

"Yes, we'll have a talk later." Dato Sri Razak could still look straight into Amy's eyes. "It's time for dinner. What do we have? Or are we going out-lah?" Dato Sri Razak returned the baby to Adila, the true repository of the precious burden.

Without answering, and ignoring Amy altogether, Adila walked back inside. They wouldn't go out, to some restaurant that served steaks to fat Americans, Dato Sri Razak's favorite kind of place. It would be that hateful nasi lemak again, rice drowned in coconut curry. At first, Amy had tried to like it, but it was too lumpy and bloated and flavorless to eat for long. It was more of a street food than a delicacy in Malaysia, and so naturally it was high on the rank of things to savor on a day-to-day basis for the Zainul-Abidins. It went well with the bland nasyid music. And the lah, lah, lah at the end of every single sentence. Lah, lah, lah! How they take advantage of me, Amy thought as she followed the Zainul-Abidins into the safety of their expensive River Oaks home, cursing Enron for treating Tun Tun Dato Sri Abdul Razak with whatever generosity of spirit it did, for she found that same attitude unbearable when he brought it over to the home, the only thing worse being when he withheld it. She almost wished the police had come, and there had been an anticlimactic scene on the street. She missed out on everything, all the fun.

GYPSY

That first morning when Baba woke up with the sticky white fluid coating his eyes, he dismissed it with contempt, as he had all his previous ailments—his joint pains, his swollen jaw, his rotting teeth. "It's nothing," he said, donning his thick brown corduroy jacket, even though it was already warm, the kind of hot June day that had the capacity to disable hundreds of frail people in Indianapolis and Chicago. It was like him to dress without rhyme or reason, almost catching the death of his cold when he ventured out once in a thin tropical shirt in the icy Indiana winter in the middle of the night when he thought he heard burglars in the pigpen.

"Nothing, Baba? It's your eyes. What if you go blind? You must see a doctor." I wished I had the courage to ask Janie, my friend who lived a few miles away, and about whom my father knew nothing, to send along a doctor to our house.

"A doctor? Who needs a doctor, Marcsa? They put a spell over you with their bad magic, and before you know it, you really are ill. It's false speech, rooted in their own diseased minds. A doctor is who you call when you have a death wish. They killed your grandfather, when all he had was a little stomach ailment. They killed your mother, when they went against her natural melancholy. It's all right to be

207

sad—the world is a sad place, but the gaźos expect everyone to be happy. It's human nature to want to survive against all odds. The body is capable of miracles. If only we'd let it…"

I listened to this speech as I had to so many others instructing me in right and wrong, warning me not to trust gaźos an inch, or they'd deprive me of my romanes faith, and leave me belonging neither here nor there. I fixed him a bowl of the barley gruel he liked for breakfast, and some strawberries, his favorite fruit, which we only rarely used to have in Hungary.

We'd come to America from Tatabanya, north of Budapest and just short of the border with Slovakia, in 1947, when with the first wave of communism it became clear that henceforth the lives of the Rom would be made even more miserable than during the World War. At least during the war there were pockets of peace, and the interference of the state was random and haphazard; you could take a chance on escaping the worst. But once the communists came to power, it was clear that everyone would have to change their old ways to some degree or the other. The Rom would be expected to contribute to building the communist state, their old customs punished and destroyed. The pictures of my father, around the time he got married in the thirties, are of a plumpish young man, with a naughty smile in his eyes. Now I felt sorry for his gaunt cheeks and sunken eyes, and the gray marking his thin moustache.

He stubbed his toe against a chair, as the cloudiness in his eyes made it difficult for him to concentrate. "Write a letter to your cousin Radka in Indianapolis today. Her father still owes me sixty thousand florints on our last big horse sale in Tatabanya. Milan was drunk that day at the market, and I covered for him, but this doesn't excuse him from a legitimate debt. Tell her he must do the honorable thing, or else… Or else…"

Or else what? What could he do? Call some sort of mafia to his aid? In America no one knew or understood or cared about his long-ago transactions, what was owed to him and what he owed to others. For that matter, I figured Baba owed any number of large and small debts to his brethren among the Rom, but here everyone seemed to have been allowed to go on with their lives and no one wanted to dredge up the past unless there wasn't any other way around it. Baba, on the other hand, still designated money in the Hungarian currency, still mixed up the Indiana state authorities, who'd been so generous with their resettlement policies, with the merciless communist apparatchiks determined to make productive wage laborers out of the most obstinate Rom. He blamed himself for the death of my mother, who died soon after arrival in the new world, of complications, following a depressive episode, that remained unclear to everyone. I couldn't be sure if Baba would have accepted slavery at a communist factory as the price for my mother still being alive, but I knew his calculus of how and why things happened was all awry.

"Later when you have time"—he paused to scratch his eyes violently, barely able to see through them now— "try to make sense of this letter." The night before, my mother's younger brother Vlad had dropped by, when Baba was already quite drunk on his favorite fruit brandy. Baba was uncharacteristic among the Rom in that, when drunk, he didn't utter profanities, violent sentiments toward stubborn women and state officials; his was a civilized kind of drunkenness, yet he was too befuddled to do anything but nod through the spiel Uncle Vlad had uttered. I wasn't supposed to have listened in on the conversation, but it was about the rights to the property in Tatabanya belonging to my maternal grandfather. The communist government was being surprisingly forthcoming in acknowledging the claim to land my mother's family had owned for generations, and was willing to put an official estimate on its value, even if no mention was made of compensation for expropriation. My father didn't need to be included in these proceedings; it was only Uncle Vlad's generosity that made him share the correspondence. But perhaps Baba thought Uncle Vlad was trying to pull wool over his eyes.

Uncle Vlad had left saying he was worried about his son being called up to fight the war in Korea. But for his son to return to Hungary was not an option. We'd taken the gaźos' shelter; we'd have to fight their wars. With Uncle Vlad, Baba never brought up memories of my mother—it was against romanes to remember the dead more than a year after their death, when their souls were finally liberated and their hold on the surviving family members released—but Baba never missed an opportunity to remind me that it was moving to the new world, something I obviously didn't resent, that had somehow caused my mother's death.

I disliked these references to my mother. Baba had buried the few pictures we had of her in her grave. The gaźo priest who came with great reluctance to perform the burial ceremony, even after pocketing a hefty bribe, backed away in fear when he saw that we were burying my mother with her favorite chair, table, clothes, and trinkets, and that the grave was wide enough to be a small home, which in fact it was meant to represent. I was nine then, and my very presence, as of other children at the funeral, drove the priest crazy. He swore he would inform on us to the authorities, but this was rural Indiana in 1949, and it was possible for Baba's friends to threaten the priest enough that he probably didn't go forward with his threat. After the burial, my mother's sister Luludji sat me down before all six of her daughters and instructed me: "You'll be a woman soon, Marcsa. Your mother may have died, but her spirit lives in you. Never think you're alone. More responsibility has come your way. How you handle this responsibility will decide if you're a good romni or not. This is a time for sorrow, but it's also a time for joy. You've become a woman earlier than you expected, but you're ready for it."

Distances, in those days, really meant something. I had been to Muncie, where Luludji and her family lived, only a couple of times, and to Indianapolis only once, when my mother was still alive. Of the latter trip, I had the memory of my father spending almost the entire day at a circus, where he concluded about the Spanish and Greek and Sicilian performers: "They're Rom, every last one of them. Rom of the lost tribes, who've slowly forgotten who they are, having lived so long with the gaźos. But you can tell by their habits and actions and character, they're Rom, even if they don't know it." I remembered a clown who took a fancy to me. A lion in a cage who tried repeatedly to stand on its hind legs only to fall down, perhaps because it was so obese. And a fortune-teller named Madam Gabor, who, in a cloud of sickly incense, insisted that my mother not delegate the duty of watching over the farm animals to the servants and that she keep a close eye on the account balances. "What farm?" my mother wondered, her sweet brown eyes full of the innocence she never seemed to have lost. "We don't own a farm. It's barely a little plot of stony ground, and I don't think anything's ever going to grow on it. The only animals around are filthy cats and rabid dogs—and a couple of pigs that won't get fat no matter what you feed them. No horses at all!" Madam Gabor reacted churlishly, getting up and furiously twirling her multiple red skirts: "Hunh! If you don't want to believe me, I guess it'll never happen. Why do you come to me if you don't trust me? You're a gypsy. Why can't you tell your own fortune? Not that your kind have a monopoly on this business. This is a free country. Everyone looks out for himself." My mother didn't get upset, saying more softly, "Where are you from, Madam Gabor? You have dark skin, and—passionate manners..." "It doesn't concern you where I'm from," Madam Gabor said. "I could be Irish or Italian or whatever. What matters is I'm born and bred American. Two dollars, please." My father was more furious that Madam Gabor hadn't admitted her true Rom origins than the fact that a real romni like my mother would seek out a fortune-teller. "It was a joke," my mother explained, which made my father start yelling about the filthy communists who stank to high heaven and wanted to rebuild the Rom's homes in their filthy image, just like the filthy Americans who stank like diseased animals but thought they were fragrant as fresh roses.

My mother had a reputation for being something of a prude, even a snitch at times, when the simmering gossip and infighting among the women got to be too much for her. She preferred taking care of the pigs and horses (we did eventually acquire a fair number of them, just as the fortune-teller had predicted) with my father, which made her all the more despised among the women, because this wasn't supposed to be women's work. My mother was also begrudged by the women for knowing the rudiments of the Hungarian script, which she'd passed on to me. Of course, now we had no more farm as such, because Baba broke his foot only a few weeks after my mother died, and it turned into such an acute injury that he took it as an excuse to get rid of most of the land, selling it to a first cousin for a marginal loss (who in turn sold it to gaźos in Indianapolis who never took possession), and counting on the cash earned that way to live for a number of years without having to figure out new methods to outwit the gaźos to make money. Now I'd turned thirteen, and it seemed to me that what my aunt Luludji had said to me on the day of my mother's funeral was a pack of lies. I'd not yet become a woman, nor did I feel close to being one. I didn't feel the spirit of my mother in me. I had a whole secret life, of which Baba knew nothing. I had gaźo friends. If the Rom were supposed to be so much smarter than gaźos, why did I feel that my gaźo friends could easily outwit Baba?

After my mother died I started sneaking out of the house more and more. I soon discovered a family of poor farmers, the Dickinsons, whom, if my father had met them, he would have called true Rom to the core, even if they didn't know it themselves. The Dickinsons gamely took care of two mad older twin daughters, on whom the doctors had given up since they were toddlers. The girls, even at eighteen, spoke only in fragments of sentences, but mostly created no more trouble than wanting to swing from the trees all day long, and swim half-naked in the dirty creek nearby. The Dickinson boy, Steven, my age, talked to me about stars and oceans, atoms and clouds, and doubled his attentions to me when he finally became convinced that I'd never gone to school, even though I wasn't crazy like his two sisters. Mr. Dickinson, a wiry man always dressed in gray overalls, complained about the "damned social workers poking their nose into everyone's private business," and lamented that America was going to hell in a handbasket because we couldn't leave other countries' business well enough alone. Mrs. Dickinson, healthily plump, liked to sew contentedly on the porch, and was always reminding her family to eat more cantaloupes and oranges to get enough Vitamin C, as if they all suffered from its deficiency. When I tried to shock her one day by telling her that my mother had probably died of lead poisoning (true, as far as any theory went), from having lived too close to a cluster of factories in Tatabanya, Mrs. Dickinson said, "If it's not lead, they'll get you with preservatives in the food. Now you make sure you eat enough oranges every day—Vitamin C will keep every disease away."

It was their daughter, Janie, a year older than me, who really took me under her wings, and taught me first the alphabet, and over time to read almost as well as herself, even if my spelling never quite made it to par. It was at the Dickinsons' that I first watched television, unable, however, to catch the drift of the jokes the fat, bald comedians spewed out in an endless barrage of invective and aggression. It was at the Dickinsons' that I learned to pet a cat, although I took care not to contaminate things at our own house, washing myself thoroughly each time I returned. Not that my father noticed much. In those days, not long after my mother died, her brothers and cousins and more distant relatives frequently used to drop by our little patch of land with its absurdly crooked ramshackle house, trying to get my father interested in this or that deal for horses or other farm animals. They even tried once to include him in a massive caravan (which later became the stuff of myth in the chronicles of the Rom of that region and era) headed all the way to California, where it was said that the mechanical and automobile repair trades had already made kings of the Rom from the Western and Southern European countries. These more ambitious Rom were building fortunes even while holding on to romanes— the well-documented decisions of the kris in the Oakland-San Francisco area were some of the most authoritative, providing the basis for judicial precedents around the country, as word spread from community to community of the need to take advantage of the sumptuous deal-making opportunities in this vast and indefinable land.

I heard that the grandparents Dickinson, who lived on the other side of the state line in Kentucky, had kept up a lifelong fight with Janie's father, because he'd spurned, according to them, any number of opportunities for success earlier in life—the time he could have invested some of his money in an automobile dealership and perhaps had a chance at a serious ownership stake later on. But Janie's father seemed quite content with fly-fishing, and fixing the barn and other farm buildings year after year, as if the repairs of the previous year hadn't taken place, and talking to his kids at length on the porch about their most mundane activities, as if they were matters of world-shaking importance. I found myself included in these deliberations, slightly embarrassed at the shameless way Steven looked at my legs or arms or neck or whatever part of my body was exposed, which somehow provoked me into revealing (as though unintentionally) some other glimpse of it which I knew was sure to tickle his fancy.

Baba, of course, knew nothing about my ability to read a little now, and I had to learn not to blurt out the contents of some emergency letter, such as from the state authorities who'd initially helped us with resettlement and were forever solicitous about our welfare and "acculturation to the American way of life." I stacked the letters on the wobbly-legged round table by the door, to be tackled once every few weeks by one of Baba's more literate cousins, who would merrily butcher the English language. Without my knowing it, a distance had grown up between Baba and me, to the extent that I refused to believe I was a "woman" now just because I had turned thirteen, and was having my periods. A few times, to spite him, I even washed the clothes I was wearing during menstruation in the same sink where we washed the dishes, and once I mixed the clothes the Dickinsons' cat had crawled all over with Baba's clothes, but I derived little satisfaction from these childish pranks and soon started honoring the rules of marimo even if there was no chance Baba would ever know of any violation. He seemed to be entering a phase of utter indifference anyway, drinking himself into a stupor with fruit brandy, just as in the last period in Tatabanya, and treating the visiting cousins and "brothers" with more and more hostility. If they ever talked about Truman's politics, which seemed to be having a direct effect on all their lives, insofar as America's wars now had widespread domestic repercussions, he went into a blind fury and blamed all of them for having sold out romanes to become lackeys of the gazos. The more his eyes clouded over with the goopy moisture that hot summer, the more he acted as if he were the last true Rom left in the world.

Then Janie fell in love around Independence Day, with a boy whose family, the McPhersons, had just moved from Ohio. The father and mother were mousy-looking and afraid in the extreme, but the boy, William, was their exact opposite, a strapping hulk with a booming voice and the kind of confidence that either leads you to be crucified or to become king. At sixteen, he knew enough to tear apart a car's engine and rebuild it, and he talked a lot about farming techniques, although Mr. Dickinson mostly ignored him, because it wasn't as if he were trying to maximize the gains from his farmland anyway. Mrs. Dickinson thought William harmless, while Steven's resentment and envy of the bulkier William was barely disguisable: "He's a big moron, is what he is! I bet he got into trouble in Ohio. I ought to write to the postmaster in the town he says he comes from, to see if he's wanted for something. I bet he'll end up robbing banks." For all his distorting jealousy, Steven had a cannier read on William than did the other Dickinsons. Janie had entered a zone of perpetual rapture, where it was always William this, William that, hushed words where secrets were conjured into existence from nowhere, plans for the indefinite future that beckoned as early as tomorrow, and a righteous willingness to set aside doubt in favor of a certainty rooted in fanatic passion. Janie changed overnight before my very eyes, and I wasn't sure how to feel about it. I resented that she spent less and less time teaching me how to read, and to work sums, and to follow the basics of physics and biology, and instead disappeared for long stretches of time into the fields, never bothered by her father as mine would surely have bothered me if he hadn't himself been disintegrating rapidly.

Looking back, it seems odd that Baba was so nonchalant about my increasingly weird explanations as to why it took me hours to walk the few miles to and from the country store, or why I had suddenly become so fond of the outdoors as to take long aimless walks at odd hours. Only once did he caution me to be careful about predators, human or animal, and sometimes he warned me never to talk to the police or anyone in uniform, because they were all agents of the state, and their only business was to get the Rom in trouble for not being wage laborers like themselves. I sneaked a few books into our house, like *Little Women*, which I struggled mightily to understand, even after some years of teaching by Janie, and *Our Town*, whose weirdness was compounded by the fact that I'd never seen a play performed and so couldn't make head or tail of the stage directions, and Robert Frost's poetry, where the need to make words rhyme struck me as more showy and silly than as something profound. If Baba had ever found out I was spending time with books, I'm sure he would have disowned me and thrown me out of the house.

As it was, he got his revenge through more traditional means. It was toward the end of the summer, when Janie had already said she was going to be "engaged" to William soon, that my father got a visit from Uncle Vlad, acting as emissary on behalf of the same Milan, Radka's father, who supposedly owed my father sixty thousand florints for the horse deal gone wrong. Radka had an older brother, Šošoj, who I'd heard was one of the most desirable bachelors among the Rom in Indiana. The speech he'd made at a cousin's wedding when he was only nineteen, full of ancient romanes wisdom, was said to have been a high point, after which the community started feeling less disoriented in the new world. Šošoj, had we been in Hungary, would have approached me directly, and tried to pass a gift along to me, perhaps an embroidered handkerchief, and it would have been easy for me to demonstrate reciprocity in his interest, had I accepted his gift. From then on, unless my father had been able to prove some overtly evil characteristic of my suitor, the marriage would have been sealed. When and how had Šošoj come to know of me? Indianapolis was a big city; there were Rom there from Catalonia and Romania and Poland and Russia, many of them doing quite well in the traditional Rom trades, horse trading and metal work, and of course fortune-telling, and many of whom had pretensions to being from the elite Rom tribes—in the new world, these matters of status had suddenly become much more fluid than before. Some owned nice houses, having switched to a more sedentary life, and some spoke English fluently, almost like natives.

"You're a woman now, Marcsa," my father said after Uncle Vlad left. "If your mother had been alive, no doubt you would already have been married. I've been negligent in my duties. It was good of Vlad to remind me of my responsibility to you. After all, I'm a sick man, and I don't know how much longer I'll live..."

"Ridiculous! Baba, you're only thirty-seven. This is considered quite young in America." I almost spilled out my secret relationship with the Dickinsons, wanting to tell him how Mr. Dickinson, at fifty-five, took part in children's games whenever he could, and ran like a hare if the mood struck him.

"Thirty-seven is old. Just because a Rom comes to the new world doesn't mean he's no longer who he was born to be. Anyway, Šošoj has proposed to you. He'll be a good husband. His father has shown himself entirely capable. These things pass on in families."

"Šošoj's father? You hate him! He owes you the sixty thousand florints still. He's a cheat, who took advantage of you. Why would his son even be interested in me?"

"Enough!" Baba rose in disgust, stunned at my aggression. "I don't want people to say old Čoro's daughter is a kurvi, a whore. I want to die in peace, an honorable man. When your mother was alive, I never did anything to dishonor her. I don't want to start a bad reputation now."

"All of a sudden, you care about your reputation? You haven't visited any of your kin in years. They think you're a loner, you don't care a bit about your relationship with them. They think you act superior, just because your wife died of sadness in the new world. Suddenly, you care about what others think of you?"

Baba was pacing back and forth in our small kitchen. At one point he seized a hold of the boiling kettle and I was afraid he would throw it at me. But then he started rubbing his eyes, and I felt sorry because another attack had come upon him.

"At least see a doctor before anyone besides Uncle Vlad sees you. At least make yourself look presentable." I realized by saying this I was hinting toward granting him authority to negotiate with Šošoj's parents on my behalf. I realized I hadn't said no. I had yielded, without putting up a proper fight. Was it too late? Could I backtrack? Did I even want to? If Janie's father had sprung such a surprise on her, she would have raised hell, speaking of the "equality" of women. But then, she had William. I had no William, I had no one. Steven was good to me, but when it came time to settle down he would no doubt choose an educated gaźo woman, at the state college where he would study agriculture, or perhaps engineering or medicine if he was lucky. My world seemed to shrink enormously. A wave of coldness came over me when I thought of the Dickinsons and people like them, unaware of how lucky they were to have been born into a world where they didn't constantly have to fear that people would want them to give up their ways. I became aware that I was after all a romni, and I would soon have to leave for Indianapolis, and deal with Šošoj's drinking and staying out late and gambling, and his insane horse deals and his mistresses who'd bleed him of all his spare money. I would be a compliant bori, the grateful daughter-in-law doing slave work in the house of the man who owed my father a ton of money, at least until a second, younger bori came along to take my despised status, and I would be relieved a bit. I would deliver children, year after year, and have to teach them to stay away from the gaźos, to mistrust and doubt anyone who wasn't a Rom, to have no respect for schools and hospitals and the police and the post office. And I would forget that I was ever friends with some gaźo girl who taught me how to read. I would, perhaps, forget how to read.

I wasn't surprised when the next morning Baba informed me, rubbing his rheumy eyes, "I already said yes to Šošoj's proposal yesterday. So expect a mangimo in a week. They'll visit to formally seek your hand, and we must treat them with respect." Of course, why had I thought that he would have waited for my consent? I served him no breakfast, and instead took the shorter way to the Dickinsons', stonier and less shady than the longer, indirect route marked by flourishing dogwood and hickory trees. I'd never been there so early in the morning. It was chaos there. William was sitting at the kitchen table across from Mr. Dickinson, his head hanging low as if he'd committed some great crime, while Mrs. Dickinson looked at me from the porch as if she didn't recognize me. Janie and Steven were nowhere in sight. Even the mad twin daughters appeared subdued.

Feeling unwelcome, I wandered around in the fields, until I became worried about a plump middle-aged farmer sneakily following me. Every time I'd catch him at it, he stopped short, fiddling with a twig in his mouth and looking down at his feet, but I knew he was tailing me. In the end, I started running, but instead of going back to my own house, I headed back to the Dickinsons'. I was faint with dizziness from hunger. I felt small and deficient, as if left alone in the world, without instructions, rules, on how to make the best of it for myself.

Mrs. Dickinson sat me down in the kitchen (William was gone by then). "Marcsa, I have some bad news. Janie is in trouble. We're sending her away to an aunt's in Wyoming. At least for the summer. You can say goodbye to her today if you want to. She's leaving tomorrow morning." I figured I knew what the trouble was, and when I went to see Janie in her room, she didn't do anything to disabuse me of my conjecture. Instead of being mad at Janie, however, for causing something that would take her away from me, I asked curiously, "How was it? Did you like it?" Janie stared at me, surprised, but happier for the moment. It was as if the distance that had crept up between us fell away, and she reached over to hug me and cried her heart out.

Afterward I felt grateful to William too for some reason. He wasn't a bad boy at heart. He could have taken precaution, of course, but at least he was around to take responsibility. I imagined the tableau in the kitchen with him and Mr. Dickinson—his probable father-in-law now. He was taking it like a man, instead of running away. What would happen to William now? I didn't know if Janie would have the baby, or if she would have it taken out. I felt it wasn't my business to know that.

Steven followed me to the end of the dirt road leading to their house. He whistled coyly. "I guess you won't be coming around here anymore."

"I guess not."

"I'll miss you. You can still drop by if you want to."

"I will."

"I could teach you to read—to write even. I mean, you don't yet know how to write well."

"Okay."

"Why won't your father send you to school? You'd do well in school. There are only morons in our school. You'd be a great student."

I had no answer to this, and I said to Steven, in my most melodramatic voice, "Goodbye for now, Steven. Take care of yourself."

A few days went by without my father and I speaking about the inevitable. Then one evening I came home to find Uncle Vlad's antiquated Model T again parked outside. He was the only one among the Rom I knew who didn't constantly make apologies for driving an automobile, didn't link it to some unfortunate necessity of adjustment instead of the ideal of riding behind a horse. I knew his wife was a very unhappy woman, but because she was so fat and vile-smelling I'd never felt much sympathy for her. She too had tried to take me under her wings by teaching me all the rules of marimo I might have overlooked, in the quest to become a worthy romni. Uncle Vlad alternated between moods of bottomless melancholy and ecstatic joy, prompted by little more than a few hundred dollars of loss or gain. He talked about scoping out business opportunities in the big cities of the Midwest, mocking, like other Rom, the gaźos' terrible business instincts. "Hear this," I'd heard him tell his sons, when we were over at their house and Truman came on the radio. "Hear this! This is the voice of the biggest gaźo of them all. He thinks just because he has the bomb, the world will do his bidding. He couldn't do a thing about the communists taking over Hungary, all our lands. He's impotent. Can't do a thing!" My father—it was in the days when he still used to engage in serious conversation—responded: "But his people helped get us over here. God knows what they're doing to our brothers in Hungary. God knows if they're alive or dead." To which Uncle Vlad replied, "The Rom will go on until the end of time. We'll figure out new ways to survive. We always have." I'd figured out that the more a Rom badmouthed America, the more eager he was to get a piece of the action he thought the stupid gaźos were missing out on.

The evening he visited, he and my father had apparently had a long heart-to-heart talk. I found Uncle Vlad drinking fruit brandy alone in the kitchen. Like my father, he never acted drunk, no matter how much he drank. It was one of the things his fat wife most admired about him.

"Look, Marcsa," Uncle Vlad said, "I've been talking to your father, and we think we haven't taken your wishes into account enough. This is the new world after all. Of course, we have to abide by the romanes ways, but you're a smart girl and we need to listen to what you say. Šošoj is a good man. He won't fool around recklessly, and he'll keep a good house. But the choice is really yours. Do you have someone else in mind?"

How could I tell him that I didn't have anyone in mind? I was thirteen, and even if Janie, at fourteen, had gone and got herself pregnant, I'd learned enough to know that this was an aberration. You waited longer in America. You learned to respect your body—your thoughts and your dreams. You learned to protect yourself, even from your closest family, even from the person you thought you might love one day. How could I tell Uncle Vlad it wasn't about Šošoj, or whatever romanes tradition was or was not good for me? It was about being able to go deep into my hiding shell of a cool Indiana evening, when the enormity of the land invited unspoken thoughts to come to the surface, so I could dissect and consider them, discard the silly ones, turn over the more profound ones for further exploration. Unexpected connections between people and things then became evident. And you couldn't do this when you felt obligated to love someone. You never could.

"Of course, the choice is yours," Uncle Vlad went on, "but your father is getting old...and he's very sick—"

"Why can't you convince him to see a doctor? You seem to have enough time on your hands—"

"Marcsa!" he said sharply, then quickly retreated. "It's not the kind of sickness a doctor can do anything about. His neck hurts, his stomach aches, his feet are swollen—what can you do? Your mother died, and he's a soft man. It's just the way it is."

"Hypocrite!" I shouted at him. "You don't care if Baba lives or dies. You act like a big shot, and you watch American television, and you say the kinds of things they say to women here, but you don't feel a thing for women. You're a Rom all the way inside, and you probably laugh at Baba for not having married a younger woman the minute my mother died. You don't understand what the past is, you don't linger over it. That's the romanes way, isn't it? And I'm supposed to sacrifice myself so a bunch of you men can feel good about yourselves! If Šošoj is so special, why can't he marry some girl he knows? He's never known me, and my father is rumored to be a strange, lonely man who no longer takes part in any mulatšagos, who has nothing to share with anyone. I don't want to marry him. You can say no to them, and if you go ahead anyway, you should know that I'll make him the unhappiest man on earth! He'll live to regret the day he sent you over as his emissary."

To which Uncle Vlad laughed uproariously, and wouldn't stop when I stalked out of the kitchen.

I refused to talk to Baba the next couple of days, even as his eyes got really bad. Friday afternoon, at the appointed time, the mangimo party arrived. Šošoj and his father came in a newer model car, with wide fins and a gigantic hood, which I later knew to be a Cadillac.

I'd hidden behind a fence to catch a look. Šošoj was stunningly beautiful, lean and muscular in a way that few Rom were after their teenage years, because they drank so much, and refused to make a ritual of keeping their bodies in shape. He also had keen eyes, and an intelligent, roving face that seemed to have less than the usual Rom arrogance.

Later, while his father Milan made elaborate speeches about how the two families would be greatly blessed if Baba gave my hand to his beloved son, and other relatives from Šošoj's side followed suit, I stayed in the next room, overhearing everything.

Finally, it was Šošoj's turn to get up and make a compelling speech in which he assured my father that if we were to be married, he would promise great fertility, many children, who would proudly carry on the two families' names in the new world. I had a tough time not laughing at this speech, which my father took in silently. In the end, Baba must have mumbled some words of assent, because boisterous cheers went up, and then the men talked over the bride price for hours, the amount my father could get for me suggestive of his status in the Rom community. To no surprise of mine, the bride price was settled at sixty thousand florints, precisely the amount from the horse deal Milan owed—not that that unfortunate event was ever brought up. I had begun to enjoy the proceedings, despite my will not to. I almost wanted to dress up and join the party, hoping that Šošoj would offer me a beautiful gift, which I might or might not have accepted on the spot.

Then I heard Šošoj say to my father, "Your eyes are very bad. You need to have a doctor look at them."

A hush fell on the room, since it was hardly the position of the just anointed son-in-law to offer medical advice to his respected father-in-law so soon.

But my father only said resignedly, "If you'll get someone you can trust, I'll see to it right away. I can't sleep all night because of the itching and burning..."

It was at that moment that I felt a final tug away from the Dickinsons and their thrall, and decided that I had to live for myself and not through Janie's fantasies or anyone else's, and that there was an unbridgeable gap between the gaźos and us, which, despite their goodheartedness (who could ascribe any malignant motive to a man as generous as Mr. Dickinson?), couldn't possibly make us one people. I felt rushing over me the warmth one feels only for blood relatives, only for family one is crazily in love with despite, or perhaps because of, their weird habits and moods, and I thought I grew into the stature of a woman then, even though I was only thirteen, vastly "underage" and "immature" according to any gaźo definition. I knew it was time for me not to treat myself as a child anymore. Perhaps I could teach Šošoj to read and write as well as I was able to myself.

I haven't moved far from the place I used to call home more than fifty years ago. I live in Indianapolis now, the reviled, bland Midwestern city that outré writers like Kurt Vonnegut have targeted for satire over these recurrently sad late twentieth-century decades. For a while I'd lived in Bloomington, in the sixties at that, when the hippie generation adopted a lot of the "unproductive," lackadaisical, minimally efficient romanes habits. But then their pretension of not wanting to be part of the "rat race" (the gaźos' own definition of their work ethic) got to be too much, and I retreated to the safer, humbler, more workaday environs of downtown Indianapolis, working for the city as a counselor to troubled youth, mostly poor white kids in the early years, then blacks, and more recently Hispanics and Asians. The daring innocence about Indiana that attracted me to the gaźos at home in it in the early days hasn't gone away, regardless of the sophisticated veneer the land acquires. The icy wind still revitalizes in the same way, and the summer still returns abruptly, making my thoughts suggestive and mystical. A huge distance separates us from not only New York, but even Chicago, a distance which makes it possible to conceive of making mistakes without paying burdensome reparations. I like it when young women with purple hair and poorly paid jobs at the video rental store go out of their way to be affectionate to slow-moving grandmothers on the streets, without the least self-consciousness. I've shed many generations of weight off my frail shoulders, without having betrayed anyone. I feel as alive sometimes in the middle of a busy day of listening to some teenaged kid's convoluted self-justifications, as I did the day I decided I was ready to be a bride, a bori in someone else's home in a big city, a woman who'd gradually establish respect and dignity in her husband's household.

Šošoj and I got married that winter, and he did well in business, before an unfortunate argument with a competitor, who claimed rights to the same plot of land Šošoj had marked

out to start a Hungarian restaurant, put an end to his life at
twenty-three. I can't say that my dream of gaining respect
as a dutiful bori in his household met with full success,
but it wasn't a bad life, and he wasn't a bad husband. Of
course, his beauty no longer held the same compulsion once
I was up close to it, and I can't deny that I often fantasized
about other men—older, more educated, mostly gaźos. In
Šošoj's memory, I slept with no other man until well after
I'd established myself in a profession, following years of
struggle as an older-than-normal student in college. Šošoj
had died before we could have a child, even if it was for
no lack of his trying. (I suspect the problem might have
been with me, although I've never gone to a doctor to find
out; this could have become a fatal problem between us, had
he lived on, the ignominy of an infertile woman too great
for the most understanding young Rom husband to handle
to the satisfaction of his parents and kin.) The one thing
that did disappoint me about Šošoj was that he showed
no interest in reading or writing beyond the rudiments
he needed to conduct business, which only drove me to a
madder frenzy of self-education—which perhaps has lasted
to this day. I swallowed everything in the public library, and
I made friends with schoolteachers, once I moved into my
own apartment in Muncie, to be closer to my father, whose
later years were relatively peaceful. I tried to be as good a
listener as I could when Baba told stories of his adventures
as a young man—this would have been in the thirties, when,
despite the worldwide depression, it was still possible to
ignore the threat of war, and the communists hadn't yet
made the simplest adherence to romanes difficult. I always
felt I had disappointed him in some fundamental way, and
he showed only token enthusiasm when I mentioned getting
some award as a teacher or counselor. He died in 1969,

mumbling that the gaźos had gone to the moon but would never be able to defeat the stubborn Vietnamese. It was in the middle of a hot summer in the seventies that I finally tried to track down the Dickinsons, but the parents had died long ago, the old farm had been demolished, and, try as I would, I never did find out what happened to Janie and Steven. I imagine Janie is alive somewhere, a grandmother nourished by despotic love, justifying her decisions as a younger person, making her past look inevitable and logical, as we all do, wherever we end up. As for myself, I enjoy getting the respect owed to a silver-haired dignified woman, with thin bones and a matriarchal face, even if I never so much as got pregnant or nursed a hungry kid of my own.

TEHRAN

Deep in the winter smog on the second of Dey, at the Shadman
Café in north Tehran, near where the Vali-e-Asr Avenue's
shops begin to thin out before the old condominiums built
in the Shah's time, there was an explosion killing ten people.
Two of the bodies were never identified. The owner of the
café, Mr. Tavakkoli, a lover of Hafez and part-time cab driver,
was spared because he was skiing that week with his male
Afghan lover in the Alborz Mountains. Among the rest were a
beautiful thirty-five-year-old pregnant schoolteacher, whose
patterned silk rusari remained intact even though her head was
blown off; a white-turbaned young cleric newly resettled from
Qom, in whose pocket was found the ungodly sum of twenty
thousand U.S. dollars; and the instigator of the attack itself
(though he was never identified as such), a Baha'i zoologist
whose friends never took claim of the body, afraid of the
reprisals for themselves. Next door in a bookstore, the power
of the blast made the thin, dusty volumes of French novelists
in Persian translation totter and fall off the shelves, although
the thicker British and Russians stayed put. The Baseej unit
first to arrive on the spot, after the late-afternoon tragedy,
was quick to note that there wasn't a single picture of Imam
Khomeini or any of the current leaders of the Revolution,

no sign whatever that the owner and the workers were of pious inclination; perhaps even this distaste couldn't quite explain the slowness of the recovery, nor the wild late-night speculation among them about the future of all north Tehran sidewalk cafés (by nature, spots where subversive activity was quick to take root). A sympathizer placed a bouquet of flowers on the curbside the following day, before a placard with Hafez's verses, appropriate to the sad occasion. A month later, the site was demolished; Mr. Tavakkoli, disheartened, decided to leave the restaurant business. A year later, a women's clothing store, specializing in elegant permutations of various head and body coverings, proudly announced its grand opening. Soon it was difficult for casual pedestrians to recall if there had ever been a café in that spot—perhaps not; perhaps it was just a fluke of imagination. In the near distance (the shimmering sun sometimes made it appear closer than it was) the smiling Damavand peak, topped with snow, challenged the restless activity with its obsolete calm.

In Mrs. Shahnaz Rasuli's two-bedroom apartment in the clean north Tehran neighborhood of Zafraniyeh, the banter between husband and wife, restrained lately by the awareness of the recent deaths of their respective fathers only months apart, was finally giving way to its usual occasionless levity.

"Mr. Rasuli," said Shahnaz, this being her usual way of addressing her pudgy husband, who thought he was capable of rolling over and dying for her at her merest whimsy, "you haven't finished your ghormeh sabzi. If you weren't hungry, you could have warned me. As it is, I have plenty of papers to grade. Or perhaps you're still thinking about the new Peykan you thought you might get for a bargain from your friend? Has

he left for America yet? Perhaps there's still hope. Although
I always say one Peykan is as good as another. Mr. Rasuli, are
you listening?"

"Khanom, why won't you let a man finish the paper?
It could be a newsworthy day."

"The paper? You call *Tehran News* a paper? That man,
that editor, what's-his-name, a royalist to the core, a man
who wouldn't hesitate to have the Shah's mummified corpse
return to Niavaran Palace to rule like a whimsical demon—
not to mention the anorexic empress, who looked only half-
alive even when she was wife of the King of Kings." At least
the Revolution had settled that; there was no going back to
monarchy. In that sense, everyone was enqelabi, a partisan of
the Revolution.

In fact, Reza never read the establishment papers with
anything like attention. He had already been twenty-one at the
time of the Revolution, old enough to remember the days when
the eternal pull of the Persian toward the hedonism issuing
from the West distorted the smallest news item, making every
event worthy of note, because it was infused with a dynamic
greed. The censors had relaxed a bit in recent years, but
they'd succeeded in permanently cloaking reality with a grim
blanket of obligation that no amount of individual heroism
could overcome. Reza only read the papers because his best
friend from childhood, Javad-Ali, was editing a newspaper
called *Asr-e-Aazadi*. This was the paper's third incarnation,
the Ministry of Culture and Islamic Guidance having shut
it down previously for its favorable reportage of student
demonstrations against the mullahs' wealth and privilege, and
for its criticism of Imam Khomeini's leadership. Reza liked to
examine the bland newspapers toeing the conservative line; it
gave him hope when he read his friend's paper in comparison,
always appealing to the Iranian sense of pragmatism.

"May I return to the paper?" Reza said. "The statistics on car production—not to mention steel—are astounding for this year."

"Always the engineer, Mr. Rasuli, always the engineer. Thank God I never understood exactly what it is you did at work, so senior in qualifications I think they let you warm your seat for your mere honorable presence."

"Shouldn't you be seeing about grading those papers?"

"I already know exactly what grade each of my students is going to get. Only two of them are getting A's. In Social Studies, Mr. Rasuli, I have to inform you that the opinions of my girls are distinctly on the tame side. You should see how they repeat the Imam's line on the war. The few that have actually been to the Behesht-e-Zahra cemetery, you can always tell who they are. They begin by exclaiming their pride at having a martyr in the family. Do you know, Mr. Rasuli, I think our Social Studies texts are due for a revision? Can your influential newspaper editors possibly move our reformist leaders in this direction?"

"In the Islamic Republic, the only miracles are effected by the people's own will—"

"Which works as slow as drops of water eroding a rock..."

"Now, now, we mustn't be impatient. You, for one, are better off because of the Revolution. You'd have been able to teach under the Shah, no doubt—but would you have had the same prestige?"

"That's because we killed off so many promising young men in the war. Because we didn't have enough air cover we forced little boys to crawl under Iraqi tanks and blow themselves up. Even now it feels as if there are too many girls in this country, not enough boys. Where are the boys?"

"The boys are everywhere." Then Reza said something stupid, trying to pacify his wife. "These things balance out over time."

Normally Shahnaz would have gone into a fit, blaming his excessively rationalistic engineer's mentality for perceiving all the tragedies of the world in mathematical terms. Instead, she became quiescent, insisting only that Reza wash the dishes and clean the kitchen when he finished. She was going out to shop for the party they were having on Friday night, to announce Shahnaz's pregnancy. Would he please also remember to put the garbage out? Oh, and not to open the door when the komiteh knocked on the door in the afternoon, as they had been doing for the last few days. They were going around asking residents in the neighborhood if they owned a satellite dish—illegal still to have in Iran—as if anyone would admit to this.

Reza took a last slow bite of the ghormeh sabzi. These leisurely weekday brunches were the boon of his life, now that the government was paying him a monthly salary of two million rials (half of what he was getting before) after the shutdown of the armaments factory where he had been employed as an engineer since he graduated from Tehran University in 1981. The plant had consistently been running losses; Russian armaments, of better quality, could be had for a fraction of what it took to make them at home, and the enterprise would show a smaller loss if it suspended operations and paid its employees partial salaries until they transitioned into other jobs. The Bonyad which controlled the armaments industry was facing tough times, as the fervor of the eight-year war with Iraq had slowly dissolved into memory, and more pedestrian concerns had taken hold. Reza had been worried about how Shahnaz would take his extended layoff; in fact, she hadn't protested a bit, and they'd decided to have a child. It had been their form of dissent against the excesses of the Revolution not to have a child during the days when the regime had done everything in its power to encourage an explosive birth rate; but now that the official policy was to discourage births, an opinion of Imam Khomeini having been conveniently discovered from when he was still alive to justify birth control, they had decided to go against the grain once again. They'd decided not to know the sex of the child. If only any of the grandparents were still alive! Without them, the pregnancy felt unearned somehow, as if they'd stumbled on it, not deliberated for years as they had.

Finishing up the chores he knew Shahnaz would appreciate his doing, Reza thought of the war, which he had been spared from joining because he had been too brilliant a student in the early going to have been put on the military track. Had it not been for the Revolution, no doubt he would have gone to America for his engineering degree; his parents, both retired government servants, could certainly have afforded it. But even though he had never shared the enthusiasm for black-turbaned clerics to decide the nitty-gritty of policy, he felt it would have been a betrayal to leave the chaos and thrill of the Tehran street for the suburban American life some of his contemporaries wrote about in their occasional letters. No, he had been better off staying; and how would he ever have met a woman as sympathetic and easygoing as Shahnaz, had he run away?

The komiteh never knocked on the door that afternoon, and Reza felt confident that there'd be a day soon when the komiteh would stop knocking on doors, and arresting people for moral violations. Javad-Ali had been producing a very tame *Asr-e-Aazadi* in recent weeks, when all indications were that, with the reformists in the ascendancy, the criticism of government institutions could be stronger. What was wrong? Reza decided to visit the offices of *Asr-e-Aazadi*, and find out. Javad-Ali had often asked him to contribute—"the scientists have a saner view of the world,

Reza, and we woolly-headed arts and humanities types could learn a lot from you"—but Reza wasn't interested in giving final shape to nebulous irritations and frustrations. The more concrete a resentment became, the more one had to sustain its daily weight. Better to get along and get by, with as little fuss as possible.

Kazim Shariati had never expected to be asked to fill in for his friend and mentor in Tehran, the learned Judge Hashim Tabatabai, in the civil court empowered to resolve marital conflicts. Yet because Kazim had already witnessed firsthand, on different occasions, the Judge's tendencies and procedures, and because the Judge reserved the right to delegate a short-term substitution in exigencies, and because one didn't refuse an older person of authority in such a situation, Kazim had no choice but to preside over the court for a few days that he hoped would be less busy than usual. Judge Tabatabai's foremost strategy was to hold his tongue as much as possible and let the antagonists arrive at a reconciliation that they would feel they had initiated themselves and that would leave both sides feeling victorious, having extracted a small taste of revenge. Kazim promised himself to do the same. Hadn't Kazim been striving for an unexpected challenge that would clarify things for himself?

What, after all, was a promising young cleric, seemingly destined to achieve the title of hojjatoleslam by the age of forty, to do in the capital city without the constant guidance and supervision he'd been used to since his early days at Qom's Feyzieh Seminary? As much as possible, Kazim had tried to isolate himself from the traditional preoccupations of the clergy once he left Qom at the end of the summer.

His goal, to offset the predictability of the daily prayers, was to let at least one unexpected thing happen to him over the course of each day. Once he started substituting his clerical outfit with ordinary shirts and trousers, he found people's attitude to him changing completely: the look of mingled respect, contempt, fear, and expectation he'd come to assume as his due for the rest of his life vanished, in favor of mere friendliness toward his delicate good looks, or at best curiosity when the slowness of his speech (one learned to speak in certain ways before the hojjatoleslams and ayatollahs, who were examining and judging when they least appeared to be doing so) gave him away as a newcomer to urban fastness. In Tehran, it seemed that if you gave the impression of having time on your hands, and looked respectable enough, sooner or later you'd be recruited to help someone. While he wore his clerical garb, he was once asked to help trace a missing mentally ill teenage girl by a pair of frantic parents. In his civilian clothes, the owner of a new café asked him, and a few other young men, to sit at one of the curbside tables all day long to make it look as if the café were busy.

No beautiful young girl had yet spoken to him beyond the bounds of taarof, politeness of a dilly-dallying kind whose relative rarity he'd come to appreciate in Qom. Now that he didn't tell anyone he was a cleric, and had moved from a neighborhood closer to affluent north Tehran than the run-down south side, he lived in constant trepidation that some girl would make an advance toward him. He'd heard that it wasn't unusual for bored girls and wives to seek nameless trysts, and that certain streets and shopping malls were well-known for the prowling activity of frustrated women. His religion taught him not to look at a woman with lust, let alone touch her in an unmarried state—what would he do if a woman approached him, and his will wasn't strong enough to do the right thing? Sometimes he wondered, sweating in his stuffy little apartment on the second floor of a Mediterranean-style building, if he wasn't turning his fear of such an encounter into a pleasurable fantasy by itself. Sometimes he wondered how different his life might have been had he not been an orphan from an early age, and something other than the existence of a seminary talabeh had been open to him. Would he have been happier? He had always been bothered by the cocksure attitude of some of the top-ranking clerics, who turned every physical sentiment of Ferdowsi and Rumi, Hafez and Saadi, the poets who had given Iran its most lasting heroes and myths, into metaphors for the love of the divine. But now his discomfort had become severe irritation. The next time a cleric talked about how the heady wine, the moonlit night of fevered embraces, the caresses of the beloved's dark tresses, all represented a helpless love of God, he would blow his top. Were the poets so afraid of public sentiment as to have apparently engaged in nothing but convoluted strategies of taarof? Perhaps they were sensualists above all, plain and simple. Perhaps there was more to the sharia than elaboration of rules of cleanliness, the rituals involving menstruation and defecation, eating and sleeping, copulation and masturbation. This dryness was tolerable only up to a point. To become elevated to the rank of ayatollah a prominent cleric had to compile questions and answers to masa'il, problems involving these very rituals of cleanliness for the most part. Yet the curious fact was that once an ayatollah died, it was nearly always revealed that he had been a lover of classical poetry, that he had himself composed in his youth verses that were so risqué they couldn't have been publicized while he was still alive. So which was more real? The hidden or the apparent self?

Of course, Judge Tabatabai, who came from a family of clerics but had chosen to practice civil law instead, would have said there was no contradiction. The surface and the depth were in harmony, if you only knew where to look. "Why don't you come and visit me at the court some morning?" the Judge had asked. "You'll see that it's not that difficult to square the apparent irreconcilables. You'll learn that the same spark of dignity flares in the most uncouth and the most polite expressions. We all want to be treated with respect, we're all yearning for freedom from oppression. It's nothing more complicated than that." And so, instead of browsing in the bookstores of north Tehran all morning, as he'd been apt to do, marveling at the ease and certainty with which well-dressed young Iranian women demanded to see this or that Western novel, Kazim had walked to the Judge's house in central Tehran, an annex to which served as his court.

The first case was one where the husband claimed infidelity on the part of the wife, yet he didn't want a divorce, although he was entitled to seek one on that basis alone. What he wanted was public admission of the woman's adultery, the humiliation that he would forever hold against her. They were affluent, both university teachers, and they could easily have settled this matter between themselves, since divorce wasn't the issue. Judge Tabatabai was about to let them go with a gentle admonition to both sides to be civil to each other, when unexpectedly the woman asked for divorce—it seemed spur-of-the-moment, and Kazim could tell that the husband was unprepared for this turn of events. "I never wanted a divorce," he appealed, to which the woman replied, "But I do—now. I've seen a side of you I never wanted to see." "Yet I forgave you for your sin," he argued. "No you didn't," she shot back, "You're unable to forgive. I can't go on in these circumstances." Judge Tabatabai called a halt to the proceedings, wanting them to think it over before returning in a couple of weeks. Later, Kazim asked him if he wasn't giving the couple all the rope to hang themselves with, since a fortnight of festering resentment might easily spell their end. "I think it's more likely both of them will see they've overplayed their hands. For middle-class couples in their position, secure in their status, it's really difficult to start over. Far better to forget the indiscretion, pretend it never existed." Kazim thought bitterly, "Ah, politeness again. Our national bane. When will we ever be able to face facts?"

The other cases were deceptively routine. A construction worker had started squandering his meager wages on his gambling addiction instead of supporting his obedient wife and four children. At one point the construction worker yelled in anguish, "Where is the Imam Khomeini now? He said for us to have as many children as we could, to fight the war against the devil enemies. Where are the devil enemies now? Why can't we fight another war so I can have four little shaheeds on my hand instead of four hungry mouths to feed? Why can't I live like a man instead of being a slave to—to them!" The children were present in the courtroom, probably because the wife wanted her husband to be shamed into accepting his obligations. Instead of warning the man that he was treading dangerously close to blasphemy, Judge Tabatabai oversympathized with the embittered man to the extent that he started withdrawing his most blatant accusations. Before long, husband and wife were apologizing to each other, and the kids were all crying. "You see, he needed to let off a little steam," said Judge Tabatabai to Kazim, when the courtroom was empty. Another couple were in disagreement over the financial settlement of their already agreed-on divorce—one of the rare ones actually granted by the Judge, instead of his having pressed till the last moment for a reconciliation—and a close rehash of the agreement revealed that in fact there was no discrepancy, only a misunderstanding about future income.

Judge Tabatabai was energized at the close of proceedings in the afternoon.

"So! You promised to reveal how things were in harmony once we looked the right way," Kazim protested. "All I see is utter disharmony. No one knows their own motivation, let alone of the person they're supposed to understand most intimately. It is all blindness and chaos. There is no order anywhere, and to pretend there is, is colossal ignorance."

"My young friend, you still understand so little…"

"What is there to understand? The sharia codes say one thing. The real world runs on a parallel track. Where do they meet? We have come too far from the conditions in which the universal laws could apply. Everyone now is interested in only his own happiness."

"I disagree. The Iranian people value sacrifice above all other qualities."

Kazim wondered if this was true. He found in himself only a rage against human unhappiness that led in no way to sacrifice—only self-expression, to use a dreaded Westoxified term. Yet he visited the Judge several more times. Then when he agreed to take over for him for a short while (did the Judge's illness really compel him to make the request, or did he want Kazim to be at the helm for its own sake?), he felt himself a hypocrite. How could he, who had never touched the flesh of a woman, know what it was for a husband and wife to feel simultaneously so full of love and hatred for each other? It was back to his discarded clerical robes for now.

Of the twenty-five hundred fiction, poetry, and drama manuscripts submitted for publication approval to the Ministry of Culture and Islamic Guidance that year, none was odder than the magical realist novel produced by Keyvan Yazdani, whose introductory letter had failed to clarify his age, religion, educational background, and degree of loyalty to the Revolution. Instead of the usual words of slavish praise for Imam Khomeini and the worthy leaders who had followed him, Keyvan had talked knowingly of the condition of postmodernity in the third world novel, which, it seemed to him, "had ended up making a fetish of obscurity for its own sake." Keyvan, the youthful intern who first came across his manuscript was shocked to discover, wanted to "reinstitute in Iranian fiction the degraded naturalist elements lost since the Revolution." So what had the Ministry been approving all these years? Mere fantasies?

Even the intern who brought it straight to the veteran director's attention was struck by the irony that Keyvan's novel was more fantastical than any submission he'd come across. The director read it over a weekend, and his first words to the intern were, "The young man has clearly got the hang of his Bulgakov. I never thought *The Master and Margarita* could be borrowed from. This is either a work of stark madness or genuine inspiration."

The intern, in a high state of alert for any unintentional misunderstanding, noted, "Definitely madness, I would say."

The director replied wearily, "That would seem to be the safer conclusion, wouldn't it? Still, I wouldn't mind knowing the young man."

"Why do we presume it's a young man? He could be very old."

The director laughed. "Only young men write with such verve, such disrespect for conventions. Writing conventions, I mean, not the conventions of social life the Republic aspires to instill in all our citizens. Old people are too baffled by their own mortality to undertake such revisions. There's a trace of Garcia Marquez here that has somehow been salted and resalted until it's aggravating in the extreme."

"So shall we send this back, stamped disapproved, and relieve the—young man—of his agony?" the intern said, already plotting the contemptuous letter with which he would spurn the ambition of so wild and unruly a writer.

"If we haven't returned any other manuscript, why should this get the special treatment? Here we treat everyone the same. I suggest you place it firmly at the bottom of your stacks of manuscripts in uncertain status. Neither approved nor disapproved."

The intern wondered at the sagacity of this course of action. Perhaps the young man who had composed the fantastic *Iran Beheaded* would rather, faced with overt rejection, make his escape to more favorable territory, America perhaps, or at least Turkey, instead of trying to inflict his agonized reflections on Iranians. The director, on the other hand, wondered long and hard what he was doing at the Ministry, if a manuscript of such genuine talent couldn't be approved. It didn't matter that the main tension in the novel was always escaping out of sight, unraveling into too many strands that petered out into nothing—the writing evoked a world of dark horror, where to be alive was to have made a fatal bargain with the devil, where to eat and talk and love and hate was to have compromised your humanity at every level.

There was in the script a butcher from Kurdistan who dreams of working as an executioner for the Revolutionary Guards, chopping off the rebellious heads of writers and intellectuals with nothing better to do than foment frustration; each slab of meat served by the butcher to his bourgeois customers is an offering to the gods of retribution, a pale substitution for the human heads he'd like to serve to these very same consumers of hatred. There was a charming housewife in Shiraz who has deviated so far from Islamic ritual that she starts her own Satanic religion, involving the torture of unsuspecting neighborhood men—why men, not children or the elderly or naïve wives? The woman ends up becoming a nun, recognized by the Supreme Leader for having devoted her entire life to the service of mankind, the care of orphans, et cetera. There was a university professor in Kerman who kills off each of his competitors in fits of jealousy, as they publish accomplished papers in foreign journals, while he, loyal to the Revolution's ideals (if not its outward forms of piety), languishes in unpublished obscurity; yet this professor regularly goes out of his way to be compassionate to the poor and oppressed around him, relieving their problems by bringing together patrons with beneficiaries in the unlikeliest of coincidences. Harboring these hyperenergetic agents, a drugged, calculating, rationally mad Iranian citizenry goes about its daily business, turning a blind eye to whatever outrageous violence has occurred the night before, refusing to believe its very senses that anything could be wrong with the revolutionary Republic. It was too much, altogether too much, this young man's ability to see through the most sophisticated delusions! He was spreading the blame equally, without hesitation. It was the sure hand of the kind of writer who came along very rarely, who'd suffered so intensely that his every word, every jotting, was a complete vision, with worlds of hells and heavens scaffolding it.

The manuscript must be destroyed immediately! The director had taken ill, failing to show up for work as he went over the events of the novel in his head again and again. Three days had gone by without his colleagues sending so much as a messenger to inquire if he was alive or dead. The director's wife had left some years ago for a younger man; this was inevitable, since she was a famous beauty, and he a mere intellectual, bald and pasty-faced, unable to satisfy her sexual voracity. The director had had a couple of homosexual encounters in his youth; this was during the late years of the old regime, when homosexuality was so close to the surface that it had almost become acceptable, even fashionable, behavior among the bourgeoisie—as long, of course, as one didn't make too much of a fetish out of it, and impose it on others. Now, among eager young interns—full of airtight theories about right and wrong in literature, absorbed from Tehran University professors who had never published a story or poem in their lives—the director felt the old homosexual tug of war with an intensity he thought had died with his marriage. Yet to act on it was laced with such danger that his throat constricted at the prospect of unforeseen consequences. What was this young man Keyvan like? No doubt he was beautiful—bony in frame, articulate in the way he moved his lips and eyes, surrealistic in how he accepted the strength of his physicality.

For the sake of the Republic, the manuscript had to be destroyed immediately! Leaving the last cup of tea he was ever to savor on earth unfinished—its cinnamon stick would be murky by the time the police captured it for examination of possible traces of drugs—the director jumped into his aging Peykan at five p.m., knowing that all his colleagues would have departed and there would be no one to question him about his arrival at the Ministry so late in the day. He put on an old Dariush tape, a remnant of the old regime that promised the flare of genuine rebellion each time he listened to the singer's sexually charged melancholy, loud and polite at the same time, and promptly ran into a colossal garbage truck which plowed over his little Peykan and made mush of his mangled body, his arms widespread, as if welcoming the encounter with the devouring truck. Dariush blared on, the cassette player undisturbed.

The secret life of Shahnaz Rasuli had grown so extensive over her years of marriage that she no longer bothered to keep track of her little lies and deceptions in the service of humanity.

Once in a while she helped arrange sigheh matches, temporary marriages she could justify as being rewarding for certain women in dire financial straits, and for preventing the overt sin that came from lawless affairs, where the woman had no security whatever, and was more likely to be used and then left discarded. She was a member of two book clubs that discussed classic Western novels, and she was friends with a set of young women who attended rare screenings of Iranian films whose release the censors were delaying. In addition to her full-time job teaching eighth graders Social Studies, she also privately tutored girls she thought had an excellent shot at doing well in higher education. She could boast of having encouraged several future Tehran University graduates, now managing successful professional lives, and others who'd gone on to study in Europe and Canada. The money wasn't so much the issue here—although that helped too, with Reza's drastically reduced layoff compensation—as the pride in doing a job well. She was circumventing the Revolution's persistent effort to flatten out distinctions amongst students: the very smart were not necessarily encouraged to express themselves, while the dumb were made to feel they were almost as good as the average. Shahnaz was picking and choosing whom to give the most attention, and that was a no-no. The principal at their school was fond of repeating Imam Khomeini's supposed edict that the Revolution had to be nurtured one soul at a time, and God never made a distinction between souls, having created them all equal.

In some respects, Reza was a stick-in-the-mud; despite Shahnaz's best attempts to humor him, he could be very stubborn when it came to following the letter of the law. He wouldn't have liked any kind of freelancing, since one never knew where the authorities stood on it. In the years soon after her marriage, when Imam Khomeini was still alive, Shahnaz had offered birth control classes to groups of young housewives, her students' mothers. If a student showed signs of neglect at home, it was a good bet that her mother would be receptive to any idea to improve her harried state of being. Once the war was over the general melancholy dissipated, the glory of having martyrs in one's family became less and less an excuse to justify the shabbiness of one's home and children, and her task became much easier. Compared to those years, when a girl Shahnaz was trying to encourage to go to college might burst into a justification for why she didn't have to put herself out, because a brother had already become shaheed in the trenches and their family was saved, this was nothing. Coming from a well-off middle-class family, with educated parents, even under the Shah Shahnaz would have had some sort of profession—although only on the Shah's cultural terms, and if she had been one of those women uncomfortable with Westernization, she would have been out of luck. But now far more women worked in the professions than ever before, and in return for Islamic modesty, they got respect from men. It was a fair bargain: women were freer; the tough years of the Revolution were already over, and whatever progress came now would have a sustained momentum. Now was the time to have her own child, so she could teach her—she hoped and prayed it was a girl, which was what Reza wanted too—never to take her freedom for granted.

Yes, this was nothing, Shahnaz thought, as she went over her to-do list for the afternoon, merging into the busy

foot traffic heading up Ali Shariati Avenue. She had a more
subversive agenda than just shopping for food and drinks for
the Friday night party to announce her pregnancy to friends
and family. Her younger sister, Sakineh, was a sucker for
gourmet French pastries, and Shadman Café was renowned
for its selection; she would go there at the end, and call
her husband from there—he appreciated knowing once in a
while where she was perambulating, even though he always
acted surprised when she called. But first she had to pay a
visit to the mother of a girl, Massoumeh, who had recently
moved with her family from Isfahan. The father, Cyrus, a real
estate developer, was Zoroastrian, but the mother, Nauroz,
had recently converted to Islam, and took every decree of
the mullahs as sacred word. In itself this wasn't a remarkable
enough fact, but Nauroz had lately been instilling a deep
sense of shame in Massoumeh about her thirteen-year-old
body. For a girl of average looks this wouldn't have been so
much of a problem, but Massoumeh's very identity was rooted
in her extreme beauty. Like all converts, Nauroz's zeal was
excessive, and she had already sent notes to Shahnaz that
Massoumeh didn't seem able to explicate the Revolution's
goals for women upon Nauroz's questioning. This had to stop,
or Massoumeh would end up a wreck.

Shahnaz hailed an orange cab rather than ride in the
back of a bus. She had almost justified the necessity of women
sitting in the back, but this seemingly trifling inconvenience
grated more on her than major disabilities. The traffic in north
Tehran was a little saner than in the central and southern
parts of the city, although it was Reza, always reluctant to let
Shahnaz drive their Peykan, who had made her conscious of
its awfulness. The reminders of the war—pictures of groups
of martyrs, often young boys, graced with Imam Khomeini's
certain declarations that they had entered paradise—were

less frequent along the wider, grassier boulevards of north Tehran than elsewhere, and the shops were becoming almost blasé in advertising Western goods, many of which couldn't be officially imported at all. Shahnaz agreed with the regime's ban on the use of women to advertise anything—although when it came to refrigerators and washing machines, it was a little laughable to see men caressing the appliances with their thick hands and awkward embraces.

At their single-storey bungalow off Vali-e-Asr Avenue in Mahmoodiyeh, Massoumeh was already expecting Shahnaz. The house was inconspicuous, as even the richest Zoroastrians' homes usually were, unlike those of ethnic Persians whose first indulgence upon pocketing any substantial wealth was a house beyond their means. No servants seemed to be in evidence.

"My mother has gone shopping—in preparation for Moharram," Massoumeh explained. "I did my best to keep her, but she barely listened."

The living room was a curious amalgam of Zoroastrian and Islamic images. A picture of the fire at Yazd that had been burning continuously for fifteen hundred years stood next to one of Imam Khomeini's portraits as a younger cleric in exile in Najaf.

"Khoob, we might as well use our time for some studying," Shahnaz said when an hour had gone by and there was no sign of Nauroz. "We can go over some English grammar."

At four-thirty, Cyrus, a handsome if somewhat portly man in a Western suit (but no tie, since this was banned in the Islamic Republic), arrived, without showing much curiosity about Shahnaz's purpose in being there.

"I'd better leave now. I'll come some other time. Khoda Hafez." Shahnaz excused herself at last when there was no sign of Nauroz, bored for once with Massoumeh's flashy control of the material. She regretted having been deprived of what had promised to be a lively exchange of ideas with Nauroz. Most women were unoffended by Shahnaz's advice. The Revolution had made everyone so used to altering the very fabric of their lives in accordance with the Republic's changing dictates that a little neighborly advice was hardly worth getting one's dander up.

It was after she left Massoumeh's home that Shahnaz first felt the burden of her pregnancy. She'd hardly noticed it before. But it was well into the third month now, and it was undeniable that something was growing inside her. Perhaps she should have taken the Peykan after all, even if Reza would have been offended. She didn't feel like going to Shadman Café to pick up the pastries, but if she didn't, it would be awkward to explain to Reza where she had been. Like all men he assumed that it took women hours and hours to shop for things men bought in minutes. Shahnaz smiled when she thought of the looks on their friends' faces when they found out she was pregnant for the first time at her late age. Always the trendsetter, she thought, even if she had never done the outrageous things her little sister Sakineh was known for.

The dirty Tehran air had already got to Kazim Shariati. He tried to stifle his coughs inside the dark courtroom (there was a problem with the wiring for the lights that no one seemed able to figure out), embarrassed that he had succumbed to a city affliction. Whenever he felt irritated by some trivial malady, he tried to remember his friends who had died or been injured in the war—so many of them, even from Qom, where they could easily have been excused for the sake of their religious studies, had they chosen to exercise the privilege. He was seventeen when the war ended, several years older than the youngest of the martyrs. Yet his teachers sheltered him from so much as a whiff of participation in the violence on the front. "Iran needs you here, in the seminary," was their refrain, and he had wondered in later years if they had noticed some fatal weakness of his that he was unaware of. Wherever he went, he found mentors willing to go out of their way to promote him. Perhaps only a woman could explain to him the peculiar hue of light his eyes and face gave off to other men: was it something to be proud or ashamed of? There was no reason why he shouldn't already have been married; had his parents been alive, no doubt he would be the father of several children by now. An unmarried cleric was an aberration; it gave rise to all sorts of suspicions, and besides, it wasn't considered healthy for a Muslim man to spurn intimate relations if it was within his power to be married. Even the temporary sigheh, often performed for the most exploitative of reasons, was considered better than to engage in more unhealthy, or even sinful, practices. Women were a mystery to Kazim, even an affable young woman like the court assistant Farkhondeh, who'd accepted his appearance in place of Judge Tabatabai as if it were routine.

"Has anyone been delegated before to do this job by the Judge?" he asked.

"No, you're the first one," said Farkhondeh. "Judge Tabatabai takes great pride in his reasoning. But you'll be fine. The cases are very routine. By this time I have them all categorized."

"Oh, and what are the categories?" Kazim said as he sat behind the low desk, on a chair that had the plump Tabatabai's bodily grooves well marked on its ancient stuffing. The first case wasn't due to be heard for a few more minutes.

"Half the time the man is clearly the culprit. He's gotten away with so much unfair advantage all his life that he's completely taken aback when the woman finally can't take it anymore and challenges him. In these cases, you must not let the man's cries for pity weaken your resolve. Be firm but considerate—"

Kazim didn't learn how else Farkhondeh would have characterized the rest of the cases, because they were interrupted by the rude entrance of the first couple, peasants who had lived in Tehran for only a few years, battling over the right to spend the money from the sale of the woman's recently deceased parents' land. While listening to their chatter, he wondered idly if at the end of the day he could have a cup of coffee with Farkhondeh, perhaps at the Shadman Café he'd already been to once: quite a shocking change from the boring, cleric-dominated cafés of Qom, as here artist and writer types smoked themselves into strained inspiration, scribbled their notes with vacant eyes, and spoke very fast, in squeaky tones that would have earned them mockery among Qom's articulate young scholars. What had Farkhondeh's training in fiqh at Tehran University been like? Now there were seminaries in Qom training women to be ayatollahs. He tried to picture pleasant Farkhondeh as an ayatollah, and could only smile. Later, his conscience was pricked: she could be an ayatollah, but she couldn't be a judge—the Revolution had stripped women of their judgeships.

The first case turned out to be easy. Their mere presence in the court softened both sides. Kazim had seen the same phenomenon over and over with Judge Tabatabai. Perhaps warring couples in Iran used the marital courts mostly as an excuse to reconcile. By the middle of the morning, Farkhondeh was passing him notes on the relevant fiqh as if they'd been doing this together for years. And he was beginning to take it easy, venturing now and then into questions far removed from the antagonists' current dispute. It was only after Farkhondeh left early in the afternoon, just before zohr prayers, to take her mother to a doctor's appointment, that the first really interesting case came before him.

These were professionals, the Moavenis, the husband a pediatrician and the wife a researcher at a biology lab, the kind of people who didn't air their dirty laundry in a religiously inspired courtroom, and who had plenty of resources of their own, parallel to those provided by the Islamic Republic for people in more straitened circumstances. Still, inflation was terrible, unemployment was rife, and no one knew what to do with the armies of educated people who couldn't find good jobs. So it was possible that even a professional couple might face conditions making them stoop low enough to come to this court.

"Our problem, you see, is that we need a reliable witness as we pass some money into a third party's hands," the woman, Shirin, said with an immediately confidential tone that Kazim didn't altogether take to. She was leaning too close, and she was one of those women on whom the most elaborate covering only seemed to be wasted as a further token of nakedness. There was no modesty there.

"I don't get it, I'm sorry."

The husband, Abbas, who had a habit of loudly clearing his throat every few minutes, put his hand possessively over his wife's shoulder. "My wife wants a divorce, and to leave the country. She's fed up. I, on the other hand, don't mind—as much. I can survive nowhere but in Iran. But my wife visited Paris a couple of times in her youth, and she still remembers. Be that as it may. They have denied her an exit visa a number of times. She can't even attend scientific conferences in Turkey and Jordan. The only way out is through Kurdistan. We have an agent ready to do the work. We could pay him ourselves, but we thought—we thought it would be safer to pass it on through an authoritative party."

"Someone like you..." said Shirin.

"So we're not here for a divorce settlement," said Abbas. "We've already agreed."

"How long have you been a Judge?" Shirin asked. "You look awfully young. Not that you don't look authoritative."

"He looks old enough," said Abbas. "I'm sure he knows how to do his job. Now, can we trust you to do this? It'd be helpful if you could get a receipt, but this man, Babak, might not give you one. Next month is when my wife can leave. Meanwhile, here's our settlement agreement, so if you could witness and sign it..."

"My job," Kazim said, stunned by the audacity of the proposition, "is to attempt a reconciliation. I'm not some intermediary to pass illegal bribes to human smugglers and act against the laws of the Islamic Republic. I am a—a Judge." How ridiculous he sounded, how pompous, presuming to know better than the parties involved what was good for them! His resolve was like the front tire on his old bicycle in Qom, liable to puncture at the least pinprick.

"We understand, but we're past all that, don't you think?" said Abbas.

"We're all adults here," added Shirin. "A man and a woman fall out of love, and that is that. The rest is process, resolution—moving on."

"Absolutely, moving on..." confirmed Abbas, although Kazim thought he could detect wetness in his eyes as he looked steadily away from his wife. "It's dark in here. What, the komiteh can't fix a little thing like that? Too busy snatching people's satellite dishes..."

In the end, after what felt like hours of deliberation, Kazim agreed. What did he have to lose? If his agreeing to sign the document and to be the go-between for the money made them happy, so be it. He asked them repeatedly if they didn't have a trusted family member or friend to do it, but they insisted it had to be someone religious, someone trustworthy, someone not part of their intimate circle. The risk of leakage was too great otherwise.

"And what makes you think I won't snitch on you?" Kazim asked.

"Oh, we hardly think so," said Shirin dismissively. "Look, it's twenty thousand dollars, so be careful. Movazeb bashin!"

"Bist Hezar! Twenty thousand!" Kazim gasped. Even for a doctor and a researcher to have saved that much money, with inflation as it was, and the government always imposing new taxes, was impressive!

"Pick a place," said Shirin. "For today if you can—the sooner the better."

Kazim suggested Shadman Café, and husband and wife were pleased at his choice, grinning at each other as if to say, Sure, we made the right choice coming here.

Locking the courtroom—and wondering how to explain later to Judge Tabatabai why he had agreed to a divorce the very first time it was brought to court—he felt absurd and yet also complete. It was time to remove himself somewhere far away and really take a look at what his future held. A posting in a village might be just the thing to get his head clear. It would be an excuse to talk to Farkhondeh about. She seemed the kind of urban woman who knew village life inside out.

There was a crack of rare winter thunder, and some rain fell, but the smog was barely affected. In Revolution Square, the cab he was riding conked out. In Iran you rode a machine, a person, an animal, until the very last moment of its capacity. Then, without warning, it fizzled, no transition to death being available.

Zoology hadn't been Keyvan Yazdani's first choice of professions. At twenty-one, having graduated from Tehran University with a degree in economics, he had been leaning toward a career in agricultural economics. His urban self could never get enough of the problems of peasants. He didn't believe in any romantic claptrap, but the failure of successive land reforms made it a tempting subject to analyze: the Shah tried it, in his White Revolution, to Khomeini's great disapprobation, then Khomeini himself tried it, when he felt secure enough with the bazaaris' support. It was the kind of profession, zoology, where people left you alone. If they thought you weren't doing anything jeopardizing the Revolution's foundations, there was little chance that the Baseejis, the Hezbollahis, the komitehs would bother you. Animals? The Islamic Republic hardly had time for them! Keyvan specialized in wildlife in the northwest of the country, Azerbaijan and Kurdistan, fretting about the environmental degradation of the land that had made their continued existence a problem, especially since the Revolution when the economy had been so lacking in opportunities that the wildlife was more prone to indiscriminate predation than ever. Animals had suffered just as much under the Revolution, although nobody cared to chronicle their miseries. His colleagues, most of them pious if not active Revolutionary party members, were fatalistic about the extinction of species, restricting their worries to the lack of availability of medical care for their elderly parents and relations, or the high price of gas (at a couple of thousand rials a gallon, the cheapest in the world, they complained!).

His colleagues knew precious little about him. Ah, secrets—their possession and honoring, their preservation and care! So much effort went into it, it almost became rejuvenating, like time-released adrenalin. Once, an older female colleague, another Baha'i as it turned out, had made things difficult for him, by coming on to him so blatantly that the Hezbollahi-sympathizing colleagues had taken notice, but other than that his true affiliations and tendencies had remained hidden from view. Much like the Hidden Imam, the Shi'ites' expected Messiah who had disappointed over and over—although some of the less literate among Iranians took Khomeini himself to be the manifestation of the Hidden Imam—the thrill was in the secrecy, the waiting, not the discovery. Few knew that Keyvan's great-grandmother was a British Jew who had traveled to Iran in the late nineteenth century and stayed after falling in love with the land. Few—or was it no one?—knew that his grandfather Bayman had been one of the most committed supporters of Shoghi Effendi, the grandson of Abdu'l-Baha', who was in turn the son of the major propagator of the Baha'i faith, Baha'ullah, the long-awaited Manifestation of God. Under the Shah, things were better for the Baha'is in Iran ever before or since; but Keyvan's grandfather chose this time to renounce any attachment to the Islamic faith, making a bigger public production out of it than necessary. The Shah's support didn't waver either way, and the family's lands around Yazd prospered. In the next generation, when the Shah's power was beginning to wane—of course, he had to choose that moment to celebrate twenty-five hundred years of unbroken monarchy at the infamous farce that was Persepolis in 1971, served by Maxim's and Jansen's of Paris—Keyvan's father promised the budding genius that he could study anything, be anything he chose to be. In the succeeding years of the Islamic Republic, Baha'is, often accused of treason because of their alleged espionage activities—a convenient way to get around even the semblance of following the rule of law, and to summarily imprison and execute anyone the regime didn't feel comfortable with—studied at their "Open University," organized by dispossessed professors and scientists and writers and journalists out of their homes, enabling many of the graduates to go on to Western universities, once they made their escape through Kurdistan or other porous parts of the border. Keyvan never had to go through this kind of humiliation. But he gave the lie to his father's promise by becoming an obscure zoologist. It seemed the least significant profession in an Islamic Republic which never bothered to condescend to animals, unlike its constant protestations that whatever medieval barbarism it was imposing on women was for their own good—the marvel being that most educated women agreed that, indeed, being segregated into "womanly" professions and activities liberated them. Keyvan's mother had been a rationalizer in the same vein.

It was difficult to know when his period of degeneration began. Perhaps it was when he was in his teens, in the early years of the war, when a younger classmate went off to the front, and conveniently died under the tanks, to make heroes of his parents. One afternoon the parents talked to the assembled school about there being no age or other limits to the need for martyrdom. It was sickening, the whole performance. He felt at that moment that he'd seen through the whole spectacle, that nothing from then on was going to fool him. For it wasn't possible that the mother of a dead thirteen-year-old child could feel only nationalist emotion at such a time. Indeed, the problem of what to do with the wayward heart was eminently solved only by autocrats and theocrats, and they did it by setting up a charmed circle of insiders. Thus the obsession with oaths. Thus the obsession with not giving oaths, as his grandfather Bayman, on the verge of greatness under the Shah, had chosen: the other side of the coin, the inescapable currency of remaining alive in a regime that thrived on death.

He was the only one of his immediate family still alive. The rest seemed to have chosen early death as the extreme form of going into occultation. The whole history of Iran seemed to be degrees of presenting two faces to the world: different faiths all pretended to love Iran above all, even as their private passions lay elsewhere—this being the path to martyrdom of the private emotions. Was it any wonder that the leading myth of the nation was Imam Hossein's sacrifice at Karbala, that the most Westernized of intellectuals reverted to Iranian myths of martyrdom to justify whatever social engineering plans they had in mind? Was it any wonder that this nation, practiced in the art of hypocritical double-talk, dissimulation, taarof, politeness, courtesy, flowery obeisance and private disobedience, was the home of the modern world's greatest theocracy? If only he could break through his own imposed shell of practicing hypocrisy, tell the world he was a proud Baha'i and be done with it!

But he wasn't a proud Baha'i. He wasn't a proud anything. So when the contact was made with him, soon after Khomeini's death—when it seemed that a heavy burden had been lifted off the Iranian nation, and things would perhaps return a bit more to "normal"—by a man who identified himself as a great friend of his grandfather Bayman's, and one of the leaders of a local spiritual assembly in Keyvan's ancestral Yazd, he was quick to respond: "I'm going to be a zoologist, so I'm hardly to be reckoned a person of any importance. I've never been a practicing Baha'i. Behind Baha'ullah's great talk of the oneness of mankind, the oneness of religions, the oneness of the Manifestations of God, himself being the latest of these, I find the same restrictions on human freedom that infect every other religion—nineteenth-century prudishness, no doubt, rather than, say, Muhammad's seventh-century anxieties. Women are equal to men, but not quite equal, or not quite the same, because…Non-Baha'is are equal to Baha'is, but not quite the same, because…This whole business of hierarchies, despite his intention to abolish them, he just gets around. So he ends up being yet another Manifestation of the same tyranny that has always existed everywhere, and I see no human solution to it. Forgive my bluntness." He'd gone on in this insulting manner, and was surprised to have had a civil response, and continuing correspondence all these years.

In his manuscript, *The Tyranny of Heaven*, later renamed *The Hands That Cause*, and finally *Iran Beheaded*, there was a domineering character, steeped in the lore of a Masonic-like brotherhood, who has immense hypnotic powers over younger men at pains to be authentic in a world of only mirrors and illusions. This character was based on his forever-unidentified correspondent, who never stopped pleading with him to publicly identify himself as a Baha'i, to register with the government as such, to work for the mission of the universal faith, to spread the word through his writings and speech, to donate money to the various funds for the educational uplift of oppressed Baha'is. Keyvan had saved every one of these letters. He hoped that the police would follow up on these in the aftermath, trace the identity of the sender (he'd had some suspicions, but each time the person he'd suspected had died, so he had to look for others). It was petty, he knew; but even pettiness can be sweet when one's spirit has been broken down.

He studied the disappearance of wild animals, tried to convince his colleagues that some species or other of buffalo or deer was about to become endangered, and that somewhere someone should do something about it, while he labored for years over a manuscript that he knew had no chance of being accepted for publication. The day he finished it, his girlfriend broke up with him, because she said he didn't need her anymore; it had only been an act of mercy on her part to see him through its completion. No, she wasn't seeing anyone, but would Keyvan, in his blindness to the needs of anyone but himself, have noticed if she was? She was a beautiful young Muslim, a pious believer who, even if she didn't cover her hair tight enough to hide every single strand of hair, did believe that the hejab allowed her to interact with men without being the object of unwanted attraction and scrutiny. "Fine, you're free—and so am I," he'd said, locking himself up in his north Tehran studio for three days, subsisting on cheap caviar and prune juice.

Something seemed to have ended in him after finishing that novel. His girlfriend had been right. The politeness of his neighbors and colleagues drove him to fury. It was then that he hatched his plan. He would wait exactly a year, no more than that, for his manuscript to be approved; that was the latest the Ministry said you should expect to wait—assume the worst if you didn't hear by then. His plan underwent many transformations, the precise method unclear to him, but in the end these seemed to him trivial maneuverings of the lost mind. Only the final act mattered. He would go out a free man— never having been married, faithless to the core, irrepressible under the most tyrannous regime. He would define freedom on his own terms. He pitied the martyrs who were doing it for something as concrete as the keys to paradise (which many kids actually wore around their necks to the front during the long war), the entrée to beautiful virgins. He reconnoitered Shadman Café many times, having picked it out as a terrific location, because he felt more revulsion toward the self-satisfied, elegant, healthy faces of the middle-class clientele there than any other place. One woman in particular, a bossy, noisily interfering schoolteacher, had the kind of glow on her face only preaching fanatics used to have in the old days; this halo was now suffusing people who worked at boring professions. She came frequently, and she smiled at Keyvan brooding over some last French nouveau roman from the fifties he had to check off, as if she knew all his manly secrets. He dreamed of men who smiled so widely from politeness that all their big white teeth showed, until slithering, venomous snakes suddenly came out of their mouths. He had been startled into total wakefulness and he couldn't get enough of it. But he was resolved. It would happen precisely one year from the date of delivery of the unpublishable manuscript. His Kurdish suppliers of the bomb materials insisted on believing that he was a partisan of their side. It was incredible how quickly the worst weapons could be procured, for amounts and considerations so small as to beggar the imagination. These were the cheapest things on sale in the Islamic Republic.

It was only in the penultimate moment before detonation—he did it precisely at five p.m., when the hateful schoolteacher had done with her selection of pastries for a party she couldn't stop talking about, in that false, blustery tone of hers—it was only in that half-moment that he wondered if he wasn't following strictly in the line of Baha'ullah, by signifying his oneness with the inveterate violence of the world, his oneness with the depredation and tragedy that compelled men to put an end to all hopes for a better world at the first sign there would be difficulties along the way. Was he one of them? Was his denial confirmation? But the thought had barely made its way around his mind when it was no more. It was his thirtieth birthday. *Happy birthday to me,* his very last thought fizzled out in his scattered synapses.

Mr. Rasuli enjoyed the gold section of Tehran's Grand Bazaar more than any other. He lingered over gold urns, gold vases, gold trays, gold spoons, and expressed notes of appreciation over the fine craftsmanship of the products. "Kheyli khoob. From Isfahan, no doubt?" he said to the vendors one after the other. They knew he wasn't going to buy, but they were unfailingly polite to him, offering him qahve at every stop. Once in a while, he did stop for coffee, the dark Turkish kind, since the majority of the Bazaar merchants were Turkish in origin, and the more rugged Azeri Turkish prevailed here rather than the sweeter Persian. How evocative of the forms and expressions of medieval exchange this vast, labyrinthine, enclosed space was! You felt somehow the dust you were treading on was sacred. True, the Bazaar itself was no more than a century and a half old, but it represented the merchant tradition—tolerant and pragmatic, never prone to extremes of emotion—better than anything else in this country. Iran felt timeless, a nation that would outlast many others now considered great, as long as the Bazaar went on as it always had. He was gratified enough to make an impulsive purchase—a gold earring for Shahnaz. He also bought a gold penholder for his friend Javad-Ali at *Asr-e-Aazadi*.

He passed a demonstration in Enqelab Square against the high price of bread without much interest, and found the offices of *Asr-e-Aazadi*, when he got there around six p.m., to be lacking the turmoil he normally expected there.

"What's wrong, azizam?" he asked Javad-Ali, one of the few intellectuals he knew who didn't really mind being overweight.

Javad-Ali had lately given up his lifelong habit of chain-smoking, and was cajoling Reza to take up running to lose the bulge around his waist. "I see you've lost some weight. Good, good for you."

"I would say I've added a few pounds. Impending fatherhood…"

"What! Is that true? My God, congratulations! This is wonderful news. I never thought you would—my God, mubarak!"

They hugged and laughed, making raw jokes, and then Javad-Ali shared the news with the first person he saw, a lovely young editor who tried her best to look happy for Reza, despite the evident strain on her face.

"Her father was a Berkeley graduate," Javad-Ali explained when she left. "Something obscure, in the sciences, otherwise he'd have been tapped for Rafsanjani's California mafia, no doubt. She's brilliant, very much a chip off the old block."

A childhood friend, whose diplomat father's career had been ruined during the hostage crisis, Javad-Ali always went to great lengths to point out to Reza the slight cracks in the regime's tight control of thought and opinion. "It can only get better, we've already been through the worst," was how he always prefaced some positive development—a movie that had unexpectedly made it through the censors and was getting rave reviews, an admission of unfair intelligence gathering or even torture by the police or Baseej or Revolutionary Guards. Truth be told, Reza himself didn't think things were all that bad—even if at times he did wonder how high his own standard of living might have been had the Shah managed to survive.

"But the office is so quiet today," Reza complained. "Other than the little commotion I've caused."

"So you've noticed...Actually, there have been a lot of staff changes. I've let go of some of the firebrand young editors, replaced them with more seasoned hands. Journalism isn't only a matter of venting your private opinions, you know. There must be some basis in empirical fact, if you're going to advocate alternative policies to what the government is pursuing. Besides, I think we've just about played out the cultural angle. Or maybe that's going too far. We can still talk about the illogic of not letting women be judges, when we treat them as adults at nine, but other newspapers are doing that. Heck, the films are doing that now, and getting away with it."

Reza kicked back in his comfortable chair. Ah, to have a nice intellectual discussion, on an otherwise lazy evening! He pictured Shahnaz finishing her shopping, and arriving home early to find him not there. She would get to work preparing dinner—morgh polow today, as he'd requested— and she would be more easygoing in bed than usual, because school would soon break, and there would be no papers to grade, no classes to prepare for. Life was about as good as it could get. If some opportunities had been lost because of the Revolution, perhaps others had been gained.

"So what will your paper write about now?" Reza asked.

"Economic policy, azizam, that's the make-or-break thing for Iran now. How we utilize resources. How we spend the oil wealth. What we produce, how much we subsidize food and essential products. And then the problem of dependence on oil—which leads to so much unemployment. Inflation— why can't we control it better? It's unacceptable to put such a squeeze on the hard-working middle-class. You shouldn't have to hold two or three jobs to make ends meet, if you're a teacher or nurse. These are the ways we can make people's lives easier, by having more rational policies."

"You should name your paper *Asr-e-Iqtisadi* then. The age of homo economicus."

"Perhaps we will," Javad-Ali said seriously.

"It would be the first time a newspaper had renamed itself voluntarily, not because the government had banned it."

"There's a first time for everything, Reza."

The young editor, covered elegantly, even if her voluptuous figure was undisguisable, came again to get Javad-Ali's approval on a short piece she had finished editing on Iran's participation in some new regional economic cooperation plan.

"Khoob, I don't have to see it, if you think it's ready," Javad-Ali said easily.

"So you're coming to the party Friday night?" Reza said.

"How could I ever miss it! Although I might have to leave early—there's a meeting of editors far out in the suburbs I need to go to. It doesn't hurt to put our minds together once in a while instead of always competing for the scoop."

"The real scoop is that there is no scoop people don't already know about, dorost?"

"Dorost, of course," said Javad-Ali. "Light will be shed on hidden things. It's just that it doesn't always come about because we push it to happen."

Perhaps he should take up running, Reza thought on his way out. But if it weren't for paunchy bazaaris who sustained the impression of everlasting Iran, one would almost have to turn to Ferdowsi and Rumi to find the resonating legends. And he just wasn't into poetry.

ACKNOWLEDGMENTS

I owe tremendous gratitude to the editors of the journals who first published the stories in this collection: Martin Tucker, Julie Shigekuni, Wendy Sumner Winter, Anthony Stewart, Brian Bedard, Sven Birkerts, Bill Pierce, Michael Croley, Maggie Gerrity, Jeff Brewer, Tom Lorenz, and Michael Tussler. The stories appeared as follows:

"Anatolia" in *Confrontation* (Spring 2007)

"Conservation" in *Blue Mesa Review* (Spring 2007)

"Dubai" in *The Pinch* (Fall 2006)

"Go Sell It on the Mountain" in *The Dalhousie Review* (Fall 2008)

"Gypsy" in *South Dakota Review* (Summer 2007)

"Independence" in *South Dakota Review* (Spring 2006)

"Manzanar" in *Agni* (Fall 2008)

"Profession" in *Harpur Palate* (Summer 2006)

"Repatriation" in *The Portland Review* (Summer 2007)

"Tehran" in *Cottonwood* (Summer 2007)

"Texas" in *Wascana Review* (Fall 2006)

"Dubai" received Special Mention for *Pushcart Prize XXXII*, for which I thank its editors.

I owe special thanks to Eric Miles Williamson, who inspires me to try to say the difficult but necessary thing, rather than settle for the easy and redundant, and who has been the force behind most of the good things that have happened in my writing life; to exemplary editors, Richard Burgin and Kevin Prufer, for being so extraordinarily supportive over the long haul; to Jay Parini, for his outstanding model of a complete man of letters; to Gina Frangello, who took a chance on me at a time when all seemed dark and lost; to Glenn Blake, for first establishing in me the sense of a writerly vocation; and to Gary Heidt, for his unwavering belief in my work.

The people at Black Lawrence Press have been everything a writer could want. Thank you to Colleen Ryor for picking my collection, to Diane Goettel for her unstinting efforts on its behalf, and to Sarah Crevelling, Adam Deutsch, and Steven Seighman for their contributions. And a huge thank you to Dan Wickett.

I would like to thank the editors of the literary periodicals who have sustained me over the years, particulary Stephen Corey, Laurence Goldstein, Wendy Lesser, John Matthias, David Hamilton, Robert S. Fogarty, Tony Tremblay, Paul Doyle, John Whale, Michael Tyrell, Stephanie G'Schwind, Keith Botsford, Robert Lewis, Richard Mullen, Wayne Chapman, John Witte, Sebastian Barker, William Ryan, J. Mark Powell, Robert Nazarene, Ian Britain, and Christina Thompson.

I thank my mother and father for their extreme laissez-faire attitude in raising me, which makes me unable to do anything but write as a living; my uncle for always coming through; Noori for the wishing flower; and Mehnaaz for being the dream companion every writer wishes he could have, day in and day out, through ups and downs, so that the struggle means something in itself.